Praise for *Thr*

'A real puzzle box of a story
salty, can't-live-with-ca
between the two sisters.
J. M. Hall

'J.L. Blackhurst brings a fresh, modern twist to the classic locked-room mystery. Three deviously clever impossible crimes propelled me to keep reading late into the night to finish *Three Card Murder*.'
Gigi Pandian

'I was gripped by this clever, intricate murder mystery.'
Louise Jensen

'A clever modern interpretation of a classic locked-room mystery, with two engaging protagonists and an ending I never saw coming. What more could you ask for in a mystery?'
Faith Martin

'Slick and sparkling, a brilliant premise executed with such panache. Twisty, tricksy and whip smart, *Three Card Murder* is huge fun and a cracking read.'
Marion Todd

'Ingenious, fun and very different from so many of the crime books out there today.'
Ajay Chowdhury

'I loved this book! It's deliciously complex. I turned the last page and wanted more.'
Imogen Clark

'The perfect summer holiday read. Filled with murders, twists, feuding sisters and a real heart.'
Derek Farrell

'What a joyous ride *Three Card Murder* is!'
T. Orr Munro

J.L. Blackhurst is a pseudonym for Jenny Blackhurst who was born and grew up in Shropshire, where she still lives with her husband, two boys and two beagles. She has written eight psychological thrillers including *How I Lost You*, which won a Silver Nielsen award and became a Kindle number one bestseller in the UK and a *Spiegel* Bestseller in Germany. She can solve a Rubik's Cube in three minutes.

Also by J.L. Blackhurst
Three Card Murder

Writing as Jenny Blackhurst
How I Lost You
Before I Let You In
The Foster Child
The Night She Died
The Perfect Guests
The Girl Who Left
The Hiking Trip
The Summer Girl

Smoke
AND
MURDERS

J.L. BLACKHURST

ONE PLACE. MANY STORIES

This novel is entirely a work of fiction. The names, characters and incidents portrayed in it are the work of the author's imagination. Any resemblance to actual persons, living or dead, events or localities is entirely coincidental.

HQ
An imprint of HarperCollins*Publishers* Ltd
1 London Bridge Street
London SE1 9GF

www.harpercollins.co.uk

HarperCollins*Publishers*
Macken House, 39/40 Mayor Street Upper,
Dublin 1, D01 C9W8, Ireland

This edition 2024

1
First published in Great Britain by
HQ, an imprint of HarperCollins*Publishers* Ltd 2024

Copyright © Jenny Blackhurst 2024

Jenny Blackhurst asserts the moral right to be
identified as the author of this work.
A catalogue record for this book is
available from the British Library.

ISBN: 9780008567279

This book contains FSC™ certified paper and other controlled
sources to ensure responsible forest management.

For more information visit: www.harpercollins.co.uk/green

This book is set in 10.7/15.5 pt. Sabon by Type-it AS, Norway

Printed and Bound in the UK using 100% Renewable Electricity at
CPI Group (UK) Ltd, Croydon, CR0 4YY

To my mother-in-law, Jen Blackhurst.
Thank you for donating me your son and your name, and
thank you for everything else you do for us xxx

Chapter One

Members of the Lewes Bonfire Council would say afterwards that the event would have been a huge success that year, if it hadn't been for the dead body.

By 7.30 p.m. on Tuesday 5 November, thousands of people milled around the narrow Lewes High Street clutching plastic beer cups, shifting for the best position along the kerb, being moved out of the closed-off road by attending police. It was a dry night, but bitterly cold, and onlookers watched those who lived above the high-street shops lounging in their bay windows in their pyjamas in pure envy.

Amy Munroe almost hadn't gone this year. She'd been so many times, and each year it got busier and busier as more outsiders found their way in. It didn't matter how early the council closed the roads, or how many of the Airbnb owners claimed to be booked up, people from all over the country descended, parking in inconvenient and thoughtless parking spaces, filling up the pubs and bars so that the people who lived there, people who spent their money there week in and week out, couldn't even enjoy their own traditions. No, Amy had been fully ready to boycott, before Steve had casually mentioned he was going, and that if she wanted to meet him outside the courthouse he'd be there at eight.

It was hard to look sexy when you were wearing a puffy jacket and woolly hat and scarf, but she'd done her hair in light waves and put some make-up on. At thirty-three, Steve was four years older than her, and she'd almost given up hoping that one day he'd stop seeing her as a work colleague and maybe start seeing her as something more. The town wasn't exactly bursting at the seams with eligible bachelors, and Amy had watched as one by one, the boys they'd gone to school with had paired off or gone away to university. Not Steve, though, he never seemed particularly interested in women. Not in an 'interested in men instead' kind of way, he just hadn't spent their shifts at Waitrose boasting about all of his conquests like the others had. He was different.

Even in the crowds of tourists, Amy had seen plenty of people she knew. Her old headmaster had been stumbling out of the pub as they battened down the hatches – they'd open for locals later but not until things in the high street had calmed down. Her sister had waved at her from across the street but hadn't joined her – thank God. That was the last thing she wanted; Kara had been stealing her boyfriends since they were teenagers. Tim who ran the fruit and veg stall at the market had told her she looked 'nice' tonight, and the woman who ran one of the gift shops had pushed past her in a right old rush, looking like she'd rather be anywhere else. Everyone knew that if you didn't want to be caught in the crowd on bonfire night, you closed up early and got the hell out of Dodge. Some even boarded up windows. Amy didn't blame the woman – Truly, her name was – for not wanting to be in the middle of all of this, though. If it hadn't been for Steve . . .

'Wotcha,' he said as Amy shuffled her way through the crowd towards him. She'd spotted him straight away, he was well over six foot and solid looking, so tended to stand out. She grinned at him and gestured her head around.

'Madder than normal, this.'

'I know, I don't know why we still bother.' He linked his arm in hers, a gesture he'd done a thousand times but for some reason, tonight, it felt different. Amy felt a shiver that had nothing to do with the cold. It was bloody cold, though.

'Because you're like a big kid on bonfire night,' Amy said, poking his ribs. Steve pretended to fold.

'Behave yourself. Which fire are we going to?'

There were seven bonfire societies in Lewes – six marching on the fifth itself – which is why it had been named the 'bonfire capital of the world'. It was, far and beyond, the most electrifying, and the most awe-inspiring sight that had to be seen to be believed. Once a year the town gave itself over to a semi-lawless tradition that dated back to the early nineteenth century, with torch-lit processions through the streets to honour the seventeen Lewes protestant martyrs burned at the stake in the 1500s. Effigies – called 'tableaux' or 'tabs' by the locals – of controversial political figures were paraded through the town before being burned as well as the traditional Guy Fawkes on the bonfires. The tabs were once of Pope John Paul but these days they were more likely to be the prime minister of the day, although 'No Popery' signs were still carried by the renegade Cliffe Bonfire Society. The effigies were always social issues statements, whether it be a protest against fracking, or war, or even the potholes in the county roads. Burning barrels were dragged through the streets then thrown in the Ouse to remember the clashes of the Bonfire Boys with local magistrate J.P. Whitfield on Cliffe Bridge. Thousands of people attended every year, with the Lewes Bonfire website warning that attendance constitutes *volenti non fit injuria* – spectators accepted the risks of injury.

After the processions through the town, people would make their way to one of the sites to warm themselves by the bonfires and continue the festivities. Amy's favourite society was Cliffe. She wasn't a member – it was a lot of hard work year round to be a bonfire society member, fundraising and a lot of drinking – but she always bought tickets to their fire site, despite being able to see the fireworks from her bedroom window. Cliffe were the rebels, the historical outcast society. Everyone knew they were a law unto themselves. They marched alone, with banners that proclaimed 'Good Old Cliffe' and 'No Popery' in black-and-white-striped smugglers' and Vikings' costumes. Cliffe knew how to put on a show.

'You know where we're going. I heard a rumour they're burning Trump this year.'

'Yeah, all right. Who's the big kid now?'

Amy smiled and as darkness blanketed them she allowed herself to fall into the carnival atmosphere of the bonfire. The shrieks of onlookers as firecrackers landed at the feet of those closest to the edge, so loud you could feel it in your teeth. By the third time around, the air was so thick with smoke that the banners and colourful costumes could barely be seen. Burning torches were tossed to the side of the road, creating mini bonfires along the kerbs that onlookers used to warm their hands until they were scooped up by the members of the procession wearing flameproof gloves.

When the procession was over the crowds moved like a tidal wave towards the top of the high street, then began to disperse to their chosen bonfire – along the way, the odd local dipping almost unseen into the pubs whose doors were locked to all but those whose faces were familiar.

The effigy of Donald Trump had been made bigger and better this year. They had made the first Trump in 2016 for the elections, and it had been such a popular choice, and much less likely to get the society in trouble (as the planned effigy of Alex Salmond almost had), that they had brought his likeness back for an encore. He had been dragged through the street on a pantomime horse and was now being unceremoniously hauled onto the top of the pyre as flaming torches were thrust into the bottom. The fire took hold and the pile of wood began to burn.

'Just popping to the loo.' Steve leaned into her and shouted over the noise of the crowd as Trump's feet began to burn. Amy gave a small cheer as one of his legs fell off into the flames, and the orange tongues licked at the papier-mâché body. Any minute now there would be a mini explosion from inside the effigy to mark the beginning of the firework display.

'Okay,' she shouted back, hoping he wouldn't be too long. God, she had it bad. Did he feel the same? Men could be so hard to read sometimes.

The explosion made everyone jump, as it did every year. Good-natured squeals and shouts rose up from the crowd. Amy joined in, cheering as Trump's body caved in from the flames entirely, and fire began to engulf his head. Instead of folding in effortlessly as the effigies usually did, however, it began to sway from side to side, almost as if it were too heavy now that the body was all but gone. Time seemed to slow down, the squeals turned to screams and it took her a moment to realize that the head of the effigy had toppled from the peak of the fire and was starting to roll now, engulfed in flames, towards where she and several others were standing. She screamed, frozen in shock, everything happening too fast for her brain to tell her to move. She felt a rough hand grab her am and yank her to one side as the flaming orange-topped head of Donald Trump landed inches from her feet.

Steve pulled Amy into his chest, and she felt his coat sticky with the beer he had spilled down himself while attempting his daring rescue. Adrenaline still surging through her, she watched as the crowd parted for two men with fire extinguishers spraying foam at the head even before they had reached her. People watched in fascination, squealing and laughing in the relief that there had been no casualties, ready to continue the party.

Then the fire went out and the firefighters' foam fizzled away to reveal the blackened, burned human head that had been inside, and the screams began again.

Chapter Two

The four councillors who had missed the meeting of Lewes and Eastbourne District Council the week before the bonfire, would forever lament being otherwise engaged. One of them had a hen do for someone she barely even knew, another had a sick cat. A third councillor had taken one look at the blustery November rain and stayed in front of the fire, and the fourth had got the date wrong entirely. It was this person who was most aggrieved – she had attended every single boring meeting for the last five years and the one that she wrote on her 'Raining Cats and Dogs' wall calendar incorrectly was the one where Rupert Millington's life was threatened.

The first forty-seven minutes of the meeting were as snooze-worthy as every other before it. Twelve councillors sat in a semi-circle, facing the twenty or so Lewesians who everyone knew had turned up for one reason only – because a motion had been tabled to cancel the Lewes bonfire procession starting from the following year. Again.

At minute forty-eight, Councillor Rupert Millington stood

up and cleared his throat, despite there being no need for him to do either – his audience was captive enough. They had come prepared for this. Battle lines had been drawn in previous years and representatives of six bonfire societies already knew what they were against – it was a fight they had been winning for two hundred years.

Rupert Millington was the epitome of the District Council: his teeth as white as his tailored shirt, a sharp navy suit and tie and a perma-tan that was trying to say 'distinguished older man' but instead squeaked 'used car salesperson'. He had a long history of taking up controversial viewpoints that he knew would garner publicity and support. One could say that Rupert's main advantage lay in his distinct lack of fear of 'cancellation'. *No one gets cancelled*, he was fond of saying to his wife. *They just gain a different kind of supporter.*

'Once again,' he said, his loud, RP accent ringing out across the room, 'Lewes finds itself in the spotlight for all of the wrong reasons.' A ripple of mutters flowed like a Mexican wave over the members of the public. Rupert was not deterred. Rupert was never deterred. 'I can *hardly bring myself* to read some of the headlines this week regarding the behaviour of members of certain bonfire societies—'

'Those issues have been dealt with,' a voice from the public called out. 'In a meeting with yourself, I might add.'

Rupert shook his head. 'While I appreciate the effort that the chair of Borough Bonfire Society has gone to to address the issues, it doesn't mitigate the fact that these things happen year on year on year. Society has simply moved on from dressing up as Zulus and burning papal images, and while I'm a huge believer of free speech, we have our reputation to think of.'

8

'Like I said—'

'You'll have your chance to speak, Fred,' Jeremy Finch, head of the council cut in. He looked at Rupert. 'Carry on, Councillor Millington.'

Rupert gave Finch a grateful smile and cleared his throat for effect once more. 'Thank you, Jeremy. As I was saying, these types of celebrations are outdated, and cost the council thousands in extra policing for the road closures and in keeping the peace on the night. Not to mention the amount of calls councillors have to take about various issues surrounding contentious costumes, and complaints about not being able to drive in and out of their own town. The whole thing is a massive burden on the town of Lewes and I happen to know a lot of locals feel the same.'

'Where are they, then?' A woman was on her feet, motioning around her. She was tall with dark curls, voluminous around her head like a modern-day Medusa. She wore baggy sage-green dungarees, cuffed at the ankles, and despite the coldness of the evening she had on only a thin denim jacket. 'All these supporters you have?'

'Mrs Donovan, you can speak when Mr Millington is finished.'

'Oh shut up, Finch, if we wait for Millington to finish we'll all be too old to march anyway. I'd like to see this "local" support our esteemed councillor has, because every Lewesian I've spoken to—'

'Lewesian?' Rupert scoffed, cutting the woman off. 'That's rich, coming from a . . .' He stopped short.

'Coming from a what?' the woman prompted, her voice rising to practically a squeal. 'From. A. WHAT?'

Millington's face coloured but he was a master of the quick recovery.

'From an outsider,' he hissed.

The woman scoffed. 'That's not what you were going to say, though, was it, Rupert? And as you well know, I'm not an outsider. My family goes back generations in Lewes, my—'

'Yes, yes, so you claim,' Rupert shot back, his eyebrows raised. 'But you pop up out of nowhere, with your quack medicine and your fortune telling and no proof that you were ever related to Aubrey Taylor and—'

The woman pointed a sharp, blood-red nail at Rupert. 'How dare you.' Her voice was low but still resonated across the room. 'How dare you! *Invechit bakri darhija sose koga parni . . . invechit bakri darhija—*'

Rupert's previously pink face paled. 'What are you doing?' He looked around wildly. 'What is she saying? Can anyone understand her? Make her stop! Tell her to stop!'

The room broke out into a cacophony of noise but no one made a move to stop the woman, her voice getting louder over the crowd as she continued her chant. '*Invechit bakri darhija sose koga parni . . . invechit bakri . . .*'

Rupert stumbled backwards as though the words were physically pushing him. One of the other councillors stood up and rushed towards the woman. 'Now come on, Mrs Donovan, there's no need for this kind of behaviour, I think that's enough for this evening.'

The woman stopped chanting. 'Your days are numbered on this council, Mr Millington, you mark my words!' she hissed, her finger jabbing in his direction once again. Rupert flinched with each jab. 'You mark my words!' She shrugged away the councillor who was trying to intervene. 'Get your bloody hands off me, Finch, I'm leaving.' She swung back to face Rupert Millington once again. 'You watch your back, Millington, or you'll be the one on the bonfire. Remember, remember, Mr Millington. Gunpowder, *treason* and plot.'

Chapter Three

DI Geoff Walker leaned over the computer and pressed 'pause'. The woman on the screen froze, her face contorted in a horrifying grimace. He sat back on the table, attempting the 'casual but still in authority' look. Standing at the back watching, DS Tess Fox thought that in his cheap grey suit he gave off more of a 'substitute teacher trying to be *down with the kids*' vibe.

'This was sent to us this morning by a member of the public. It's a recording of the Lewes and Eastbourne District Council meeting, held on Friday 1 November. This captures the last known sighting of Councillor Rupert Millington, now believed to be the skeletal remains recovered from last night's bonfire fiasco. We're treating this as a murder, for obvious reasons. It's unlikely our victim put himself on top of the bonfire.'

'Who's the woman threatening him?' someone else asked. DI Walker checked a Post-it on his clipboard.

'We don't get to see her face because the person taking the video was in the row behind her but I'm told her name is Donovan. Local resident. Says here that she and Mr Millington had a bit of previous; a couple of low-level reports from the wife making complaints about her turning up at their house to give him grief. I went round to the address we were given for her as soon as we got this, but she wasn't there. I left a card saying we wanted to speak to her, but I'll keep trying. Given the nature of the threat and how close it happened to the murder, she's definitely a person of interest.'

'You think she'd really kill him over him wanting the procession stopped?'

Tess looked at who'd spoken, a young DC she didn't recognize. Couldn't be particularly local – anyone who had lived in Sussex for a while knew how heated things could get over the bonfire night celebrations. Pun intended. If it had been two of the big burly men scrapping over the procession she might easily believe it could have been a fist fight gone too far, ending in manslaughter, perhaps. But Tess couldn't see this woman hauling Millington's body onto a bonfire without help.

'. . . over less,' Walker was saying, and Tess realized she'd been tuning him out as usual. She really was going to have to learn to pay attention to him now that he was her boss. 'There are at least thirty people in that room, I want a statement from each of them attesting to the threats. Barnes, Judson, you can get a list of names from the council minutes.'

The two officers nodded. Walker closed the laptop and directed their attention back to the board.

'So. Rupert Millington, local councillor, running for member of parliament for the Conservative Party, was last seen at this meeting. His wife, Leodora, was staying with a friend on the night of the council meeting, and didn't return until the following evening. She went to bed assuming that

Rupert would be home late; apparently, if he came home too late or too drunk he would sleep in the spare room. So it wasn't until the following morning when she discovered that he hadn't returned that she started to worry. She reported him missing on Sunday the third. As Mr Millington was an adult, and not known to be vulnerable, we filed a report and began contacting hospitals, got a list of known acquaintances, et cetera, but it wasn't exactly the manhunt of the year, I'll admit. It being a Sunday, and a couple of days before bonfire night didn't help.'

Tess had to stop herself from rolling her eyes. Why was Walker going over what they all already knew about Rupert Millington's disappearance? Why were they standing around watching home movies of council meetings when there was a murder investigation to be getting on with? Not for the first time, Tess had to fight to keep the disdain for her senior officer off her face. It had been six months since Walker had been promoted over her and her tongue was showing signs of wear and tear from the constant biting.

'Do we know for certain this bonfire victim is him?' one of the DCs asked.

Walker shook his head. 'Definitely not. But it has raised a considerable amount of press since the discovery last night, and I would assume that if Millington could just come home with his tail between his legs smelling of perfume, then at this point he probably would. We're waiting on tests, of course visual identification is . . . unavailable.'

'Any other suspects?'

Walker shook his head. 'Like I say, Millington wasn't a high-risk missing person until this body showed up in the bonfire last night. We're upping his missing persons inquiry, and we're also investigating the possible murder of our John Doe, but as far as the press are concerned, they are separate cases at this moment in time. Johnson, speak to whoever made this video,' Walker said, standing up to indicate the briefing was over. 'I want names and statements from everyone who was at that meeting. Richardson, I've got the chair of this Cliffe Bonfire Society coming in the next hour. Get the names of everyone in the society and prioritise the volunteers who worked on the Trump tab. If they weren't personally responsible they might at least know how a body got inside the bloody thing without anyone noticing.'

Richardson nodded. 'Yes, sir.'

'Burton, you can come with me back to the fire site. I need to put some pressure on the fire marshal to release the scene for forensics, not that there will be much that wasn't already burned up or washed away.'

Burton nodded. Tess zoned out as Walker gave out the important jobs to everyone around her. God, she hated that man. Ever since he'd won the promotion he'd been lording it over her, giving her the most menial tasks he could find. PC Heath had gone back to the beat, despite all the promise he had shown, and Fahra was on a six-week training course in Coventry. Now she and Jerome were all that remained of their little gang and they were probably going to be stuck making the coffee. Or worse, door-to-door.

'Fox, Morgan.'

She started at the sound of their names. 'Sir?' she said, the word stinging her tongue. Walker gave a satisfied smirk and she knew that despite herself she'd sounded hopeful.

'Door-to-door.'

Chapter Four

That evening, in the sweltering Cairo humidity, Sarah Jacobs sat at the hotel bar, sipping on her third cocktail. Around her, wealthy Americans knocked back whisky chasers, tipping ten- and twenty-dollar bills like they had printing presses in their five-star hotel rooms, and laughing loudly at one another's unfunny jokes.

'Maybe I'll just move here,' she said to her sister who sat at the bar next to her. 'The place is loaded with marks. I could run a few simple tricks in here and walk away with a week's wages.'

Julia flicked her huge dark eyes around the tables and gave a shrug. 'It would be quicker to steal from them than it would be to trick them,' she said. 'Look at the way they leave everything on the tables: phones, wallets, designer jackets slung over chairs.'

'I never steal when I can con,' Sarah argued. 'It's so much more satisfying when someone hands their money to you.' It basically wasn't even stealing, especially on short cons which purely relied on her knowing the odds of her street games better than her mark, and playing to them. The same as a bookie's, really.

'I tell you what,' Julia said, her eyes flashing conspiratorially. 'You try some of your cute short cons, and I'll go on the take, and we'll see who can get the most together in a couple of hours.'

Sarah's first instinct was to tell her sister no. They were in Cairo to search for the mother Sarah had believed almost her whole life to be dead, and getting arrested in a foreign country was not on the agenda. The first, and undoubtedly biggest reason being that Julia Jacobs was currently on the run for murder. Not one murder, in fact, but three. The first two victims being men who had attacked Sarah fifteen years ago, the last victim being the three women's shared father, Frank Jacobs, although Julia swore that Frank's murder had been a mistake. Tess couldn't understand how Sarah could travel the world with Julia at her side knowing she was responsible for the death of their father. But then Tess wouldn't, would she? *Her* mother was still alive. She wasn't an orphan. If there was even the smallest chance that Julia was telling the truth about their mum, Lily, still being alive, then Sarah had to put her anger to one side until they found her. She didn't want to think about what would happen after that.

'I don't know,' Sarah said, shaking her head. But *I don't know* wasn't the same as no, and they both knew it. The thing was, as much as Sarah loved and respected Tess and her straight-and-narrow ways, Sarah and Julia shared the same moral compass. Well, almost – Sarah's was kind of broken and

Julia's had been flung in the sea a long time ago – but they both needed the thrill of breaking the rules.

'Come on, I'm bored,' Julia whinged. 'And we're all dressed up. May as well make a night of it.'

She was right, they had both made an effort this evening. Though with her huge dark eyes and pixie face, slender curves that looked more comfortable in evening dresses than in pyjamas, Julia would still look beautiful in a bin bag. Sarah knew she looked okay, but next to Julia she still felt like one of Cinderella's ugly sisters.

'Okay, fine.' Sarah picked up her handbag. 'Two hours. We'll have to go to the other hotels in the resort, I can't con money from someone if you've just stolen their wallet. I'll meet you back here at the poolside bar; it's closed now and there are a couple of tables around the back where we won't be seen. Don't get caught. Egypt is not somewhere you want to spend time in prison, and Tess isn't here to fix anything for us.'

Julia scowled at the mention of her half-sister. Tess was a police officer, the officer in charge of finding Julia and putting her behind bars for murder. It was a skewed family dynamic, to say the least.

She got to her feet and clapped her hands together. 'Yay! I was starting to think we were going straight,' she said, a little smile on her face.

'Julia, you stole everything you're wearing,' Sarah said, her tone exasperated. 'I could tie you to a six-foot ruler for the rest of your life and you still wouldn't be straight.'

'Three, two, one, go!' Julia waved and darted off. Sarah tutted and rolled her eyes. She should have said no. Tess would have said no. Still, it would be a chance to show Julia that Sarah was just as clever as she was.

'Oh, does that mean I've won?' Sarah pretended to look surprised as the rest of the table scowled and handed over their money. A short, thin man with a full suit on, despite the heat, nursing a non-alcoholic-looking drink, narrowed his eyes at her in suspicion and she knew it was time to move on – the airhead hustle only got you so far. In the last hour, she'd enjoyed herself with some cute little-odds bets, the penny on the cigarette trick and some bumbles with the dice she always kept in her purse. She'd made a couple of hundred dollars, then a hundred sterling on that last poker game, but nothing near the amount that Julia would have been able to rack up in the same timeframe. Short cons were fun, long cons were lucrative, but out-and-out stealing was probably always going to come out on top. Sarah wasn't above lifting the odd wallet or piece of jewellery – she had years of practice and had learned from the best – but it was usually done as part of a con, to get hold of an ID card for a building, or to become a woman's new best friend by returning her 'lost' bracelet. She was no longer Aladdin, needing to steal to eat, her father's investments had made sure of that.

Back at her hotel bar she pulled another couple of three card montes – her dad's favourite trick – then ordered six drinks. She took them over to the closed-off pool bar and found a place to sit and wait for Julia. She had thirty minutes to waste so she pulled out a book and took advantage of the silence.

'You're finished early, too?' Julia's voice came from behind her, ten minutes before their two hours was up. Sarah put down her book as her sister walked up to the table and placed a stack of notes, three watches and a couple of necklaces in front of her. Sarah whistled.

'Impressive,' she said. 'Maybe a thousand there? Not including the fencibles which we can't keep, by the way.'

'I found a man who will buy them for two hundred,' Julia said. 'We actually tried to steal the watch at the same time – funny story. So, how much did your card and dice tricks pull in?'

Sarah frowned. 'Just three fifty.' She shrugged. 'I knew I wasn't going to win so I slacked off a little early. I got us drinks – the bar was about to close so I got three each.'

Julia looked at the three pints and the three whiskies and frowned. 'Are you going to drink all three of those?' she said, gesturing to the pints. 'We'll be here all night.'

'Don't worry,' Sarah said. 'I'm a really fast drinker.'

Julia scoffed. 'Three pints of beer? An hour at least. I'm tired.'

Sarah sat up straight. 'I tell you what,' she said. 'I bet I'll have finished my three pints before you're finished your three whiskies.'

Julia laughed. 'Don't be ridiculous.'

'Honestly!' Sarah said. 'I bet I will. If I'm wrong you can have everything I made tonight.'

Julia grinned. 'Fine. And if you can't, you can have everything I made.'

'But you're not allowed to touch my glasses,' Sarah warned. 'No moving them.'

Julia swept a hand impatiently. 'Yes, yes, I'm not going to touch your glasses.'

'Fine.' Sarah picked up her first pint and began to down it. Julia picked up her whisky and sipped, her eyebrows raised in amusement as Sarah gulped noisily. When she had finished her pint, and Julia had finished her first whisky Sarah looked green.

'Oh God, that's disgusting,' Sarah said, screwing up her face. 'I don't remember beer tasting that bad.'

'Two more to go,' Julia smirked, picking up her second glass and taking a gulp. Sarah smiled, turned her empty pint glass upside down and placed it over Julia's last whisky tumbler. Julia put down her drink and frowned. 'What are you doing?'

Sarah picked up her second pint and began to drink at a leisurely pace. She took a mouthful then wiped the foam from her lip. Julia drank her second whisky and went to remove Sarah's glass to drink her third.

'Um, I don't think so,' Sarah said, wagging her finger. 'You're not allowed to touch my glass, remember?'

Julia's mouth dropped open. Sarah reached over the table and picked up her sister's takings for the night and added them to her pile. She glanced at the watch. 'And by my reckoning I still have three minutes left.'

She took another sip of her drink. 'And that, dear sister, is how you make more from grifting than from stealing.'

Chapter Five

Tess dragged the semi-conscious man through the door, down the poky hallway and deposited him half on, half off the battered old sofa. She cringed at the stench of alcohol and body odour that immediately filled the living area of her flat and prayed to any of the thousand gods that he wouldn't vomit on her carpet. She surveyed him lying there, his floppy black hair hung over his face and a bruise under his eye that was beginning to flower. He was a mess. After a fruitless day of door knocking, this was the very last thing she needed.

'Wes?' She shook the man lightly but there was no response. 'Wes?'

Nothing.

Tess took the few steps from her living room into what was supposed to pass for a kitchen and poured a glass of water. What the hell was she meant to do with him? Wes Carter was not supposed to be her problem. She pulled her phone out of her back pocket and pressed call on the last number dialled. The dial tone was insistent but there was no answer. She carried the glass of water into the living room and threw it at Wes's face.

He jumped up like he'd been hit with a bullet.

'Jesus!' Wes shouted, wiping the cold water from his eyes. 'What was that for?'

'Sorry, I slipped.'

Wes scowled. 'Like hell you did.' He looked around. 'Where am I?'

'Welcome to my humble abode.' Tess gestured around.

'I'd say humble is an understatement,' Wes muttered, his eyes following her gesture.

'Ten seconds ago, you were passed out on my sofa, now you're critiquing my interior design?' Tess went back to the kitchen to get more water. Wes saw the glass and flinched.

'Don't worry, this one's to drink.' She handed him the glass and he downed it greedily.

'Thanks. How did I get here?'

Tess took a seat across from him. 'Bar tender called me. Tim, is it? Good hair, boxer's nose?'

'Et tu, Tim?' Wes muttered. 'Bloody Judas.'

'What, you'd have preferred he call the actual police?' Tess asked. 'You were so drunk I had to get my neighbour to help me get you out of the car and drag you up here. God knows what you might have let slip if a real police officer had turned up.' Wes hung his head. She guessed not.

'How did Tim know to call you?' he asked, his tone sulky.

'Because last time he called the actual police, Mac called me to deal with it. I thought I'd give Tim my number and told him to call me if you caused any more trouble. What the hell are you playing at, Wes? You told me you'd cut it out. You promised.'

Wes looked up at her through his long lashes, his blue eyes full of faux remorse. 'I'm sorry, Tess.'

'You are not. Do you have any idea how much trouble I could get in for covering for you? Let alone if my boss found out who you work for . . .'

'Who I used to work for,' Wes corrected, the pain clear on his face. And that was what this was all about, of course. Frank Jacobs. Specifically his death. Tess felt her temper soften. Wes had taken Frank's death hard. Tess sighed.

'You work for Sarah,' Tess reminded him. 'Or you did last time I checked.'

'And when was the last time you heard from our fearless leader?' Wes asked, a little louder than he usually would, the alcohol making him bullish. He had a scowl on his handsome face. Tess hated seeing him like this. Wes was usually the nicest guy you could ever hope to meet. Quiet but funny, super intelligent and most of all, loyal. In the short time Tess had known him she'd come to like him a lot. She'd also come to witness his sad decline after the death of the man he had always thought of as a surrogate father. Her own father, in fact, except Wes had had a far longer and less turbulent relationship with the late Frank Jacobs.

'She text me yesterday,' Tess replied, recalling the photo Sarah had sent her, pretending to hold up a pyramid. Had it irritated her that Sarah – who was supposed to be on a mission to find her mother – was messing around taking silly pictures with their murder suspect while she, Tess, was left behind to explain to her superiors how that suspect had got away under her very nose? Yes, of course it had.

'Enjoying Rome, is she?'

'Egypt, actually.' Wes raised an eyebrow.

'Don't try and pretend you actually approve of what she's doing. Or who she's doing it with,' he added. Tess turned away so she wouldn't have to lie to his face.

'She's doing what she has to do,' she said. 'And I wasn't about to stop her. She lost her dad, too, remember. If there's the slightest chance that Julia is telling the truth—'

'Which there isn't.'

'And Lily is still alive—'

'Which she's not—'

'Then I certainly don't blame Sarah for wanting to find her.'

'Which she won't,' Wes finished.

Tess sighed. What could she say when she believed the same herself? That Julia Jacobs – Sarah's sister and Tess's half-sister – was a liar and a psychopath who was leading Sarah on a wild goose chase around the world to find a mother who most likely died when Sarah was three, just like her father had said.

'She'll come back, Wes,' she said, her voice gentle. 'And when she does she's going to need her family around her. Sober.'

It was Wes's turn to sigh. 'I know,' he said, closing his eyes and lying back against the sofa. 'I just kind of needed her here myself.'

She waited until he was snoring gently then dialled the number once again. This time a gruff voice answered. 'Tess? Is Wes with you?'

'He's here, Mac,' Tess replied. 'Sleeping off a session on my sofa.'

There was a muttered curse at the other end of the phone. 'Sorry about that – I know you can't be involving yourself with us. I'll come and get him now.'

'Leave him until morning,' Tess said, looking down at the young man. 'He's struggling, Mac. First Frank, now Sarah. He's adrift.'

'The whole crew is adrift,' Mac admitted. 'I know I shouldn't be telling you this but things are falling apart without either of them to direct us. It feels like the heart of the family has been torn out, and instead of sticking around to hold us together, she's gone off chasing ghosts.'

'You think Lillian Dowse really is dead, then?' Tess had never asked Mac how much he knew about Sarah's mum; she'd barely had any contact with the crew since she'd let Julia and Sarah go.

There was silence on the other end. Mac knew far more than he would ever tell.

'She needs to come home,' he repeated.

'Then tell her,' Tess urged. 'Call her and ask her to come home. She needs to know how bad it's getting, otherwise she'll have no business to come home to.'

There was silence on the other end. 'I'd have thought that was what you wanted,' Mac said at last. Tess bit her lip.

'It should be,' she admitted. 'I should want nothing more than to watch Frank Jacobs's criminal empire crumble.'

'But you don't.' It wasn't a question. Tess frowned.

'No,' she said. 'I don't. Frank was my father, Sarah is still my sister. I don't want to see her lose everything.'

A pause. 'You did a good thing, letting her go, you know?'

Tess's heart sped up at the words. They had never discussed the fact that she had allowed a killer to escape, that she'd trusted a con artist to bring Julia back to justice once she had the information she needed. It certainly hadn't been the right thing for her, for her career. The promotion she had worked so hard for had gone to someone else, and she woke up every morning with the dread inside her chest that Julia might have killed someone else. If just one more body turned up after Tess had had the chance to arrest her, then the blood would be on Tess's hands.

'A temporary stay of execution,' Tess reminded him. 'When they get back she's mine.'

'I didn't mean Julia,' Mac said quietly. 'I know how hard it was for you to let Sarah go when she'd just come back into your life.'

Tess tried to scoff but it came out more like a strangled noise. 'Good riddance. That woman is a menace.'

She heard Mac chuckle. 'Well, there's something we can agree on. I'll come and get the boy in the morning. Thanks again, Tess.'

'You're welcome,' she said, but he was already gone.

Tess pulled a spare blanket from the drawer under her bed, took it to where Wes was snoring less gently now, and tossed it over him. She tucked it in around the edges and hoped Sarah made it back soon.

She was just about to climb into her own bed and try to salvage what was left of the night when her phone rang. She debated leaving it – she wasn't the boss anymore, not even acting, and she wasn't on call – if she didn't answer, the team would have to try someone else. She was probably only getting the call because Jerome had ignored it.

Except there was no way she was going to leave it and her DI knew that. Despite it not being her shift. She muttered a curse then put on her work voice.

'DS Fox,' she said, emphasising the 'DS'. She resisted adding 'on her night off'.

'Fox, you're needed at Lewes station.'

Tess bristled. 'I think there's been a mistake, sir,' she said, as calmly as she could muster, and without the slightest hint of caustic emphasis on the 'sir'. 'I'm not on duty tonight. I think it's DS Morgan, actually.'

'I know that,' came the sharp reply. 'But we've located that Donovan lady from the council meeting and she says she's not talking to anyone but you.'

Tess sighed. 'Geoff—'

'She's also the only person of interest in a murder inquiry. But if you're currently warming someone's bed . . .'

Tess inhaled sharply through her nose. How this misogynistic, useless sack of – one, two, three . . . She wanted to tell him to shove it but she knew she wouldn't. It wasn't every day a person of interest in a murder asked for her by name, especially as the only murderer she knew on a first name basis was currently out of the country. She was intrigued, as DI Geoff Walker had known she would be.

'No, sir,' she said, through gritted teeth. 'I'll be right there.'

'Right there' was still an hour from Chichester to Lewes, even in the middle of the night. Lewes Police Station, unassuming from the outside, was generally used as the headquarters for the Sussex and Surrey Major Crimes Team. Samantha Kirk looked up from the booking desk as Tess entered the near-empty station. Sam smiled. 'Hey, Tess.'

'Hey. Geoff called, said you had someone asking for me?'

Sam raised her thick black eyebrows. 'Not just anyone, Tess, it's that witch woman. The one who put the curse on Rupert Millington before he went missing. One of those pagans or what have you.'

Tess rolled her eyes. She was too tired for this shit. 'I don't believe in curses, Sam. Geoff said she asked for me by name?'

'Yeah, said she wanted to speak to you or she wouldn't say anything.'

Tess shook her head. She was furious that Walker was shoving this one onto her. It was bad enough that she was still known around the station as 'Sheila Holmes', and that she had endured months of invisible man jokes all thanks to the three impossible murders she'd been in charge of as acting DI earlier in the year – now she was expected to deal with a suspect accused of witchcraft?

'She's not under arrest, right?' Tess said, trying to sound neither impatient nor desperate. 'I'm just here to take a statement, Geoff said. What's her name again?'

Sam checked her notes. 'We've got Donovan here,' she said frowning. 'But there's a note to tell you she used to go by Dowse. Am I saying that right? Lily Dowse.'

Chapter Six

The impossibility of that name hadn't faded as Tess made her way down the corridor to the interview room where her father's ex-wife, Tess's *stepmother*, Lily Dowse was waiting. It had taken every ounce of the Jacobs blood running through her veins to maintain a poker face when Sam had said the name, not to look around for the hidden cameras or ask if Jerome had set this up. Because, of course, the woman that Tess's half-sister was in Egypt looking for was in her station, asking for her by name. Suspected of murder.

Tess paused outside the interview room, wondering what the hell she was going to say to the woman inside. She had so many questions for the infamous Lily Dowse, and few had anything to do with the murder of Rupert Millington.

Tess had only ever seen one picture of Sarah's mother, taken many, many years ago, and yet she recognized her the moment the door swung open.

Lily was sitting in the chair facing the door, staring straight at Tess. Her long brown hair had a thick streak of white running from root to tip, with a heavy fringe framing huge dark eyes. Julia's eyes. She was wearing a floor-length forest-green dress, covered by a long, tatty grey cardigan that she had pulled tight across her chest. Around her neck hung an assortment of brightly coloured crystals and pendants, rings adorned her fingers. She was quite beautiful. The room smelled of incense.

Tess took a seat opposite Lily, and for a moment, neither spoke. The two women didn't know one another, but between them sat a lifetime of history.

Lily was the first to speak. 'So you're Frank's other daughter.'

It hadn't occurred to Tess that Lily might feel hostile towards *her*. Tess was born before Frank and Lily had met. She was surprised Lily even knew about her – Tess had tracked down Frank Jacobs a long time after Lily had died, or as was clear now, gone missing.

'And you're Sarah's mum,' Tess said, loading as much disapproval as she could into those words. Lily had the decency to look ashamed. Sarah had believed her mum dead from the age of three until just a few months ago. How could a mother do that?

'I know what you must think of me,' Lily said, her voice quiet. 'To abandon my daughter. It was inexcusable.'

'It doesn't matter what I think of you. I'm here to take your statement about what happened between yourself and Rupert Millington at the council meeting on Friday the first of November. You and I don't have anything else to discuss. That's between you, Sarah and Julia.'

Lily's eyes widened.

'What do you know about Julia?' she asked. 'Does Sarah know about her? How is Sarah?'

'We know barely anything about Julia, thanks to your secrets and lies. In the space of two months, Sarah found out she had a sister, lost her father, then found out that her mother was alive and a pathological liar. It's fair to say she's a tad unsettled.'

'At least she found you again,' Lily said. She twisted the ring on her middle finger. 'You're good for her, Tess. She needs you.'

'You don't know me,' Tess said, stabbing a finger at Lily. She could feel anger rising inside her now, anger on behalf of Sarah, and on behalf of their shared father, Frank. 'You don't know anything about me.'

'I know more about you than you think.'

Tess scoffed, sitting back in the uncomfortable chair. 'Oh, is that because you're a psychic? Some kind of witch? You've really got your neighbours fooled, you know. We've got thirty statements swearing you put a curse on Rupert Millington the night he went missing. What exactly were you yelling at him in that meeting?'

Lily shrugged. 'I have no idea. I'm from a Showmen family, we don't speak Romany. I picked up some words from some travellers we met on the road once – I think one of them was "animal", maybe "liar" but there are about thirty words for that depending on where you're from and I probably got it wrong. Point is, I was making it up, shouting whatever I could remember just to scare the racist old bastard. He was more than happy to believe the 'gypsy' woman was putting a curse on him.'

'And it's a coincidence that he ended up dead just days after your fake curse, then, is it?'

Lily raised her eyebrows. 'So it's really him?'

Tess hesitated. This was all so surreal – she'd come to the station to speak to a woman who had threatened a murder victim and come face to face with her stepmother. Did that make a difference? She couldn't assume Lily was any less of a suspect just because she was Sarah's estranged mother.

'The victim's identity hasn't been confirmed yet,' she said, deciding to give nothing away. 'But if it is Millington, you can expect to have some more questions to answer.'

'The police don't believe in curses,' Lily scoffed.

'No, but they believe in threats,' Tess countered. 'And at that council meeting you told Rupert Millington that his days were numbered.'

'*On the council*,' Lily stressed. 'His days *on the council* were numbered. Good Lord. And everyone's seen that video, Tess. As you can imagine, I already have somewhat of a reputation in the village for being a little . . . eccentric.'

'Surely not,' Tess said, dryly.

'Apparently it's all over Facebook, me standing there cursing the political figure who was days later burned on the bonfire. I'm sure you've seen the accusations. Like I'm Guy Fawkes or something. Then I get summoned here to be questioned . . .'

'Guy Fawkes was the one executed for treason,' Tess reminded her. 'I'm not even sure who you'd be in that situation. Parliament? But it does make a nice comparison, given how his body was found.'

'And that's what matters, of course. The story. Never mind the poor, innocent old lady who's going to be hung for a crime she didn't commit.'

'You threatened a man who ended up dead, Lily. We wouldn't

exactly be doing our job if we didn't follow it up, would we? And usually I'd say if you didn't do it you don't have anything to worry about, but this is DI Walker's first murder since his permanent promotion and he's going to want to close such a high-profile case pretty quickly.'

Lily sat back in her seat and just glared.

'I take it you know about Frank,' Tess said, her voice low and gentle. Lily started at the sudden change in subject. She closed her eyes and nodded.

'Yes, I know. And I also know that Sarah didn't kill him – which I'm sure you know too.'

Tess was shocked. Clearly Lily didn't know that her eldest daughter, Julia, had been the one responsible for the murders in Brighton – including Frank's. Tess certainly wasn't going to be the one to tell her. She'd find out soon enough, when Julia was arrested.

'I don't know how you know anything about Sarah whatsoever,' Tess snapped. 'She could be a mass murderer for all you know.'

Lily flinched, but recovered quickly. She'd prepared herself for this confrontation – but was she prepared for Sarah?

'I need to get a statement from you,' Tess said. 'If you're not going to tell me about your involvement with Millington then stop wasting my time, I'm tired.'

'I'm not saying anything on the record.'

'Then why did you drag me all the way down here?'

'To make sure you knew I didn't do it!' Lily exclaimed. 'To ask for your help! As—'

'Don't say it,' Tess warned. 'Don't you dare say it.'

'As family,' Lily finished. Tess let out a breath. 'If you don't help me, they're probably going to arrest me for murder.'

Tess pushed back her chair and stood up.

'Whatever mess you've got yourself into, Lily, you're going to have to find someone else to sort it out for you. In fact, I hope Walker does arrest you. As far as I'm concerned, the sooner you're in prison and away from Sarah the better.'

She turned in the doorway to look back at her stepmother who suddenly looked much less sure of herself. 'So thank you. Because killing Rupert Millington might have been the biggest favour you could have done me.'

As she walked down the corridor, Tess heard her call, 'I didn't kill Rupert Millington.' As she rounded the corner she heard her add, 'But I'm not sorry the bastard's dead.'

Tess stood outside of Lewes Police Station, her phone clamped to her ear, listening to the international dial tone on repeat. Where the hell was Sarah? It was the middle of the night, but Sarah was used to answering her phone at odd hours. She hung up and stared at the useless pile of metal and glass in her hand, willing Sarah to call back.

And what are you going to tell her? a little voice asked. *That you've found her dead mother?*

That was exactly what Tess had been about to tell her, of course, but it dawned on her now that it might not be the best of ideas. For one, Tess didn't just want Sarah to come home. No, she needed Julia to come with her. It was clear now that Julia had been lying to them all along – she never had any intention of helping Sarah find Lily – if she even knew where Lily was. She'd taken Sarah first to Venice, then to Rome, and now they were in Egypt for reasons only the Devil knew.

So if Tess got hold of Sarah to report that she had found Sarah and Julia's mum in Lewes – what exactly would Julia do? She wasn't going to get back on a flight just to be arrested and thrown in prison with said mother. No, she was going to go on the run . . . and running from Egypt would give her a hell of a head start.

Could she trust Sarah not to tell Julia that her mum was in custody? Earlier in the year, they might have been getting to the point where Tess could possibly have said yes. They had begun to build a bond, despite the difference in their vocational choices – and that was a mild way of putting it – and it had almost felt like they were sisters for a while. But now, with Sarah having so much time around Julia . . . she wasn't so sure. Okay, so Julia had killed Frank, and Sarah was bound to hate her for that, but Julia was a world-class psychopath and manipulator – Tess definitely wouldn't put it past her to have convinced Sarah to let her go. Sarah liked to think she was worldly and streetwise, but in reality, most of the time Tess could still see that scared seventeen-year-old girl just yearning for approval.

Maybe, thought Tess, the best thing to do would be to let Sarah and Julia come back in their own time. That way, she could have Julia Jacobs in handcuffs before Sarah had the chance to help her escape custody a second time. What was it Sarah had told her? A grifter had to always be two steps ahead. Well, it was about time they learned that Frank Jacobs's blood ran in *her* veins, too.

Chapter Seven

Tess stood shivering on the side of the street in Chichester. She was waiting for Jerome to pick her up after dropping her car in at the local garage, but he'd called to say he was going to be another half an hour. The guys from the garage had offered for her to wait inside but the fumes from whatever they were using had been giving her a headache.

She tapped away on her phone, checking the day's headlines. The body in the bonfire was obviously front-page news, alongside the disappearance of the local councillor. The papers already had almost as much information on Rupert Millington's life as the police did, it was so readily available these days. They were obviously looking at the disappearance through a political lens, and Tess had to get to the second page to see if Lily Donovan was mentioned. She was skimming the article when she heard the commotion from the end of the street. She looked up to see a group of five or six clowns and a man on stilts walking towards her.

'Join the circus!' one of the clowns was shouting. 'Come and join the circus!'

Tess snorted. Perhaps that's what she should get Sarah to encourage Julia to do – run away with the circus. It would solve most of her problems.

'How about you, love?' one of the clowns said, approaching her. Tess cringed. She was not in the mood for this. 'Fancy joining the circus?'

'No thanks,' she said, looking back down at her phone and hoping the clown would take the hint.

'What's the matter, no talent?'

Tess's head snapped back up. 'Well, that's just bloody rude.'

The clown laughed. The others had moved on down the street but this one had decided to risk their life taunting Tess. It was impossible to tell their gender under the baggy bright red suit, the garish purple, pink, red, blue and yellow wig, and the thick make-up, but Tess thought from the bone structure it was probably a woman.

'Not to worry, we can use you in the lion act,' the clown continued. 'We need bait. Or maybe,' they pressed on before Tess could argue, 'we could shoot you out of a cannon. Want to try my wig? Go on.'

The clown pulled its wig off and long blonde hair spilled over her shoulders. Tess groaned. Without the wig obscuring half of her face, it was quite clear who the irritating clown was. Tess reached into her handbag and pulled out a pack of hand sanitising wipes and Sarah set to wiping off her make-up.

'Thanks, guys!' she called to the other clowns who had been waiting a bit further up the street. 'See you later.'

'Tell me, did you see a bunch of clowns walking around

and decide to commandeer them to irritate me?' Tess asked. 'Or was that entire display a set-up?'

'All a set-up,' Sarah replied. 'Just some colleagues. They love a chance to dress up.'

'Am I going to get back to the station to a dozen reports of pickpocketing clowns?' Tess asked.

Sarah grinned, her face almost totally clean now. 'Probably, yeah.'

'How did you know where I'd be?'

Sarah shrugged. 'We followed you from your house.'

Tess sighed. 'So you came back then?'

'For now. Julia says—'

'Where *is* Julia?' Tess interrupted, as though she expected her half-sister to jump out at her any second.

'What, no "I missed you, Sarah", "Great to see you, Sarah", "How was your trip, Sarah"? Just, "Where's Julia?"'

'Where's Julia, Sarah?' Tess repeated.

'She's not here this precise minute. God, you don't have to look so worried, she doesn't start murdering people as soon as I slip off to the bathroom.'

'That might be funny if she wasn't an actual fucking murderer, Sarah. I knew I shouldn't have left her with you.'

'It must be exhausting to constantly have to second guess all of your life choices. Julia is fine and she hasn't killed a single person while we've been away. I've made her a little board that says DAYS SINCE LAST MURDER and I feel like it's really helping.'

'That last murder you're actually joking about was our dad, Sarah.'

Sarah's face crumpled and Tess regretted her words

immediately. Of course Sarah hadn't forgotten. Her flippancy and jokes were her suit of armour, it was how she had managed to spend the last eight months searching for a mother she thought was dead alongside the woman who killed her father. By pretending that life was a cabaret and if you just had a magic act and a singalong number, it would all be happy ever afters.

'I'm sorry,' Sarah whispered. 'I know what she is, who she is. So why can't I let her go?'

'Hey, come here.' Tess pulled her sister into her arms and Sarah buried her head into her shoulder. They stayed there until Sarah said, 'She thinks we should try Cambodia next. She remembered something Mum said about—'

'Wait, what?'

'What, what?' Sarah looked confused.

'I thought that's why you came back? I thought you knew . . . Sarah, your mum is here. Well, in Lewes. She lives there. She asked for me in the station when she was being questioned.'

Sarah took a step back. 'She what?'

'Yeah, there's been this murder and . . .'

'How long have you known this?'

'Since Thursday. I tried to call you but—'

'Three days? You've known for three days that my mother, who I have been travelling around the world looking for, is alive and living down the road, and all you did was "try to call"?'

'Sarah, I'm sorry. I don't know what to say.'

'You could say that you didn't tell me because you needed me to bring Julia back into the country.'

'Very astute.'

Sarah shook her head. 'In Lewes? For how long? Never mind, what did she say to you? Did she know that Dad had told me she'd died, or did she just not care enough to ask?'

'We were a bit preoccupied with the murder everyone is accusing her of.'

'Murder?'

'Apparently, the people in the village she lives in are accusing her of killing her neighbour, Rupert Millington.'

'The guy who rolled out of Trump?' Sarah asked. Tess nodded.

'That's one eloquent way of putting it. But yes, he was the body found on bonfire night. We just got confirmation back that it was definitely him. He was quite a big deal in Lewes, apparently.'

'Why would Lily kill him?'

Tess noticed that Sarah wasn't questioning whether Lily was capable of killing someone, only her motive for doing it. Was this how their life was now? Living with the knowledge that anyone they knew could be a murderer?

'She was heard threatening him a few days before the bonfire, and . . .'

'And what?' Sarah pushed.

'And apparently, the villagers think she's a witch.'

Sarah's eyes widened and a grin returned to her face. 'She's a grifter!'

Tess laughed. 'Bloody hell, Sarah, wait until you meet her. She's . . . she's pretty much you with some silver streaks.'

That conflicted frown was back on Sarah's face. Another member of her family who had let her down. Tess wanted to shake every single member of the Jacobs family who had contributed to her little sister's pain. But she supposed she'd have to shake herself too. After all, what had she done if not abandon Sarah years ago because of her own pain and guilt? She'd left Sarah to grow up far too fast, without a mum and in a world surrounded by criminals.

'She might have had a good reason for leaving,' Tess tried, feebly.

'What's a good reason for leaving your child?' Sarah asked. 'I was three. What could I have done that was so wrong?'

'Oh, sweetheart.' Tess hugged her again. Even after the death of their father, Tess wasn't used to seeing Sarah so vulnerable. She'd taken off days after the funeral to find her mother, her emotional armour firmly in place. 'You didn't do anything wrong. Whatever happened wasn't your fault. And you don't ever have to see her if you don't want to.'

'Well, that will be difficult,' Sarah said, 'if we're going to solve the murder case where she's the prime suspect.'

Tess shook her head. 'There's no "we" this time. It's not my case. Not my circus, not my monkeys. I'm just on the sidelines. Besides, you're not a police officer – your involvement almost got me fired on my last case.'

'Well, then that's my demand,' Sarah said, with a shrug, as though she'd ignored what Tess had just said completely.

Tess was confused. 'What do you mean, your demand?'

'Well, I've got your murder suspect, haven't I? I was just going to ask for Taylor Swift tickets as my ransom demand, but this is much better. You solve this case and keep Lily out of jail, and I'll hand Julia over, no questions asked.'

Tess let her words sink in. Anger rose in her chest, but she bit back her words. Sarah didn't mean it when she said these things, she was a joker, a grifter. She wasn't really going to renege on their deal.

'The deal was, Julia helped you find Lily, then I arrest Julia,' Tess said. 'There was no mention of Taylor Swift tickets or solving cases.'

'If you're worried you can't figure it out then let me help you,' Sarah said. Tess gritted her teeth.

'I'm not worried I can't figure it out,' she lied. 'It just isn't my case. I'm doing bloody door-to-door. And it wasn't part of the deal.'

'Neither was me helping you arrest Julia,' Sarah pointed out. 'You said you'd let her go, and once I'd found Lily you'd arrest her. So go ahead.'

'Excellent, where is she?' Tess realized as soon as the words were out of her mouth. 'You're not going to tell me.'

'Nope.'

'Because that wasn't part of the deal.'

'But it could be.'

'If I investigate Rupert Millington's murder.'

'Got it.'

Tess clenched her fists and tried to concentrate on not punching anything or anyone. 'It's not my case. I'm just doing what I'm told.'

'Secret,' Sarah whispered theatrically.

Tess sighed. There was no point in arguing with a person who didn't operate in the real world. 'I can't promise to solve it. No one can promise that.'

'Fine. Done. We look into it, we solve it together. Done.'

'I never said "together". I never said that.'

'It's part of the deal.'

'No deal.'

'Good deal, if you ask me. Tess is the hero all round.'

'Well, I do like the idea of being a hero . . .'

'SuperTess . . .'

Tess raised her eyebrows. 'Fine. Deal. But I get to choose my own costume. And no clowns.'

Chapter Eight

It was midday and Tess and Jerome had spoken to over forty people in Kingston, the village outside of Lewes where Rupert had lived, and they had been given forty differing opinions on everything from parking zones to fly tipping. Tess had heard so many complaints that she was starting to think she worked for the council rather than the police force – which was, of course, exactly how Walker wanted her to feel.

'How about we take a lunch break?' Jerome said as the local pub, the Juggs, came into sight.

She shrugged. 'Why not?'

Usually this early in a murder case, they wouldn't stop for food, or drinks, or for the toilet sometimes, but Tess was completely fed up and doubted Walker would even notice. He hadn't even wanted her on the case, but the Major Crimes Team was too small to snub her entirely, so he'd stuck her on foot patrol as a clear message – this is *my* case. Walker was looking into a political angle: local councillor burned on the bonfire as a political message. He was bringing in every member of every anti-establishment protest group they knew of in Sussex. That's why he had Tess traipsing around Kingston – although he knew that Lily's threats needed following up, he didn't believe for a second that there was a local villager responsible for this murder.

The Juggs looked from the outside like any of the large cottages in Kingston, and on entering the picture didn't change a great deal. Exposed oak beams and an open fire completed the home-from-home look and the woman behind the bar glanced up at them as they walked in. She appeared to be in her forties, tall and thin with a mass of curly light brown hair. Her face was void of make-up and she wore a simple navy T-shirt and jeans with a clean but greying apron over the top. She smiled at them as they approached.

'Morning,' she said, glancing at her watch. 'Sorry, afternoon just about. What can I get you?'

'Pie and mash, please,' Jerome said without waiting for Tess. 'And a side of chips. And a Coke.'

Tess didn't even flinch. She was well used to Jerome ordering multiple side dishes by now. He didn't usually finish them, so she got to.

'What sandwiches do you have?' she asked. The woman reeled off a list. 'BLT, please,' Tess said. 'And a sparkling water.'

Tess took her drink and a spoon with a number two Sharpie'd on to it and left Jerome to pay. He didn't object, just followed her to the table she'd chosen and pulled out the chair opposite hers.

'Got to love a village pub,' he commented, as if he lived in some huge city. The truth was, Jerome lived in Burgess Hill which was barely bigger than a village itself. 'Cosy, isn't it? Makes you want to get a dog and do some hiking.'

'The day you get a dog and do some hiking is the day I give up police work and become a country and western singer.'

'I've heard you sing,' Jerome replied. 'And for the safety of everyone's hearing I think I'll stay away from hiking and pet ownership.'

'You absolutely haven't heard me sing,' Tess said. 'And you never will.'

Jerome grinned. 'So where's the legendary Sarah Jacobs? Isn't she supposed to be your Watson now?'

'She had some family business to attend to,' Tess replied. 'And don't start with that Watson and Holmes shit, it's bad enough Walker can't let it slide.'

Jerome held up his hands. 'Sorry, boss. Family business, though? Shouldn't you be there for that? Seeing as it's your family too?'

Tess flicked him the 'V'. 'For all her bluster and bravado I think she's nervous about coming here. She's going to have to face Li—'

Tess stopped at the sound of raised voices – no, Tess thought – *screams*, coming from outside. The door to the pub burst open and Lily Dowse flew through it and hurled herself at the bar.

'For God's sake, Harriet, don't just stand there!' Lily screamed. 'She's gone mad!'

Tess was on her feet moments before the pub doors opened a second time and a woman was at the bar, grabbing Lily by the arm and spinning her around.

'You think you can come in here and I won't make a scene?' the woman shouted. She was a tall, sturdy-looking middle-aged woman, wearing cream jodhpurs and a long-sleeved navy T-shirt with a dark green gilet over the top. Lily had ditched the flowing skirt and crystals and was dressed down in cream linen trousers and a loose-fitting white shirt.

'Good Lord, Babette, will you just leave me alone!' she shrieked.

'I'll leave you alone when you undo whatever curse you've done, you horrible witch!'

'All right.' Tess approached the two women and Lily's eyes widened. 'What's this all about?'

'Oh, Tess, thank goodness. This mad old bag is trying to screech me to death.'

The other woman barely glanced at Tess, just continued to glare at Lily. Her dark blonde hair was pulled into a bun but strands had escaped and were sticking out around her face – the effect was quite scary.

'Stay out of it, Blondy,' the woman warned, turning her glare on Tess. 'This is between me and Grotbags.'

Lily laughed. 'I'll have you know, she's a police officer.'

Babette raised her eyebrows. 'Well, that's saved me a job. This woman is a murderer! You need to arrest her, with your handcuffs and whatever.'

'Mrs Donovan hasn't even been made a person of interest in Mr. Millington's murder yet,' Tess replied, but Babette waved her words away with an air of impatience. She was a large, imposing woman with a booming voice and next to the petite Lily she looked like a giantess.

'I'm not talking about Rupert,' she snapped, glaring back at Lily once more. 'Although we all know that she cursed *him* too. I'm talking about my cattle.'

48

Tess took a step back from the women, confused now. 'Your what?' She noticed that Jerome was still sitting at the table, surveying the situation with an amused look on his face.

'My. Cows. This *bitch*' – she spat out the word – 'put a curse on them and one of them died this morning. The vet thinks it sounds like foot and mouth but there's been no cases round here for years. The whole herd might end up having to go.' Her voice broke on the last sentence, and Tess realized in horror that tears were running down her cheeks. Lily looked as alarmed as Tess felt at the woman's abrupt change in demeanour.

'Now, now, Babette.' A man came running out of the kitchen and put his arm around Babette's shoulder, Harriet from behind the bar trailing behind him. She'd obviously gone to fetch him while the commotion had been occurring. 'It might not be that bad. Paul's on his way as fast as he can. He'll do what he needs to do. You should get back to the farm, hear what he has to say.'

Babette looked as though she wanted to stay and shout at Lily some more, but after a few seconds she hung her head in defeat, nodded, and let the man lead her outside. Lily let out a breath at the same time as Tess.

'Phew!' Lily said, grinning. 'That was intense. Lucky Reg was on hand to get rid of the barmy old bird.'

Tess glowered at the woman, amazed at how she could still be smiling after that performance. She grabbed her arm and dragged her back to where Jerome had remained seated the whole time.

'Thanks for your support, partner,' Tess hissed. Jerome shook his head.

'Look, you step into an argument between two women and it's all fine. I step in and it becomes an *escalated situation*. I am a black man in a small village. Strapping white women like Babette don't like me telling them what to do.'

'He's right, you know,' Lily agreed. 'Babette "battering" Ramsey goes through life asking to see the manager. She only knows one phone number better than her lawyer's and that's her vet's.'

'I take it that's the Paul that the chef mentioned?' Jerome asked.

'Paul Carrington. Local cow whisperer.'

Tess took a sip of her drink. 'What did she mean about you putting a curse on her cattle?'

They looked up as Harriet brought over their food and laid it on the table in front of them. Lily reached out and picked off a chip.

'My apologies, Harriet,' she said, taking a bite off the end of the chip and realizing it was steaming hot. She blew on the end. 'Whole village has gone bloody crazy.'

Harriet nodded. ''S'okay,' she said, her voice quiet. She looked like she was about to say something else but instead just bit her lip and muttered, 'Enjoy your meals.'

Lily looked back at Tess and Jerome. 'I didn't say anything about her bloody cattle, you know. I called *her* a mad cow. I'm as psychic as Sarah is – you know it and bloody Babette knows it too. She's just jumping on this curse thing as an excuse to blame someone for her bad farm management.'

'Sounds to me like you're in the habit of putting curses on people you don't like,' Jerome said, a slightly amused look on his face.

'Works a damn sight better than a cease-and-desist letter.' Lily gave him a sly grin and winked.

'Mrs Dowse,' Tess said, her tone warning.

'Donovan, these days,' Lily corrected.

'Mrs Donovan. Have you forgotten that a man is dead, and you were heard threatening him the night of his disappearance? Just because you haven't been arrested yet doesn't mean you won't be. In your shoes I'd be cutting the comedy act.'

'Just because a man is dead doesn't mean I have to be sorry about it,' Lily snapped. She folded her arms across her chest in a gesture of defiance. 'And just because I'm not sorry about it doesn't mean I killed him.'

Jerome raised his eyebrows. 'Ma'am, you're talking to police officers now. Your logic has no place here.'

Tess shot him a look that quite clearly told him to shut up. She could tell that Jerome was having far too much fun with Lily Dowse, and she was worried it was catching. Tess could see what Mac had meant when he said that Sarah's mother had been charming. Although her charm hadn't won her any favours in Kingston, it seemed. The village had been mighty quick to believe that she had been flinging out curses the way Oprah gives away cars.

Lily sighed. She reached out a hand and placed it on Tess's. Tess yanked her hand back as though she'd held it against fire. Lily looked hurt but didn't mention the slight. 'You don't believe in curses, Tess. You know I'm not responsible for Rupert's death, or for old Battering Ramsey's mad cows. But you've said it yourself, I have history with the, um, with the *deceased*. It was well known that we didn't get along. His wife thought I was harassing him which I absolutely was not, by the way.'

'Then you haven't got anything to worry about, have you? Walker thinks there's some kind of political motive. He's only got people looking into you to cover all bases. You don't need my help.'

'Ah,' Lily said, looking much less cocksure now. 'And if there was, perhaps, another motive that turned up?'

Tess scowled. 'What other motive, Lily?'

Lily shook her head. 'Oh no, there isn't anything else, I was just playing Devil's advocate.'

'Let's say I believe you, which I shouldn't, and that I want to help you, which I don't. Who else should we be looking at? What motive would anyone else have to kill Rupert Millington and harm Babette's cattle?'

Lily snorted. 'Have you ever spoken to either of them? Rupert Millington was a bigger shit than all of Battering Ramsey's cows' produce put together. And you saw old Babette in action herself – show me one person in this village who wouldn't like to send her packing and I'll show you a liar.'

Tess sighed. 'I'll tell you what I told Sarah,' she said, pausing to take a bite of her sandwich. Lily waited impatiently as Tess chewed slowly and swallowed. 'It's not my case. I've been put in charge of gossip and tittle-tattle duty.'

'Haven't you ever watched *Father Brown*?' Lily asked. 'That's how these village cases get solved, gossip and tittle tattle.'

Tess didn't know what to say to that. Between a sister who compared her crime scenes to magic tricks and a stepmother who compared evidence gathering to an episode of *Father Brown* she was beginning to think her family didn't take her job seriously at all. But a tiny thought nagged at the edges of her mind. Walker had put her on door-knocking because he'd thought it would keep her out of the way, and to demean her, humiliate her in front of people who were calling her 'boss' just a few short months ago. What if there was some truth in what Lily was saying? What if the incident with Babette's cattle was linked to Rupert's death in some way? If she wasn't going to be allowed to play at the table with the big boys, perhaps she could sneak in under the table. Or whatever the right analogy would be there. Maybe she'd take a leaf from Sarah's book and steal the table out from under their noses.

Jerome tossed down his knife and fork in what appeared to be record timing for pie-and-mash eating. Tess was only halfway through her sandwich but she pushed it to one side, her hunger for the case seeping back in.

'Lily,' she said. 'If I'm going to prove you didn't kill Millington, I'm going to need you to give me all the information you have on him, and everything else that goes on in Kingston.'

Lily shot a glance at Harriet, who was drying glasses behind the bar. 'Fine,' she said. 'But not here. It's bad enough they think I'm a witch, I don't want them thinking I'm an informant too. Follow me to my house. At a distance, if you don't mind.'

Lily's house was a small cottage – exactly the kind that Tess would expect to find the local witch living in. Sage hung in dried bouquets around the burnt-red front door, and ivy crept up the walls. There was an unused bird bath, its body in the shape of the head of Baphomet and the stone bowl at a skewed angle. The whole place looked at once unkempt, and yet not untidy, as if nature had stepped in to beautify what humans had left to decay. Jerome had to duck his head to get through the low front door. Inside was a wrought-iron umbrella stand, and a large, slightly wonky, black iron coat rack. The floors were cold stone but there was a runner woven in purples, oranges and reds that stopped it from looking uninviting.

They made their way through to the kitchen where it smelled of patchouli oil and rosemary. It was a large country kitchen that looked as though it had been built around its main feature, the sprawling black AGA beneath a panoramic window that looked out over the Sussex hills. Plants featured as heavily inside as they did out – almost as if you could forget that you had even ventured inside. Plants that tumbled from their planters, ones that stood up straight like sentries and those which looked battle worn and weary, slumping in a mishmash of pots. Nothing matched in Lily's kitchen, not the chairs around the long slab of wood that was used as a table, not the crockery or the mugs, not even the cutlery. It reeked of a life collected, everything kept for a reason, a story waiting to be told about every piece. Of course, it could just as easily have denoted the life of someone who never felt settled enough to buy matching furniture, or a full set of knives and forks. Someone who never really felt as though they would be here long enough for any of those things to matter.

'How long have you lived here?' Tess asked as Lily filled a wrought-iron kettle and placed it on the AGA.

'That's part of the story,' Lily replied, taking down mugs from completely different cupboards, sometimes opening three cupboard doors before she found one. 'And I don't want to tell the story. Not before I've told Sarah, at least.'

'So you're asking for my help but you're not willing to give me any information?'

Lily gave a small smile. 'I'll tell you anything I know that relates to Rupert Millington's murder, which isn't much.'

'Okay,' Tess said. She took a seat at the long wooden table and pulled out her notebook. She could sense there was no point in arguing. Besides, Lily was probably right on that score, Sarah should know the truth first. 'Tell me everything you know about Rupert Millington.'

Chapter Nine

Sarah opened the heavy iron lock and wrestled with the old, rusted gate of her crew's headquarters, an abandoned warehouse building on the outskirts of Brighton. She kept meaning to replace the gate but it wasn't just a case of calling someone in, this place was supposed to be condemned, out of use completely. A normal contractor would ask too many questions and she didn't want to have to up and move so soon after making it fit for purpose. They had chosen the building for its location, remote enough that no one would notice them coming and going. It had taken months of recon to ascertain that no one ever came over this way – even dog walkers and ramblers didn't bother to make the walk.

Setting the warehouse up to use as their crew's base of operations had been an interesting task. They hadn't been able to employ just any building firm because they would question why they had to dress up as government officials and council workers, and why they were setting up offices on the underground level of the warehouse instead of using the vast, empty first floor. Thanks to her dad's contacts – her contacts, now – they had made the building secure and safe. Well, safe enough for them.

Sarah couldn't wait to get back to work. Grifting was her life, and her team were her family, although it hadn't escaped her notice that she'd driven to Chichester to play a trick on Tess – even having to call in favours to rustle up some clowns to meet her there – before going to see Mac, Gabe and Wes at the unit. Despite loving the three men to pieces, it was Tess she'd been desperate to see.

She gestured for Julia to follow her across the gravel courtyard. Her sister let out a tiny squeal, sounding like a little girl at her first princess party.

'God, I can't wait to see this place.' She clapped her hands together. Sarah stopped her just before the door.

'Look, this is my workplace,' she said, trying to implore Julia to understand the importance of what she was about to show her. 'You can't mess around here. It might look like fun and games but these guys are the best in the business. They aren't tricksters and carnies. No offence.' Not to mention that Julia wasn't exactly popular in a place where Frank had been king. No one would challenge her directly – not when Sarah was with her – but they wouldn't like her presence.

'None taken,' Julia said, and Sarah knew she meant it. Julia was incredibly difficult to offend. Sarah shook her head and let them into the warehouse, leading Julia over to the lift. The lift doors still retained their old, decrepit looks but the mechanics had been completely replaced so that none of them had to worry about plunging to their death on their way to work.

As the doors opened at the bottom, Sarah's eyes widened

in shock. The warehouse was near silent, there was no hum of activity coming from every corner, no groups of grifters practising on one another. Last time Sarah had been in here there had been at least thirty people picking up props, dropping off cash, engrossed in research on the bank of computers against the wall. Now there were less than half that number, and no music playing, no laughter and worst of all, no buzz.

She was relieved to see the faces of the people in the room lift in surprise and pleasure as she walked through. On some, it looked like relief. Becky threw her arms around Sarah's neck and kissed her cheek, others were more muted but still clearly pleased to see her return.

'Hey, can someone get some music on in here, please?' she called, and almost immediately the sound of nineties pop – which they all knew was her favourite – filled the air.

'Becky,' Sarah said, gesturing around. 'What's going on here? Where's Ceri, Fred? Where's Mark?'

Ceri was their betting expert, Fred ran the pyramid schemes and Mark was their master forger. Sarah glanced around. And they weren't the only three missing . . .

'Mark had some work in Salt Lake City. He's been under a while now, actually – we're starting to worry. The others . . .' She stopped as though she didn't know what to say. Sarah saw her glance furtively at Julia.

'Don't worry,' Sarah said. 'Who else is here?'

She wanted to ask if her family were there. If she still had them on her side. It was starting to look like her decision to search for her mum so soon after her father's death had done more damage than she had anticipated.

'Wes, Gabe and Mac have actually been in the office all

morning. They don't spend too much time here now but there was some talk about someone being followed on a pigeon drop.' Sarah felt her stomach plummet. It was all falling apart.

'Okay.' She turned to walk towards their office but Becky placed a hand on her arm to stop her.

'They don't go in there now,' she explained, her voice low. 'They've set up in the room next door.'

Sarah nodded and turned to Julia who was talking to Lewis, one of their best street thieves. As she laughed and threw her head back, letting her long dark hair fall against the man, she pushed her chest out slightly and Sarah saw her arm move a fraction. She went over to them.

'Julia, why don't you wait in there, it's our old office. Try not to break anything. Or steal anything,' she added, taking Lewis's wallet from her sister's handbag and handing it back to the stunned grifter. She took a deep breath and headed towards the 'new' office.

Three heads looked up when she pushed open the door, and all conversation stopped instantly. Mac, Gabe and Wes were looking at her like they had seen a ghost.

'Sarah,' Gabe said, after a long pregnant pause. 'You're back.'

The usually flamboyantly dressed costume designer was dressed head to toe in black, from leather trousers to a flowing black cape over a black polo neck.

'Gabe,' Sarah said. 'You look . . . different. No offence, but aren't you a bit old to be going through an Emo phase?'

'He's worn black every day since Frank died,' Wes replied. 'Which you'd know if you'd been here.'

Sarah ignored the jibe. She raised her eyebrows at Gabe. 'Do you think Dad would have wanted you to lose your Technicolor on his account?'

Gabe's head dropped. 'It's a mark of respect,' he said. 'I'm still in mourning.'

Sarah looked at Mac who shrugged. 'Well, as the head of the family, I declare your mourning period over. It's time to move forward now, Gabe, and as much as I adore the Professor Snape look, it ends today. None of us want to do this without him, but none of us want his legacy to die with him either.'

She looked around at her closest friends, her crew, her family. 'I'm sorry I wasn't here for you all,' she said. This is my fault, I shouldn't have left. But I'm back now and we can salvage this. It's not too late to put the team back together.'

Wes snorted. Mac had yet to speak – a fact that Sarah found most disconcerting of all.

'Problem, Wes?' Sarah asked, a dangerous edge in her voice.

'Oh no, no problem at all, boss. Just don't open the door to Frank's office, you might let the elephant out.'

'You mean Julia,' Sarah stated.

'Unless you brought an actual elephant back from your travels.'

Sarah sighed. 'Of course, the Julia situation is . . . complicated.' She couldn't help but notice that the other three were now avoiding her gaze entirely. Gabe still had his head bowed as though in silent prayer, Mac was studying a crack in the wall as if it were a leak in the Hoover Dam, and Wes was solving and unsolving a Rubik's Cube so fast it made her dizzy to watch. 'But what happened with Dad, it was a mistake. She had no idea it was him in that hotel room. She thought she was taking out one of our rivals.'

'One of our rivals?' Wes's head snapped up to glare at her now. 'Have you heard yourself? We are thieves, Sarah, not gangland murderers. We don't "take people out" because they're our competition. And the fact that you are defending what she did . . .' His words tailed off but he'd made his point clear.

'I'm not defending her.' A pleading note had leaked into Sarah's voice. The truth was, her feelings about Julia were more complicated than she could ever explain.

'Then what is she still doing here?'

'She's valuable, Wes. Look what she pulled off all by herself. As part of a team she could help us double, maybe triple our income. When we were in Venice she pulled off the most amazing badger – all by herself. It's in her blood, Wes, if you just spent some time with her . . .'

'Jesus, Sarah,' Wes snapped, his face full of disgust. 'I don't want to spend time with her and I can't for the life of me work out why you want to either. If you think this team has any chance of surviving while the person who killed our father is sitting in his chair drinking smoothies then you are deluded.'

'My father,' Sarah snapped, then instantly regretted it. Wes's face fell. Without saying another word he slammed the Rubik's Cube on the desk and got up to leave.

'Wes,' Sarah said, reaching out to stop him. He yanked his arm away and stormed from the room.

'Let him go.' Mac grabbed Sarah's arm. 'He's hurting. And he's confused about the Julia situation.'

'I think we all are,' Gabe chimed in. 'What's going on, Sarah? You know no good can come of her being here. She's too . . . shall we say volatile?'

'She's a bloody liability, and I know it,' Sarah groaned. 'But I needed her to help me find my mother.'

'Tess already did that, Sarah,' Gabe said quietly. 'And Julia is still here.'

Sarah sighed. She owed her family an explanation, but the truth was she had nothing to give that she thought they would understand. It was a decision that couldn't be undone and she just wanted a little longer before betraying her sister. She knew what she had to do but she couldn't help herself. She liked having a sister. Just like she'd loved being back in touch with Tess in February, except with Julia she didn't have to feel guilty for who she was. Hell, she was the moral compass of the two of them, and that was a novelty indeed. Not to mention that Julia was impulsive and fun. She literally didn't understand the concept of consequences, which was so different to Frank who had been all about risk assessment and weighing up the risk versus rewards of their enterprise. It was almost like being with the opposing half of her father, like she had always imagined her mum to be. Julia felt like the missing piece of her family, and she wasn't ready to give that up right now.

'You sound like Tess,' Sarah said, her voice glum. 'She wants me to make good on my deal to hand Julia over.'

'Well, even a broken clock is right twice a day, sweetie,' Gabe said. 'You need to listen to Tess and give Julia up. I understand that she's your sister but to everyone else she's the woman who killed Frank.'

Sarah looked up at Mac whose face was a blank slate, as always. 'And what do you think?' she asked.

Mac's blue eyes fixed on hers and she could see he was struggling. 'I think you shouldn't have brought her here. You're playing with fire, Sarah, and it's going to end up burning all of us. Keep her away from the people who hero worshipped your father, and maybe you shouldn't come back until you've decided which branch of your family tree you want to climb . . . and which should be cut off.'

Sarah fought back tears. She looked helplessly at Gabe, who avoided her gaze altogether. Julia, Tess, Wes . . . they were all her family. How was she supposed to do the right thing by all of them? She looked through the glass to where she could see Julia in Frank's office, making paper aeroplanes out of fake ten-pound notes. If this was leadership, she wasn't sure she wanted it anymore.

Chapter Ten

'Rupert Millington was a colossal prick,' Lily began. 'Imagine someone with money, a real charmer, smooth talking, silver-fox good looks, a way with the ladies, wicked sense of humour. Women want him and men want to be him. That's how Rupert acted. *Acted* being the magic word.'

'Best to leave magic out of this,' Jerome said. 'Given the circumstances.'

Tess rolled her eyes. 'Go on.' Lily's description of Millington matched that of everyone she'd spoken to on her door-to-doors so far. Mostly.

'What more is there to say? He was an arrogant, self-serving, slimy—'

'He wasn't totally unfortunate-looking,' Tess cut in. 'If you like that kind of thing . . .'

Lily held out her arms. 'Look, I only slept with him once.'

Jerome looked surprised, but Tess wasn't. She'd known that the kind of disdain Lily seemed to have for Rupert Millington rarely came from nowhere.

'And how did your affair with Mr Millington end?'

Lily scowled. 'Let's just say only one of us reached the finish line. And if you call it an affair again, I'll put a curse on you.'

'I think we've established that I don't believe in curses, Mrs Donovan. Would you say your, um, split with Mr Millington was acrimonious?'

'Firstly, can we drop the "Mrs Donovan" crap, please? And secondly,' she said, 'there was no split. There was no affair. There was a one-off . . . well, I don't even want to use the words again. It was bloody terrible. One minute we were shouting and screaming about bonfire night, the next he's pouncing on me like an inebriated rabbit and I thought, why not? I think he thought it might happen again but I told him that I was glad he'd got that out of his system and if he didn't want his wife to know, it would be best if he dropped the idea of cancelling the bonfire procession and left Cliffe alone while he was at it.'

Tess had been taking a long sip of tea, and at this new information began to choke.

'Are you saying you blackmailed the victim?' She slammed down her cup. 'Fucksake, Lily, you couldn't have led with that nugget of information?'

'It's hardly a story if you come right out with the twist at the start,' Lily said. Tess looked at Jerome in absolute shock but she could see that he was trying not to laugh.

'Do the police know this?'

'Well, they do now,' Lily said, gesturing at Tess.

'Oh, for God's sake. I knew this was a bad idea. How am I supposed to keep this from my senior officer?'

'Probably the same way you've kept your father's identity

from them for fifteen years, amongst other things,' Lily suggested. At the words 'other things' she raised her eyebrows, and not for the first time Tess wondered exactly how much her stepmother knew about her past.

'Who's Cliff?' Jerome asked. Lily frowned at the abrupt change of subject. 'You said you wanted Rupert to "leave Cliff alone". Who is he?'

'Good lord,' Lily said, shaking her head. 'Do you know nothing about the Lewes bonfire night? Cliffe isn't a person, it's a society. *The* society, actually. The oldest in Lewes, and the only ones to do it properly.'

'I thought Lewes Borough was the oldest bonfire society?' Tess asked, her voice innocent. Lily scowled.

'Don't start that nonsense or pretty boy here will be investigating *your* murder.' She turned back to Jerome. 'Bigger bullies than Rupert Millington have tried to get good old Cliffe shut down, believe me. But Millington wasn't just going for Cliffe this time, he wanted the entire procession shut down. Said it was dangerous and costs too much, what with all the police and road closures and all that.'

'Okay. Was that the reason you put a curse on him?'

'I *did not*—'

'Fine, fine.' Tess waved a hand dismissively. 'Was that the reason you threatened his life?'

'I told you, I didn't threaten his life.'

'You said he'd end up on the bonfire.'

'Unfortunate wording. I meant as a tableau, not *in* one. I'll make sure I make my threats more specific in future.'

Tess sighed. She wasn't sure she wanted to be part of this conversation anymore.

'So he'd promised he was going to rescind his proposal on account of the blackmail . . .' Tess said.

'Not in so many words. But I assumed he would. Then he came to that meeting saying he was going to get the procession cancelled altogether. So I decided I was going to get rid of him as our councillor. Overthrow him like William the Conqueror.'

'Who killed his enemies,' Jerome reminded her.

'Well, maybe not exactly like William the Conqueror, then. But his days as representing Lewes were numbered.'

'Why did you care so much?' Tess asked. 'Not hugely on-brand for you, is it? Patron of the town traditions and all that.'

Lily shrugged. 'Actually, the society was the closest I've got to making friends in a long time. I don't have a heart of stone, Tess, as much as you think I must have to do what I did to Sarah. When I left Sarah and Frank to go back to the fair, it didn't ever feel the same. Then when I found out I couldn't go back because Frank had killed me off . . . I was alone. I bounced around with other fairs, other showmen families, and it was all fine, but it wasn't until I settled in Kingston and they let me into Cliffe that I really felt like part of something again. And that bastard was trying to get it all cancelled.'

Tess was a little taken aback. Of course it made sense that Lily would want to feel part of something, accepted some-where. Wasn't that what most people wanted? It was what she'd always craved. 'So you were going to go through with your threat to make it public that you'd slept together?' Tess asked. Lily snorted.

'Good God, no, you think I want anyone to know about that? Besides, everyone in the village knew about Rupert's affairs, including his wife. It wouldn't have made the slightest bit of difference, that's why my gentle persuasion hadn't worked. No, I was going to share some of my "predictions" to convince people that their future was going to be terrible if we didn't get a new councillor.'

'Genius,' Jerome said, nodding his head in respect.

'Thanks. So that was what I meant when I said his days were numbered.'

Tess sat back in her chair. *Oh, what a tangled web we weave*, she thought. Who would have known that small town politics could be so vicious?

'Okay,' she said, and she took a deep breath. 'So you say that Rupert's wife knew he slept around?'

'If she's got half a brain she does – he wasn't exactly discreet. Although she married that arsehole so she might not even have half a brain to work with.'

'How many affairs were there?'

'I know of two women – and before you ask that doesn't include me because I told you, it wasn't an affair. There was Harriet from the pub . . .'

Tess wrote down Harriet. 'Last name?'

'At the pub,' Lily replied. 'She's Harriet at the pub. That's how I know her, anyway.'

Tess sighed. It would be easy enough to find out.

'And how do you know this?'

'Harriet came to me looking for some kind of love potion.'

'I thought it was against the witches' code to make love potions,' Jerome said. Lily looked at him as though he'd said something particularly stupid, which Tess could see he had, even if he couldn't.

'I'm not a witch, you idiot, and there's no such thing as

a love potion. Anyway, poor simple Harriet had the same concerns. She thought maybe it would be against my moral code to make someone fall in love with her against their will.'

'Wow, they say the Devil's greatest achievement was making people believe he didn't exist,' Tess said. 'Yours would have to be making people think you had a moral compass.'

Lily looked pained but didn't try to defend herself. 'Harriet assured me it was for *mental clarity*,' she said, 'not to make someone love her but to realize they did already love her. She was sure, you see, that the recipient was already in love with her. I couldn't help myself, I had to know who her mystery man was, so when I made her concoction I added something extra that would give the drinker a lovely blue tinge to their tongue for a few days. Of course, then darling Rupert turns up looking like he's fellated Papa Smurf. It was obvious after that, all the secretive glances that none of us had seen before.'

'So did it work?' Jerome asked. 'Did Rupert get "mental clarity"?'

Lily scoffed. 'Millington's head was so far up his own arse that the only way to induce mental clarity would be to administer an enema.'

'And the second woman?'

'Hehehe.' Lily gave a snigger. 'Hehehehehe.'

'All right, Lily, we're already a captive audience. Get on with it.'

'The second was Babette,' Lily said, her voice full of relish. 'Babette battering bloody Ramsey.'

Chapter Eleven

Sarah opened the door to Frank's office and took a deep breath. She understood completely why the rest of her family had chosen to stay out of there since her father died. It wasn't just that it smelled of him, or that there was a picture of him on his own desk. It was the memory of him in every inch of the room, from the sofa where he sat upright watching the warehouse whilst the rest of them took a break, to the bookshelf where he kept a small bottle of whisky hidden in a hollowed out copy of *The Art of War* that he thought Sarah didn't know about. As if there wasn't a book on that bookshelf she hadn't read while waiting around for her father as a bored teen.

She crossed the room to the desk where Julia was sitting now, holding the photo of Frank from his desk.

'I thought this was Frank's office?' she asked, not taking her eyes from his face as Sarah approached.

'It was.' She wanted to say 'it is' but there was no point in any of that sentimental stuff. It wouldn't bring her dad back.

'Then why does he have a photo of himself on his desk?'

Sarah smiled. 'We always used to joke that you should have a photo of the most important person in your life on your desk. I got that for him one Father's Day and he didn't stop grumbling about it. Still put it on the desk, though.'

'Is that how you felt, that he always put himself first?' Julia asked. Sarah wondered if she could sense disappointment in her sister's voice and it made her angry. Julia didn't get to be disappointed in a father she'd never known. And would never know, thanks to her own actions.

'Absolutely not,' Sarah snapped, taking the photo from Julia. The other woman looked surprised. 'That was the joke. Dad *never* put himself first. Not once. His family was everything to him. He would have died for us – he did die for us.'

'What do you mean?'

Sarah turned away, still not quite believing she was having this conversation with her dad's killer. 'Haven't you wondered why Frank swapped places with Harry Derwent? He could have easily let Harry go himself, or warned him that his life was in danger.'

'I've wondered every single day,' Julia said, and Sarah absolutely refused to look back at her, to give her an ounce of sympathy or reassurance.

'Two reasons,' Sarah said, looking out of the panoramic window to the warehouse beyond. 'One, if you managed to kill Harry, that day or any other, and it was linked back to us for any reason, we would all have targets on our back. And Dad wouldn't have stood back and let that happen. And two' – Sarah turned at last to look at Julia – 'because he knew you were his daughter.' Sarah tried not to imagine how Julia must have felt when she turned up on Frank's doorstep to tell him she was his daughter and he'd turned her away, telling her he didn't believe her. She loved her father and always would, but she wished to God he'd handled the situation better. 'He knew you were who you said you were, and he knew it was you behind the killings. So he went to that hotel instead of Harry; maybe he thought he could catch you in the act and talk to you, put an end to your mad tribute to him, I don't know. But he went there to protect us, and to protect you. So don't ever ask me again if Frank Jacobs put himself first, because he was the most selfless man I ever knew.'

Julia put down the photograph. 'Sorry,' she said, and Sarah didn't know whether she was apologising for killing Frank or insulting his memory.

'Julia,' Sarah sighed. 'What do you think happens next?'

Julia frowned. 'Next?'

She walked over to the sofa and sat down on it, gestured for Julia to join her then motioned between them. 'Between us. Next. You see, the deal I made with Tess was that once I found Mum, I would hand you in, and you would stand trial for murder. That's what we agreed.'

'I agreed to help you find Mum if you helped me get away from the police. I don't remember agreeing to hand myself in willingly when we found her,' Julia said. 'You shouldn't have made Tess promises you couldn't keep.'

'So what are you going to do, go on the run?'

Julia folded her legs underneath herself on the sofa and put her elbows on her knees. 'I was hoping I wouldn't have to,' she admitted. 'I was hoping you could talk to Tess, make her realize that I'm sorry for what I did, and—'

'Are you?' Sarah cut in.

'Am I what?' Julia asked, her brow furrowed.

'Are you sorry for what you did? Because it doesn't exactly keep you up at night. I've heard you snoring.'

'Shaun Mitchell and Callum Rodgers were horrible little shits. Are you sorry they're dead?'

'Well, no, but I didn't kill them.'

'Tess killed one of them.'

Sarah flinched. It was true, fifteen years ago Tess had killed a man. His name was Darren Lane, and Sarah had been pulling a lone con, trying to impress her father. Darren, Shaun and Callum had caught on to what she was doing, and would have killed Sarah if her sister hadn't shown up to rescue her, but Lane had been killed as Tess had struggled with him to release Sarah. It was the reason Tess had left the family and joined the police – to live her life on the side of good. And Julia had come along and muddied the waters once again. 'That was self-defence. We didn't plot to kill someone to impress our family.'

'You never had to,' Julia muttered. Sarah could see that this wasn't going well.

'Fine,' she said. 'I can see you're not sorry for Shaun or Callum. And I'm not really sorry they're dead either. But Dad?'

Julia stood up. 'That's not fair,' she said, pointing a finger at Sarah. 'Frank was a mistake and you know it. Are you going to hold it against me for the rest of our lives?'

'You killed my dad!' Sarah shouted. 'And for months I haven't said one single word about it. How long did you think I could go on like that, avoiding the fact that you are the reason that everything is broken?'

Julia looked crestfallen. 'So it was all an act? You told me we were going to be sisters, that you were going to teach me about the business and we could run it together. You were lying to me this whole time?'

The problem was, Sarah had no idea if it had all been an act or not. She had enjoyed the time with Julia; it had felt like one big adventure, the two of them had bonded like real sisters, the way she had with Tess. But just like with Tess, there was always a barrier between them, something unspoken that stopped them getting too close. And while Sarah's and Tess's differences were purely professional, it was slightly more complicated with Julia. Because no matter how much fun she was, and how incredibly close Sarah felt to her, at the end of the day Julia was a murderous psychopath with absolutely no moral compass whatsoever. And she had killed their father.

Julia, who had clearly been waiting for a quicker, pithier answer than Sarah could give, nodded her head once and turned to walk away.

'Julia, wait,' Sarah called, but her sister didn't turn back and Sarah didn't know what she'd say if she did.

Chapter Twelve

'Babette Ramsey,' Tess repeated, looking dumbfounded. 'The same Babette Ramsey whose livelihood was ruined earlier today?'

'Well, if you believe a word that mad old cow says, then yes, I suppose,' Lily replied. 'But I highly doubt her cattle have foot and mouth. If you ask me, I think she's got Munchausen by proxy, or something.'

Jerome snorted once more, and Tess rolled her eyes. 'Munchausen by proxy affects mothers, not farmers.'

'Well, she's just a bloody exaggerator, then. I don't know.'

'But if she's not exaggerating and someone has deliberately spread foot and mouth to Babette's cattle . . .' Tess said slowly, 'then we have five people involved in an affair—'

'I hope you're not counting me as one of those.'

Tess ignored the interruption. 'One of whom is dead, one whose livelihood is ruined and another who is potentially being framed for murder.'

'So you were counting me.'

Tess bit her bottom lip. 'Which leaves two people in this pentagon. Harriet at the pub, and Rupert Millington's wife.'

A slow smile spread across Lily's face. 'My money's on Harriet,' she said with a wicked grin. 'Good with knives. Although,' she said, shrugging her shoulders, 'you know another name for a five-sided shape.'

She gestured around and Tess was suddenly aware of them everywhere, in wind chimes and on plant pots, even the teacup she was holding had a little one painted on. 'A pentagram,' she said, and Tess got the feeling that Lily was quite enjoying this.

Sarah wandered aimlessly down Lewes High Street, desperate to put off what she had to do. Because today she was meeting her mother.

She hadn't truly let herself believe that Lily might be alive, despite what Julia had said – not until Tess had told her that she'd found her while they were running around Egypt. Sarah knew Tess wouldn't lie to her.

She pushed open the door to a gift shop full of handmade trinkets and pictures in box frames, cards and money boxes, sarcastic wall hangings and wooden signs that said things like WINE O'CLOCK and WHAT IF THE HOKEY COKEY REALLY *IS* WHAT IT'S ALL ABOUT? Even the shop's name was twee: Truly Yours. Sarah perused the shelves and wondered if she should get her mother a gift, then silently scolded herself for thinking something so stupid. What would the card say – 'Happy back from the dead day'? It certainly wouldn't be 'Mother of the Year', or even 'Decent Human Being'. Sarah sighed. Things had been an awful lot easier before missing members of the Jacobs family started showing up.

'Can I help you?' the woman behind the counter asked. Sarah looked over. She was pretty, mid-thirties with long dark hair and a thick sweeping fringe. She was wearing a coat despite the shop being quite warm, and her sleeves were pulled down over her hands. As she spoke, her fingers picked at the dry skin on her palms. 'Are you looking for anything in particular?'

'I was just browsing, thanks,' Sarah said, then added out of politeness, 'You have some lovely gifts.'

'Thank you,' the woman smiled. 'I make all the handmade bits myself.'

'Is it your shop, then?' Sarah asked. The woman nodded.

'I'm Truly. Yes, I know,' she said, smiling slightly. 'It's corny. But if you're stuck with the name of that woman from *Chitty Chatty Bang Bang*, the least you can do is turn it into a gimmick.'

'I like it,' Sarah said. 'It's sweet. I was maybe looking for something for my mum,' she added, although she had no idea what possessed her to say such a thing. Lily Dowse had stopped being her mum the day she walked out and Sarah certainly didn't want to buy her a gift. Perhaps she was just trying the word on for size.

'I've got these.' Truly pointed to some photo boxes, pictures made with rocks stuck to the inside with cute sayings like 'You're my rock' and 'Better Together'. Sarah shuddered. She couldn't imagine presenting a woman she didn't even know with anything like that.

'Actually,' she said, 'I probably won't. We're just meeting for the first time. It's a long story.'

One she didn't have a clue why she was sharing with

a complete stranger. And one she couldn't finish because 'my dad told me she was dead for nearly thirty years' was such a bad look.

'Well, whatever the story, I'm glad you're getting to meet now,' the woman said. She suddenly looked incredibly sad. Sarah wondered what her story was. 'Does your mum live here, then?'

'Kingston, just down the road,' Sarah said. The woman raised an eyebrow.

'Oh yes? That's where I'm from. Has she lived there long?'

'Her name's Lily,' Sarah blurted out. 'Lily Dow—Donovan.' She wasn't sure what had made her say it, except maybe that she desperately wanted to find someone who thought her mother was a good person. Julia had refused to talk about her on their travels, saying that she wanted Sarah to form her own opinion. Then she gets back and finds out that her long lost mother was a suspect in a murder, which would've been less believable if she hadn't found out she had a half-sister who was a psychopath only this year. Though any hope she had of the woman from the gift shop telling her that Lily was a saint seemed like a long shot as she saw her face darken.

'Do you know her?'

The woman shook her head quickly. 'No,' she said. She chewed on a piece of skin at the side of her thumbnail and looked down to see blood blooming from where she had ripped a piece off. She covered it again with her sleeve and put it down behind the counter. 'It's not as small a place as people think it is, though. I hope everything goes well for you.' And she turned around and disappeared into the back of the shop before Sarah could ask any more questions.

Sarah sighed. Was she ever going to find a branch of her family tree that wasn't rotten to the point of snapping? At least there was Tess, she supposed. A little ray of goodness in her otherwise bleak ancestry. Of course, Tess was only half a Jacobs – so her goodness could be solely from her mother's side. Which left Sarah without a single speck of hope that there were good, wholesome genes somewhere inside her, or that she could ever be anything but one of the bad guys.

Chapter Thirteen

Babette's farm loomed large at the edge of Kingston, just past Ashcombe Mill. To most people who lived there, the Ramsey Farm denoted where the village began. Today, two old, rusted navy trucks blocked the entrance and the machines lay silent, no staff to be seen anywhere. Tess stopped the car in the lane and looked at Jerome.

'Looks like a ghost town around here,' she remarked. 'Did he definitely say he was here?'

'He said he'd be here all day. Called it a potential government emergency.'

Tess thought back to the foot and mouth crisis of 2001 and how millions of cattle were culled to stop the spread. She pictured Babette's devastated expression in the pub the day before. Yes, in Babette and Paul the vet's world it was an emergency. The questions Tess had to answer were was it intentional, and did it have anything to do with Rupert Millington's death?

'Wish I'd thought to put my wellies on,' Jerome grumbled

as they got out of the car and walked towards the farm, their sensible shoes crunching against the gravel driveway. Tess smiled at the thought of her partner even owning wellies – she just couldn't imagine it. He couldn't look less at home in the farm environment, with his spotless black shoes and perfectly fitting suit, his nose wrinkling at the smell.

'What do you want now?' a voice boomed across the farmyard and Tess recognized it as the indomitable Babette Ramsey. 'Come to arrest me for conduct unbecoming a lady?'

'We came to talk to you about your cattle,' Tess said. 'And to see if you're okay.'

Babette gestured towards her cattle shed. 'My entire farm is being tested for a disease that rips people's lives apart. Rupert is dead . . .' She let out a huge sigh and her shoulders shuddered as if this was the first time she'd allowed herself to register that thought. Tess considered how much this woman was going through, her lover dead in horrifying circumstances and her not being able to grieve for him in public. Now her livelihood threatened just days later. Tess wondered if anyone had even asked her if she was okay.

She turned to Jerome. 'Why don't you go and ask the vet some questions?' she murmured. Jerome looked at Babette and, possibly sensing a breakdown, gave a nod.

'Babette, isn't it?' Tess asked, reaching out to put a hand on the woman's arm. 'I'm really sorry about your cattle. I'm sure Paul will do his best and with any luck it won't be as bad as it seems.'

Babette took in a deep breath and shook her head. 'I've seen it before. If it's foot and mouth, I'll be lucky just to lose a couple. I could lose them all, and we've had a bad enough year as it is. It could finish the farm off.'

'It must be devastating, on top of everything else you've lost in the last week.'

Babette looked at her with suspicion and Tess thought for a minute she would keep up the act and deny everything. Instead, her face crumpled and she began to cry. Tess almost stepped back in shock – Babette Ramsey was at least six inches taller than her but she seemed to deflate in front of her eyes. For such a strong woman to disintegrate . . . it felt . . . uncomfortable.

'God, I must look like such a fool!' Babette wailed, covering her face with her hands. 'Everyone knows, don't they? And I look like a foolish woman. It wasn't just sex with Rupert, I loved him!'

Tess wasn't sure what she'd been expecting but a declaration of love hadn't been it. With Babette's defences down, this was probably going to be Tess's only opportunity. She moved closer to the other woman and gave her a quick hug.

'I'm sure he felt the same, Babette,' she said, rubbing the woman's back. She held her at arm's length and squeezed the tops of her arms. 'Now we need to bring his killer to justice.'

'Well, if I'm relying on that idiot Detective Inspector Walker to get him justice, Rupert will be turning in his grave fast enough to give him whiplash.'

Tess almost laughed, then remembered that DI Walker was her superior and she should probably remember to show him respect. Still, Babette seemed like a strong, intelligent woman. What was she doing playing mistress to a cad like Millington?

'Was Rupert worried about anything, Babette? Surely he would have confided in you.'

Babette shook her head. 'I was told he had that fight with

Lily Donovan at the meeting but I didn't go – there were plenty of society members to represent us, and I never saw him again after that.'

'Us?' Tess asked. Babette sniffed.

'Cliffe. The bonfire society.'

'You're part of Cliffe Bonfire Society?' Tess asked, her voice sounding more incredulous than she'd intended. Babette allowed a small smile.

'What's the matter, can't picture me dressing up and charging through the streets with flaming banners?' She sighed. 'It was my late husband's thing, really. He was so proud of being involved in something so spectacular, a real part of history. Have you been?'

'I worked it a few times as a PC,' Tess said. 'It's really amazing. I always thought it must be incredible to be a part of it.'

'Walter was so proud.' Babette nodded. 'That's why the society let me take his place.'

'But Rupert wanted to put a stop to it.'

Babette nodded. 'We've had a few controversies over the years, but nothing like what's gone on the last couple. Rupert thought the procession did more harm than good in Lewes. Most places have to close early to board up their windows and a lot of pubs and restaurants only let the locals in. The council warn against outsiders travelling here on bonfire night, they stop all the trains and close off the roads so some people say the town doesn't even benefit from the added tourism. He was just doing his job.'

Tess wondered which part of the job required him to sleep with half of his constituents, but she bit her tongue. It was clear that, although Lily claimed that half the village knew about Rupert and Babette, Babette certainly didn't know about Harriet from the pub. It would be best kept that way for as long as possible.

'Did you think about asking him not to go ahead with his plans, considering your relationship?'

Babette shook her head. 'He was as bull-headed as me when it came to things like that. Besides, I was only doing it for Walter, like I said. And if his wife couldn't change his mind . . .'

'His wife? Leodora Millington was a supporter of the bonfire procession?'

Babette pulled what looked like a yard of tissue paper from her sleeve and blew her nose. 'Not just a supporter,' she said, raising her eyebrows conspiratorially. 'Leodora was the Southover Society secretary.'

'Excuse me?'

'Well, Rupert wouldn't care about that, of course. He always used to tell me that he and Leodora were together for appearances only,' she said. When Tess raised her eyebrows Babette waved a hand. 'I'm not stupid, I know all men say that to their mistresses. But he said not to worry about her, she had plenty to keep her busy. And I said, why don't you just divorce, plenty of people do. But he just smiled, and said she was more likely to kill him than give him a divorce. Why don't you come in for a drink, now you're here.'

The farmhouse was built from beautiful red bricks and Tess could see where it had been extended from the original building to something much grander, with a long gravel drive and potted conifers either side of a large entrance. Instead of using the oak-beamed, glass-fronted entrance way, however, Babette guided Tess towards a door at the side of the house that led into a small mud room, then opened out into a Shaker style kitchen.

Despite the grandeur suggested by the outside of the house, it was clear that the inside had seen better days. At least ten of the burnt-orange floor tiles were cracked and the paint had peeled from the walls in several places. Despite the more ramshackle look, the kitchen was tidy and well kept. Babette's home, it seemed, was just like her life: full of contradictions.

'Do you mind if I use your bathroom?' Tess asked. Babette waved her towards a door behind which were the steepest stairs Tess had ever come across, carpeted in ruby red with a gold diamond-pattern print that made her feel slightly woozy. At the top of the thin stairway there was an equally narrow hallway, the floorboards uneven. There were three doors on one wall and a large window across the other. Family photographs were hung on the walls, Babette with a man and boy, arms around one another, beaming. This must be the old part of the house, Tess thought. The original bedrooms and bathroom. The kitchen below her had been opened out, probably to encompass the original living room, which was why it was so large in comparison to the upstairs. It gave the house an offset, wonky feel.

Tess pushed open each of the doors in turn to find two smallish bedrooms and a toilet-slash-shower-room. No bath, and no master bedroom. Perhaps the extension had a separate set of stairs. The bedrooms looked as though they hadn't been used in years and had a musty smell. The first one she looked in had a faded pink duvet and a frilly white valance, the other a lilac version. There was a heavy-looking torch on one of the beds but nothing else of interest. Tess opened the bathroom cupboards looking for medication, or anything that might be considered useful, but there was nothing except a few half-empty bottles of products. It looked as though this was the guest wing, and no guests had visited for quite a while. Tess pretended to wash her hands in the bathroom sink then returned to the hallway where she looked out of the window. The view was without a doubt the best part of the original farmhouse, encompassing the entire village: Tess could see the village hall, Lily's house and even Rupert Millington's home. There were no cars on the drive and Tess wondered where Rupert's wife was staying. With family perhaps? They didn't have children but Tess didn't know if the grieving widow had siblings.

She made her way down the stairs, itching to get a look at the newer part of the house. It wasn't that she thought there might be anything pertinent to the investigation there – Tess had already decided that she didn't believe Babette killed Rupert – but large, posh houses held a fascination for her, probably because her own entire flat was the size of Babette's kitchen.

'Please, have a seat.' Babette motioned to the long wooden table and crossed the kitchen to put on the kettle. She leaned against the unit and covered her face again.

'Eurgh,' she moaned through her fingers. 'Eurgh. What a bloody mess.' She put down her hands and looked at Tess. 'What must you think of me? Some crazy woman screaming her way around the village. You'd be right, I suppose, don't think I don't know what they call me around here. Battering Ramsey.' She said the words as though they left a bad taste in her mouth. 'They just don't understand me because I'm a strong woman and not a simpering porcelain doll like *her*.'

Tess didn't get a chance to ask who 'her' was before Babette carried on. 'Well, more fool her because Rupert hated that. He said that's why he loved me. Because he loved how strong I am. Not that I had a choice after Walter died. Two dead lovers in the space of two years. Perhaps I'm the curse.'

Tess was making a mental note to find out how Walter Ramsey died when Babette said, 'Left me on my own to look after this place. I'm not too proud to admit I've been struggling. Probably why this foot and mouth thing upset me enough to make a show of myself in the pub yesterday.'

'Do you really think Lily Dowse was responsible for your animals' deaths?'

Babette shook her head. 'Milk and sugar?'

'Milk, one sugar, please.'

'No, I don't really believe in curses. When Harriet was warning me about upsetting Lily, I thought she was being an idiot – Harriet is an idiot if I'm honest; simple girl, you know? Not too quick. But then I got home and Martin – he's my son – told me he thought one of the cows was infected and I just lost it. Not my finest moment, I'll admit.'

It took Tess a minute to figure out what Babette had alluded to. 'Wait, Harriet from the pub, she was the one who told you that Lily could curse you?'

Babette made a scoffing sound. 'Said she was a witch, that she'd bought spells off her before and that Lily knew things that she couldn't possibly know unless she was psychic. I've annoyed myself, rising to it and acting like some hysterical woman but she was really very convincing.'

As I'm sure Lily was, Tess thought. If she was going to go around selling spells and cold reading people, then it really was no wonder they were branding her a witch.

'Did she say what the spells were for?' Tess asked, suddenly. 'The ones she'd had from Lily?'

'No,' said Babette. 'And I asked her enough times. She just said it was something to do with her heart. I said, if she had heart problems she wanted to see a real doctor, not a snake oil peddler.'

'So I take it you don't believe she cursed Rupert either?'

'I don't believe she cursed him,' Babette replied. 'She very clearly threatened him, we all saw that. But Lily Donovan wasn't anywhere near the making of that Trump figure. And she's so small! Even if I believed that a witch could curse someone to have some kind of seizure or heart attack – which I don't – there's not a curse out there that could lift Rupert's body up and shove him in a paper mache tosspot without anyone noticing.'

'Very true.' Tess smiled, realizing that she quite liked Babette. The villagers who referred to her as 'Battering' Ramsey might only have seen one side of her; the brash, loud farmer woman who was all front.

'So it probably wasn't Lily. And I assume you don't think it was, or you wouldn't be here.'

'Actually, I just wanted to check you were okay,' Tess lied. 'You seemed very upset at the pub. With good reason,' she added quickly. 'And I do happen to think . . . I do think that the timing of your cattle getting infected seems quite suspicious.'

Babette looked at her sharply. 'So you think it was done on purpose?'

'I'm not saying that,' Tess said. 'But it's a possibility, isn't it? Where were you when Lily threatened . . . I mean, when she mentioned mad c— foot and mouth?'

'We were at the village hall,' Babette remembered. 'There was a bric-a-brac sale, Lily was doing tarot card readings. I asked her to read mine and I told her that she wasn't the only one who knew things. I knew she was trying to seduce Rupert.'

Tess took a sharp intake of breath and tried desperately not to let anything show on her face. 'What made you think that?'

'The fact that I had eyes. She pretended not to like him – it drove him crazy but of course that's what she wanted, I'm sure.'

'What did she say when you told her you knew?'

'She laughed.' Babette looked furious now. 'She laughed at me and that's when she started talking about mad cow disease.'

'Do you remember exactly what she said?'

'No,' Babette admitted. 'I was wound up by then.'

'So she might have been telling the truth when she said she called you a mad cow?'

'I suppose. Still, like you said, coincidence, isn't it?'

'It is,' Tess mused. 'Who else could have heard her, do you think?'

'Oh God, anyone who was there. Anyone in the village, I suppose.' Babette shrugged. 'It's one of those places.'

Tess was about to ask her next question when there was a pounding on the door.

'Oh, do you think that's your hunky colleague?' She crossed the kitchen and swung open the door. Jerome filled the doorway, such a stricken look on his face that Tess couldn't help laughing. The front of his expensive, tailored suit was caked in mud and Tess could only guess what else. There was a streak of dirt on his face – at least she hoped it was dirt.

'Babette, you're needed at the cattle shed,' he said, and Tess thought for a second she might be about to see her hardened partner cry. Babette must have sensed it too because her tanned face turned several shades whiter. She slammed down her mug and pushed past Jerome without uttering another word.

Chapter Fourteen

The two women sat across the kitchen table looking at one another, neither knowing where to start. Eventually, Sarah took a deep breath and said, 'Did you know?' Just as Lily took a deep breath and said, 'I'm so sorry.'

'Did I know what?' Lily asked. Sarah looked down at her nails, the floor, anywhere but her mother. After all these years apart, she'd thought she would want to soak in every detail of her, and yet she felt like a voyeur, caught peeping when she shouldn't be. Was it possible to hate someone and need them at the same time? She supposed it was – after all that had been how she felt about Julia, how she still felt about Julia. But at least she could tell herself that Julia's betrayal had been an accident. Lily Dowse had run away and left her when she was three years old. There was nothing accidental about that.

'Did you know that Dad had told me you were dead?'

Lily's eyes filled up with tears. Sarah glanced at her quickly then looked away again. She refused to feel sympathy. Of all the feelings she was having now, sympathy was the least welcome. 'Not at first,' Lily replied. 'At first I went back to the fair. I didn't look back, Sarah. I don't want to make excuses; I told myself at the time I was leaving for your own good, because I was a terrible mum and you would be better off with Frank, but I left because it was too much pressure and I didn't like pressure.'

'But you left Julia with the fair. So you went back to her.' She supposed it made them equal – Julia had Lily, Sarah had had their dad. What kind of family could they have been all together? Sarah, Julia, Frank and Lily, even Tess eventually. Her life would have been so different growing up with a sister, and probably so would Julia's – it seemed so unfair that they had both had that option taken from them by the woman sitting in front of her.

'Julia was being raised by my aunty, so she was with the fair, yes, but we didn't always travel together. And when we saw each other it was as cousins, her a little girl and me just another relative. I left the fair when Julia was nine or ten.'

So Julia hadn't had Lily in her life any more than Sarah had when she was younger, not really. Julia would have been six when Lily ran away from Sarah and Frank. Lily would have been a stranger to her. Sarah shook her head.

'When did you find out, then? That Dad had told me you were dead?'

'When I contacted him to ask to see you,' Lily said. The words struck Sarah harder than anything else she could have said. Finally she looked up and into Lily's huge brown eyes.

'You did what?'

'I contacted Frank. It was about two years after I left my family's fair for the last time and it had just been your ninth birthday. I remember because I bought you a birthday present every year, and that year it was a huge teddy, took up a whole chair in my apartment. It had a smaller bear attached to it, and I imagined telling you it was me and you.'

'But Dad said you couldn't see me.'

Lily nodded. 'That's when I found out he'd told you I'd got sick and passed away. I was angry at first, obviously, but the more I thought about it, the more I realized that he'd done it to make it easier on you. It was hard enough to lose a mother at that age through illness, if you'd had to grow up knowing that I'd left you, you might blame yourself. You wouldn't have seen it for what it was: a selfish woman so scared of getting motherhood wrong that she made the ultimate mistake and walked away from it altogether. You might have seen it as your fault, thought that you were unlovable, that you weren't enough. Frank never wanted you to feel that way, so he lied. He lied to cover for me, so you could grow up thinking that you'd had an amazing mum who would never have left you out of choice.'

Sarah thought about her dad. His gruff voice, his strong, warm arms. How she'd always felt a rush of affection every single time she saw him, even if she'd only seen him a few hours earlier. She couldn't even entertain being mad at him now he was gone. If he'd been alive she'd only have managed to be furious for a couple of days, maximum. Whatever he did, he did it out of love for Sarah. That was the one constant she could hold on to.

'I understood why he did it,' Lily continued, 'but it was like he'd carved a piece of my soul out. I'd always told myself that we'd see each other again one day and you'd be angry but you'd understand. And maybe I could be your mum again. The day he told you I'd died, he took that away from me. Coming back after I selfishly ran off would be one thing, coming back from the dead – even Frank wouldn't have been able to afford the therapy fees. So from that day I knew you'd never see me again.'

'You mean *we'd never see one another* again,' Sarah said. Lily took a breath and closed her eyes. When she opened them again, her face looked as though she had come to some sort of decision.

'You may as well know everything,' Lily said. 'If we're ever going to braid each other's hair and make friendship bracelets.'

She stood up and crossed the room to an oak cupboard stained with candle wax and opened one of the doors. She slid out a box and carried it over to Sarah where she laid it on the floor and opened the lid. She pushed it towards Sarah, inviting her to take a look.

Sarah knelt down on the floor next to it and picked out the first thing on the top. It was a folded piece of paper with a logo on the front that Sarah recognized as her primary school's. Large capital letters on the front read OAKFIELD PRIMARY Y5 PRESENTS *WIND IN THE WILLOWS*. She opened the paper gingerly, her eyes scanning the cast list. She didn't have to look far, her name was right at the top: TOAD OF TOAD HALL PLAYED BY SARAH JACOBS. God, she remembered that play. She'd loved playing the artful conman Toad as he stole his motorcar and evaded the police. She could still hear the laughter from the crowd as she yelled, *BEEP BEEP*.

'Did Dad give you this?' Sarah asked. There was another option, of course, but that was impossible . . .

'I was there, Sarah,' Lily said. 'I sat in the back row and watched the whole thing. You were brilliant.'

'But . . . how?' Sarah whispered. 'How did no one see you?'

Lily smiled. 'Plenty of people saw me. No one knew who I was. I'd never been introduced to any of those people as your mum, so Frank could say I was his sister or whoever to get me a ticket. If I'd been a man sitting alone at a school play maybe it would have raised a few eyebrows, but no one looked twice at me.'

Sarah started taking more things out of the box: a programme from her first (and only) dance recital; pictures of her on sports day holding a second place medal, aiming the world's biggest scowl at the girl who had come first; rosettes from subsequent sports days; crappy bits of pottery that Sarah presumed she'd made . . .

'You were there for all this stuff?' she asked, looking up at Lily, but the other woman had looked away, her face filled with pain.

'Your dad said he couldn't let me be part of your life but he wouldn't stop me from seeing you grow up. He let me go to everything.'

Something else dawned on Sarah. 'So he'd known where you were all this time? He must have, to tell you where I was.'

'On and off. I don't want you to think that I was always there, Sarah, because I wasn't. For years I would travel as I pleased, joining up with one fair or another, up and down the country. Some of those photos I was there for, some your dad sent me. I'm not trying to paint myself as some kind of guardian angel watching over you. I'm no better than the thousands of absent fathers all over the world.'

'And at no point did you wonder if I could perhaps handle the truth now?' Sarah slammed down the photograph she had been holding so tightly it had creased. 'Maybe when I was like twenty, twenty-five? Thirty? When Dad died?'

Lily scoffed. 'I'd seen and heard enough about you over the years to know that you wouldn't just run to me with open arms,' she said. 'I'm a coward, Sarah, I always have been. I've wrapped myself up in words like "traveller" and "free spirit" but I haven't travelled anywhere in years. I'm old, and settled and I could have done it sooner. The truth was, and always has been, that I don't handle pressure well. I run from it. I ran from motherhood and I didn't stop running until I came here. Even after Frank was killed, I was afraid. The minute you found out about me I would cease to be the loving mother, tragically taken too soon, and I'd become what I really was – a coward.'

Sarah looked at the lifetime of memories in front of her, crammed into an IKEA cardboard box. Part of her wanted to shred them, to toss them into a fire and watch Lily's fake motherhood burn to ash. Because that's what it was, fake, phoney. Not one of these photos showed her with her face red and snotty as she bawled over a scraped knee, or throwing her dad's favourite cologne in a bowl with flowers and bits of grass and calling it 'perfume', or having to be picked up by Mac because she'd climbed out of the window on a bad date. It was a box of shallow platitudes, an edit wand waved over her childhood. Had Lily been hiding in A&E when she'd fallen out of a tree trying to rescue their neighbours' cat? Doubtful. Had she been watching from the DJ booth when Sarah had been attacked by Darren Lane and his friends fifteen years ago? No.

'But when you did settle, it was near me and Dad,' Sarah said, annoyed at the note of hope in her voice.

'Wherever I went I was always drawn back to the two of you. I just wished I'd been brave enough to admit my mistakes and reconnect with you earlier. And with Julia.'

'How did Julia find out you weren't her cousin?' Sarah asked.

'I think maybe your nan told her after Aunt Jean's funeral. She came to find me and asked a lot of questions. We got along. You'd like her, you know, under other circumstances. She's a good girl, lot of fun.'

A good girl? Did Lily honestly not know what Julia was capable of?

'She's a psychopath,' Sarah shot back.

Lily frowned. 'She's not a psychopath, Sarah. She's different, yes—'

Sarah would wonder afterwards if it was Lily's defence of Julia that had made her say it, jealousy perhaps, or the anger she'd been harbouring towards her mother since the day she'd found out that their separation had been a choice – that she'd grown up without any women in her life to navigate periods and boyfriends, hormones or hairstyles. Both, probably.

'Different?' She spat the word as if it had a bad taste. 'Different? Your precious daughter murdered two men in Brighton in cold blood at the beginning of this year. And then she killed my dad. Julia isn't just "different", Lily. She's a murderer.'

Chapter Fifteen

'What the hell happened to you?' Tess burst out laughing as soon as they were back in the car. 'This thing just got out of the garage this morning, now I'll need to have it fumigated to get rid of that smell!'

'I bloody tripped over, didn't I?' Jerome muttered, his voice sulky. 'Straight onto my knees in six inches of cow shite. And I got zero information from it. Well, apart from the entire history of foot and mouth disease, that is.'

'Oh great, that's all I need,' Tess said, trying to breathe through her nose to stop the smell from choking her. '"100 ways to identify early warning signs of foot and mouth" as our next Friday night entertainment.'

'I'll have you know,' Jerome replied, 'that's the bit of general knowledge I was missing for quiz night.'

Tess rolled her eyes. 'Go on then, enlighten me. Are Babette's cattle infected?'

Jerome let out a sigh and looked genuinely upset. 'At least four of them are ill. They will run tests to confirm foot and mouth but Paul's going to advise that she have them destroyed, and the entire place needs sterilising so it doesn't spread further. That's best-case scenario.'

'And does he think they were infected deliberately?'

Jerome shrugged. 'There's literally no way of knowing. Foot and mouth can be spread so easily – that's why so many cattle were lost during the 2001 outbreak.'

'So it could be a complete coincidence,' Tess muttered. 'Brilliant. Half a day wasted.'

'Didn't you get anything out of old Battering Ramsey?' Jerome asked. Tess flinched. She didn't know why but she felt quite protective over the woman. Perhaps it was because she'd never met someone who'd lost as much as she had and still been able to keep a business afloat.

'Not really. Oh, actually, there was one thing but I don't know how important it is. Rupert said that Leodora was more likely to kill him than give him a divorce.' Jerome raised his eyebrows.

'Interesting,' he said. 'But not worth ruining one of my best suits for. There's no way the smell of cow shit is coming out of this. I'll have to burn it. You'd better torch the car while we're at it. I've been telling you to get a new one for years; we can do it as an insurance job.'

Tess looked at him, then back at the road. 'The problem with you,' she said, shaking her head, 'is that I never know if you're joking or not. At least when Sarah says these things I can be sure she means it.'

Chapter Sixteen

Lily's face creased into a frown and she shook her head. 'No, no, she couldn't . . . she wouldn't . . .'

But even as she was saying the words, Sarah could see that the woman knew Julia could, and would.

She opened her mouth, not knowing what on earth you were supposed to follow that revelation up with, when *Danse Macabre* began to chime through the house.

Sarah looked around, confused. 'What the hell was that?'

'My doorbell,' Lily hissed, jumping to her feet. 'Oh goodness, it's Elma bloody Chew. Quick, hide.'

'Who's Elma Chew?' Sarah asked. 'And why hide? Just ignore it. Pretend you're not in.'

'She won't leave,' Lily said, shaking her head. 'Elma Chew is the local busybody. She has more questions than a game of Trivial Pursuit, and I'm not in the mood for them. If you cut out her tongue, that woman would tap gossip out in Morse Code.'

'Fine,' Sarah sighed. 'I'll just go in here.' She opened the nearest door which happened to be a coat cupboard and sat down on the floor, surrounded by shoes. She heard Lily answer the front door and try to convince the woman on the other side that it was a bad time. Sarah thought it had perhaps been incredibly good timing, the family reunion had hardly been going swimmingly.

'I won't stay long.' The voice got louder. The woman must have invited herself into Lily's living room. Sarah resisted the urge to open the door a crack to get a glimpse of Elma Chew.

'Thanks so much for agreeing to see me,' Elma was saying. Sarah raised her eyebrows, imagining Lily's face. As far as Sarah had heard, Lily hadn't agreed to anything.

'Oh no problem, Elma, anything for you, you know that. What can I do for you?'

'I wondered if you could do me a quick reading? My daughter-in-law is acting ever so strange and I wanted to know if you could see if she's up to anything.'

Sarah heard Lily sigh. 'That's not really how it works, Elma,' she said. Sarah couldn't help but smile. Lily was no practising Wiccan and Sarah didn't believe for a second that she placed any stock in card reading. So why was she sticking to imaginary rules for this woman? Probably Lily just didn't appreciate Elma's meddlesome nature.

'Well, just have a look anyway,' Elma replied. There was a long silence and some banging while Lily presumably set herself up. Then, just when Sarah was starting to think they'd both left the room, Lily said, 'Oh yes, actually, this is quite interesting.'

'What is it?' Elma said, her voice urgent. 'What does that mean?'

'The cards are saying that there has been some kind of

misunderstanding, Elma. That you are mistaken about something. The daughter-in-law you're talking about, it's not Carl's wife by any chance?'

'Yes, actually, it is. It's just that—'

'Well, look here, these cards are saying that it's actually Carl who you need to concern yourself with. Got a job now, has he?'

'Not exactly, he does odd jobs when he finds the time but—'

'And the four of pentacles, well, very interesting. His wife, Linda, isn't it?'

'Yes.'

'She works, doesn't she?'

'Well, she's got that little cleaning job, I suppose . . .'

'And she does some shifts at the shop in Lewes?'

'Well, only three times a week, I think.'

'Four, it says here, see?'

'Okay,' Elma's voice sounded less certain. 'Maybe four.'

'Looks after the kids then, does he, Carl?'

'I don't really see how—'

Despite her anger, Sarah smiled. She didn't think Elma was going to be popping round for a reading again any time soon.

'Well, it says here, on this one, the two of swords, that you look after the kids while Linda's at work.'

'Well, I like seeing my grandchildren, I don't think there's anything wrong with that.'

'Nothing wrong with that at all, Elma. The cards think you're a wonderful grandmother.'

'Oh, that's nice . . .'

'And that Carl could do with getting himself a job, help Linda out a bit. What you're probably sensing from your daughter-in-law is exhaustion. You seem very sensitive to the feelings of others, Elma. Do you think that's what you might be picking up?'

There was a pause. 'I suppose . . .'

'You're practically an empath, I think. Was there anything else you wanted me to ask the cards about?'

Sarah waited to see if Elma would be brave enough to ask another question. She was surprised when Elma's voice said, 'Well, there was one thing.'

'Really?' Lily didn't sound surprised. Elma Chew had obviously not come around to find out about Carl and his wife's babysitting issues. She wanted the dirt.

'Yes, well, it's probably nothing, but it's about poor Mr Millington.'

'Rupert Millington?' Lily had dropped the ethereal voice now and just sounded startled. 'What about him?'

Elma's voice was low. 'I think he's come back.'

'What do you mean, come back?' Lily said. Sarah could hear something odd in her mother's voice. 'You mean come back from the dead?'

'Come back as a ghost,' Elma said. 'As you know, my house is at the end of the lane leading to Rupert's house. Leodora, his wife, she hasn't been there for days. But every night for the last three nights, the lights have started flickering in one of the upstairs bedrooms. I saw it when I was at Carl's house. But there's been no one in that house. It must be Rupert. It must be his ghost.'

Sarah heard her mum tut. 'It's probably problems with the electricity,' she said, her voice impatient. 'Maybe Leodora forgot to pay the electricity bill. She's had a lot on her mind.'

'At the same time every night?' Elma's voice was hushed.

'Carl said it's happened every night since his death. Ten o'clock sharp.'

'It's not a ghost, Elma, trust me. Rupert Millington is dead and he isn't coming back.'

'Well, I'd want to believe that, too, if I were you.'

Lily's voice was sharp. 'What's that supposed to mean?'

'Well,' Sarah heard Elma say, 'if the ghost of Rupert Millington turns up, he might just let on who killed him.'

There was a stunned silence, before Lily coldly informed Elma that her reading was over. While Lily escorted Elma to the front door, Sarah let herself out of the cupboard and slipped out of the back.

Chapter Seventeen

'Flashing lights? You want me to go back to Walker with flashing lights?' Tess kept her voice low so the other officers in the room couldn't hear her.

'And poisoned cows,' Sarah said, as if that made it all okay. Tess groaned.

'Don't be bloody ridiculous,' she snapped. 'This is actual police work, Sarah, not one of your Golden Age novels. If Lily doesn't know anything watertight then it's best to keep her name out of it.' She looked up as Walker entered the office, signalling his team to follow him into the murder room for another briefing that could be an email. Tess sighed. 'I've got to go. Our feckless leader has summoned us. Look, can you get hold of a map of Kingston for me, please?'

'No worries. Are you going to at least mention the cows?' Sarah asked.

'Am I flip,' Tess muttered. Sarah snorted. She hung up and Tess followed the team into the briefing as slowly as she could, making sure she was at the back.

'. . . be releasing a statement today to confirm that the body found on the fire was that of Rupert Millington,' Walker was saying. 'So prepare for the extra press coverage. The memorial for Millington is tomorrow. I'll be attending with a select group, you have already had an email if your presence is required.'

Unsurprisingly, Tess had not had an email.

'As you can imagine, the autopsy was, um, unconventional. We did manage to get some tissue samples, but nothing very useful. The remains of the bonfire were searched; they found most of the rest of the body, save some fingers, I think, but there was very little flesh left, mostly just bones. The head of Cliffe Bonfire Society, Arnold Page, said that anyone in the society had access to the effigy, it was kept in one of their outhouses. Yes?'

Someone in the group passed a phone to the front. 'One of the society members gave us this. It shows the head being fixed onto Trump the evening of the procession. Apparently they made it separately because it had this weight inside that made it sway around like Trump's real bobbing head.'

'So there was what, maybe a half-hour window for the body to be put inside the effigy?' Walker frowned. 'Any more videos from this get together?'

'Not yet, sir. Although the person who made that video said that there was a crowd around the effigy all evening. They said whoever put Millington in there must have been—'

'Don't say it,' Walker snapped, and Tess had to suppress a gleeful smile. 'Do not say invisible. There is a rational explanation for how that body got inside Donald Trump and we are going to find it.'

Tess noticed that he hadn't looked at her once. He went around the group asking about the results of their various jobs, sightings on CCTV, results of licence plate look-ups. Eventually he got to Tess.

'And you, Fox? Anything useful from your door-to-door?'

'No, sir,' she said, and Walker widened his eyes in mock surprise.

'Nothing at all? Two days' police work from our superstar DS and nothing to show for it?' He was being extra callous because of the pressure, Tess knew that. Still, it stung. 'Well, obviously the best man won.'

Tess felt her face burn. 'Poisoned cows,' she blurted out, before she could think twice. 'On the farm, Babette Ramsey. Her cows have been poisoned, she thinks it's deliberate . . .' Her words got quieter and trailed off as she realized how pathetic she sounded. What had she been thinking? She'd told Sarah it was a stupid idea to bring up Babette and her cattle issue, and from the look on Walker's face she'd been right the first time. He looked delighted.

'Poisoned cows?' he repeated, unable to keep the glee from his words. 'Well, Miss Holmes, tell us about your poisoned cows . . . what was the motive – were they playing their moo-sic too loud? And who is on your suspect list? Father Brown?'

There was a ripple of laughter and heat flooded Tess's entire body. Once upon a time she'd have told Walker where to go, made a snarky comment about his love life or his mid-life crisis or his paunch or thinning hair, but the last seven months had knocked the wind out of her sails completely. Losing out on the promotion to this sack of crap had had her doubting if she was cut out for the police force at all, and now it seemed to be confirmed. He was right – two days of police work and she'd not so much as dragged up a witness or a single workable lead. She glanced at Jerome who was looking thunderous and gave a small shake of her head. She didn't need him to step in and lose his job on her account.

'No, sir,' she muttered.

'Well, then,' Walker boomed, his confidence returning as rapidly as if he were sucking Tess's away, 'you'd better follow it up, hadn't you? Will the—' he looked around theatrically, 'bovine "victim" be having an autopsy?'

More laughter. Tess narrowed her eyes, wishing that she could manifest a giant snake to fall from the ceiling and rip out Walker's throat. 'The vet is doing tests.'

Walker gave an evil smile. 'That's your next job then, Fox. Pop along to our second victim's autopsy and report back your findings. Oh, and Tess?'

'Yes, sir?' Tess asked through gritted teeth.

'Don't forget your rubber glove.'

Chapter Eighteen

The day of Rupert's memorial was grey and overcast, sombre weather fitting the occasion. Leodora Millington, resplendent in a black Dior lace dress and a short black veil, had insisted that a funeral would be held at the first opportunity, despite the fact that whatever remained of Rupert Millington's body had yet to be released by the coroner. She stood by the side of the grave as they lowered what everyone knew was an empty coffin into the ground. It was what Rupert would have wanted, she told everyone, though they all knew that the ultimate reason for this show was to get it done before the attention of the nation's media waned.

'What are they actually going to do with his body, when it's released?' Sarah asked Tess as they stood at a distance, watching the memorial. 'Dig the coffin up?'

'I think she's going to have him cremated,' Tess said. She pointed at finger at her sister. 'Don't you dare make a comment.'

Sarah's eyes widened in pretend shock. 'What must you think of me?' she said in mock hurt. 'To think that I would make a comment about Rupert Millington already being barbecued. That would be disgraceful.'

'And yet . . .'

They looked over to where the mourners were gathered, a sea of black against the lush green cemetery. There had been no request for bright colours and celebrations of life at Rupert Millington's funeral, the order of the day was sombre, professional, dignified.

Despite Rupert being described by almost everyone Tess had spoken to as a pompous arsehole, the funeral was a sell-out show. Whether people were in attendance from a sense of duty, morbid curiosity, or because they actually liked the deceased, Tess had no idea, but she had a feeling that Rupert would have been more than happy with the turnout had he been here to enjoy it.

'I wish you'd let me bring my black umbrella,' Sarah complained.

'It's not raining,' Tess told her for the third time.

Sarah groaned. 'I know, but imagine what a stir that would have caused. A lady dressed in black standing in the distance under a tree, holding a black umbrella. I would have looked like a grieving mistress, or a vengeful ex-wife or something juicy.'

'As if we don't have enough of those at the funeral already?' Tess scanned the crowd for where Harriet and Babette were standing only feet apart, Harriet in a shapeless black dress and Babette in a black trouser suit. It looked from Tess's vantage point that Babette was doing a good job of keeping herself together, and if Tess didn't already know that Harriet had been sleeping with Rupert, she wouldn't have guessed today. She came across like any other mourner, stoic and silent. A man Tess presumed to be Harriet's husband – the same man who had rescued Lily from Babette's wrath in the pub – stood next to her, his arm around her shoulder and Tess took the opportunity to get a good look at him this time. Reg, Lily had said his name was, was taller than his wife, but not by much. He was stocky with a square head, not improved by short, mud-brown hair sticking out at all angles. His suit was ill-fitting and he didn't look comfortable in it. One arm around his wife and one hand shoved in his pocket, he didn't look comfortable at all for that matter. Tess longed to ask the man what he knew about his wife and the pretend occupant of the empty grave in front of him, but from the way he was holding on to Harriet, she doubted she would get the truth out of him anyway. Even if Reg knew about his wife's affair, he had decided to stand by her and would probably deny any knowledge of it if he was confronted.

'I can't see Lily in the crowd,' Tess commented. Lily was the type of person to stand out, no matter how large the gathering.

'She text me and said she wasn't going to come,' Sarah said. 'Said she didn't want people looking at her like she was Sideshow Bob. People still think she's a curse-wielding murderer, remember?'

'An unusually astute and wise decision for your mother,' Tess remarked. 'God only knows what kind of costume she'd have shown up in.'

'She's devastated over the news about Julia, you know,' Sarah said. 'I feel like a prize bitch springing it on her like that but I was angry, you know?'

'You have every right to be angry,' Tess said. 'She abandoned you.'

'Look who's here,' Sarah said, changing the subject abruptly and gesturing to where DI Walker was standing on the outskirts of the crowd with two other officers, wearing actual sunglasses in the November gloom. His presence was the reason Tess and Sarah were stalking the edge of the cemetery instead of joining the crowd. Jerome was on the other side of the cemetery; none of them were exactly invisible but at least if Walker spotted them she could make the excuse that she had been casually passing by and stopped to look.

Tess turned her attention away from DI Walker and back to the grieving widow. Leodora Millington was tall and slim, with salon highlighted hair styled and hairsprayed to within an inch of its life, and make-up that looked so professionally done you could hardly tell she was wearing any. She had obviously anticipated that there would be camera crews in attendance. Her black lace dress looked expensive yet understated. She looked every inch the MP's wife. A man in an equally expensive and well-tailored black suit stood next to her, his arm around her shoulder. Tess knew from the news reports that this was Rupert's brother. She noticed another man standing equally as close at the other side of Leodora but without touching her. He was well put together in an expensive suit and looked incredibly well groomed, even from this distance.

'I wonder who that is next to Leodora?' Tess asked.

Sarah looked to where she was looking and raised her eyebrows. 'Window shopping at a funeral? And you say I'm the shameless one.'

Tess ignored her remark. 'I wonder if he's a family member? He's standing very close to not be.'

The crowd was starting to shuffle now and Tess wondered

if the vicar had concluded the service. Drinks and food were to be served back at the Juggs.

'Looks like that's my cue to get to work,' Sarah said. Tess looked at her questioningly.

'Work?'

'They were looking for temporary staff at the pub tonight, given the "special occasion". I applied. Obviously got the job.'

'Obviously, given all your previous bar skills and experience,' Tess said, her voice sarcastic.

'That's what my professional-looking and completely fake CV says.' Sarah grinned. 'Today, anyway. I felt like it would do me good to be closer to any action. And I don't suppose you'll be able to be there, what with Walker keeping such a close eye on things.'

'Just make sure he doesn't see you,' Tess warned. 'I take it your face will be loaded up with plastic?'

'Yeah, best I can without Gabe's help, anyway. Besides, once I've got my wig and short skirt on, your DI won't remember me from Adam.'

'Wait,' Tess said slowly as Sarah turned to leave. 'Are you getting paid for this job?'

'Obviously. Not many bar staff work for free.'

'So you're telling me that this is your first real, paying, legal job?' Tess widened her eyes in fake disbelief. 'Oh, Sarah, I'm so proud of you!' She threw her arms around her sister.

Sarah shook her head and pushed Tess away with a grin. 'Laugh all you want but it's cash in hand and I'm not paying tax on it, so there.' She stuck out her tongue and turned to go back to the car.

Chapter Nineteen

Sarah was surprised to discover that she actually quite liked working behind a bar. And despite everything on her CV being a complete and utter lie, she was actually quite good at it. Although she hadn't tried to pull a pint of Guinness yet.

Contrary to the glum atmosphere at the funeral, wakes in England tried a little bit harder to fit the mould of a celebration. People were expected to tell amusing stories of the deceased, offer fond memories and generally lament their loss whilst simultaneously getting plastered before 8 p.m. Rupert's wake was no different, the people doing the reminiscing were more likely to talk about Rupert's love of hunting small furry animals, and remember that time in university – he studied business or politics or something equally as rich white male, Sarah hadn't been listening – when he drank someone else's urine from a shoe for a dare. Sarah had found out many things that she didn't need (or want) to know about Rupert Millington, but nothing that could help her understand why someone might want to kill him. Well, she thought, apart from just being a political figure. But those murders were committed by unhinged members of the public, in the streets with a knife or a gun, not meticulously planned as Rupert's had been.

An hour and a half into the wake, Sarah realized that she hadn't seen Rupert's widow for a while. Babette Ramsey had presumably gone home straight after the funeral, and Harriet and Reg were working the bar as though it were any other shift. Leodora had spent some time talking to Rupert's colleagues, seemingly not bothered about visiting the table occupied by his family, and then disappeared.

'Hey, Harriet, would you mind if I took my break now, please?' Sarah asked, already taking off her apron. Harriet looked around and nodded.

'They'll be tucking into the buffet for a bit yet,' she said. 'Me and Reg can handle this.'

Sarah didn't give her a chance to change her mind and took off to find Leodora. She glanced out of the window that overlooked the beer garden – no sign of the grieving widow. She was about to head out of the front of the pub when she heard a faint noise. Was that sobbing? There was a door next to the toilets with a brass plaque on that read CELLAR. Sarah pushed it open and found herself at the top of a staircase. The noise was clearer now that the door was open. Sarah went back into the bar and grabbed two glasses, then she made her way down the stairs into the gloom below.

'Hello?' she called, her eyes adjusting to the half-light. It was as you would expect a pub cellar to look, barrels lining the walls, connected to the pump system upstairs, then, on the far wall, a row of wine bottles and a cabinet full of spirits.

In the far corner, Leodora sat on a wooden crate, a crumpled tissue in her hand and two tear tracks in her otherwise flawless make-up. 'Mrs Millington?'

Leodora waved a hand dismissively. 'I'm fine,' she said, barely glancing at Sarah. She swayed slightly. 'I just needed to escape for a minute.'

'Me too,' Sarah agreed. She held out a glass. 'I brought you this.'

She went over to where the bottles of spirits were lined up in a cabinet on the wall. 'What's your poison?'

Leodora looked uncertain, but Sarah raised her eyebrows. 'You're paying enough for this shindig to get a glass of something strong on the house, no?'

Leodora gave a humourless smile. 'I've paid enough for Rupert, yes. I still am, actually. And will be for some time, I suppose.' She sniffed and, getting closer, Sarah realized she was already very drunk. 'So you may as well make it a whisky. An expensive one.'

Sarah opened a bottle of whisky and carried it over to where Leodora was sitting. She poured a generous glug into both glasses. Had Rupert left Leodora in debt, then?

'I know the feeling,' Sarah said, shaking her head. 'My husband left me with debt, too. He was a gambler, owed to everyone we knew. I was so humiliated when he did a runner and left me to sort out everything.'

'You poor thing,' Leodora said, and she looked so sympathetic that Sarah almost felt bad lying to her. Almost. It was her job, after all. And it had confirmed what Leodora had been hinting at.

'It was thousands,' Sarah said. 'I was calling the bank

constantly begging for more time and to stop adding crippling interest. I lost a load of friends because I couldn't pay them back fast enough. I wasn't sure I'd ever get out of it.'

'But you did?'

Sarah looked down at her feet as though she didn't really want to disclose any more. She took a sip of her drink. 'Yeah. Eventually.'

Leodora put a hand on Sarah's arm and swayed again. 'We do what we have to, dear,' she said, and took a gulp of her whisky, cringing at the strength of the alcohol.

'It wasn't the money that bothered me,' Sarah said. 'Not so much. That was just money. After he left I found out he'd been sleeping with two other women.'

Leodora shuddered. 'Well, that's men for you.' She drank the last of the whisky and pulled a face – Sarah wouldn't be able to tempt her with another.

'Yep. Don't know why we bother with them. Shall I open a bottle of wine?' She lifted the top of a dusty crate, hoping to find a bottle that wouldn't be missed for a while. Bingo, the crate was full of wine. Leodora looked at what Sarah was holding up and put up her hand.

'Oh please, whatever you do, don't open that stuff.' She pulled a face. 'I don't even know why Reg has still got that down here. That crate,' she pointed a wobbly finger towards the crate at Sarah's feet, 'is what got us into such a mess. That and those blasted toys. Rupert's idea, as usual! He was going to pay off his gambling debts with the pig swill in those bottles. Except it was indrinka . . . unedi— wait . . .'

'Undrinkable?' Sarah suggested.

'Worse!' Leodora swayed. 'It was undrinkable!'

'Oh dear,' Sarah said, eyeing the four identical crates. 'Did he sell much of it?'

'Crates and crates of the stuff. Reg himself bought galleons of the piss water.'

'You mean gallons?'

Leodora looked confused. 'Anyway, it wasn't just disgusting. It made people sick. I know, I know all wine makes people sick' – she laughed at her own joke – 'but this stuff was imported . . . no checks. Lucky no one went blind like that Russian vodka. Although someone spent three days in A&E. And the dolls . . . oh, God . . .'

'How have I not heard about this?' Sarah mused. A local councillor supplying dodgy wine, that was at least worthy of a local news headline.

'Paid them off, didn't we? Me and Reggie boy. Could've lost the pub if we hadn't. Then Rupert went and got himself killed and I've been left with his mess. It was only a matter of time before someone did him in, after what he did. He's in hell, you know? You can't do the things Rupert did and not be in hell. I'll go there too. There'll be no escaping the bastard, even in death. It's the only reason I haven't killed myself. Just to get some time away from the bastard. Bastard!' She sat down on the floor, her back resting against two barrels, and closed her eyes. Sarah picked up one of the bottles of Rupert's wine and crept back up the stairs, leaving Leodora snoring gently on the floor of the cellar.

Chapter Twenty

Sarah worked the rest of her shift without incident, keeping an eye on the comings and goings of the mourners. The man who had been at Leodora's side during the funeral appeared at one point to inform everyone that Rupert's widow had been taken home, the grief just too much for her to bear. Sarah made a note to find out who he was, but for the last half an hour she'd been running the bar on her own. Despite the sizeable turnout at the funeral, the crowd at the wake was dwindling – obviously people were running out of things to say about their former councillor.

'Everything okay?' Harriet appeared next to Sarah at the pump. She had changed out of the dowdy black dress she'd worn to the funeral and into jeans and a T-shirt with a faded red apron over the top.

Sarah nodded. 'Who was that guy? The one taking Leodora, um, I mean Mrs Millington home?'

Harriet tried to peer out of the pub window but the car containing Mrs Millington had already left. She shrugged. 'No idea. Maybe one of her family members?'

'He was standing next to her at the funeral,' Sarah remarked, and instantly realized her mistake. Harriet raised her eyebrows.

'You were at the funeral? How did you know Rupert?'

Sarah's blush was real, but luckily she was well versed in turning her natural reactions – in this case, her embarrassment at making such a rookie mistake – to her advantage.

'I didn't,' she said, truthfully. 'But obviously I knew about what happened to him and I just wanted to be nosy. Awful, aren't I?'

Harriet shrugged again. 'No worse than most of the other people there. Half of them didn't know him and the other half didn't like him.'

'What about you?' Sarah asked. 'Did you like him?'

Harriet opened her mouth to answer at the exact moment a small woman came to the bar to be served. She made the drinks with a far more expert hand than Sarah, and turned back to her. 'I didn't really know him,' she said. Sarah thought about what Lily had said, about Harriet wanting a love potion for the murdered man – to give him clarity. 'Much like his wife.'

'He was a bit of a Romeo, I heard,' Sarah commented, not missing the note of malice in Harriet's voice. She seemed to visibly cringe at the word 'Romeo'. *Interesting reaction*, Sarah thought. Was it the idea of him being found attractive, or the idea of him sleeping with other women?

'What, you don't think so?'

Harriet reached under the bar and pulled out a clean rag. She began drying the wet glasses from the wash-up, and Sarah mimicked her actions. 'Personally, I thought he was a slimy toad who had all the sex appeal of a rotten cucumber. In fact,' she said, lowering her voice and checking none of the stragglers from the wake were listening, 'I'd rather have a rotten cucumber up my you know w— Reg!' she said, looking past Sarah and at her husband who had emerged from the kitchen.

'I thought we'd close the kitchen now – there's enough food out, don't you think?'

Harriet nodded rapidly, clearly eager to agree with whatever her husband suggested so he didn't ask what they had been talking about. Sarah noted the way Harriet's whole face had changed. She was acting strange, like she was afraid of her own husband. Was this a domestic abuse situation? Sarah couldn't see any bruises on Harriet, and she was wearing a short-sleeved T-shirt, but she was well aware that domestic abuse wasn't always visible, and psychological abuse nearly never was. Harriet wore no make-up and always seemed to keep her eyes to the floor, despite being young – maybe mid-thirties – and having a beautiful bone structure and striking eyes. Her light-brown curls could have been magnificent but instead hung in frizzy waves. She had the look of a defeated woman. Sarah would have to ask Tess to look into whether there had ever been any call-outs to the pub, or if Reg had a record for violence.

'You can go, Tina, was it?'

'Thanks, Reg,' Sarah said, tossing the tea towel on the bar. He opened up the till and handed her a brown envelope. She had almost forgotten that she was being paid. She'd seen it as a recon mission and it had been fun, it was quite the novelty to get paid for an honest day's work.

'We could put you on the books, get you some regular shifts, if you like?'

An image of the last time she had seen her crew crossed her mind, Wes mad at her, Gabe broken and Mac so muted. Were the days of the family business well and truly over? Would she ever get their respect back?

'Thanks, Reg, but no,' she said, shaking her head. 'I already have a job I need to save.'

Chapter Twenty-One

Tess pushed open the door to her flat ready to collapse onto the sofa and watch *Below Deck*. If she were heading up the team, she'd have had them all back at the station, reporting on the day's efforts, but DI Walker preferred to go out for a pint and would be content to get the update first thing tomorrow. She tossed her bag down in the hallway and—

'Holy shit!' Tess jumped in shock at the figure on the sofa. Sarah looked up, her eyes bloodshot and her face puffy.

'Oh, it's you,' she said, her voice flat.

'Well, who exactly were you expecting?' Tess asked. 'And how did you get in – actually, never mind. I actually don't care. Why have you been crying? Surely a day's work wasn't that bad?'

Sarah let out a massive sigh and Tess tossed her notebook onto the coffee table, dropped her handbag on the floor and motioned for Sarah to get up for a hug. Her sister collapsed into her arms and buried her head in her shoulder. Tess dropped a kiss onto the top of Sarah's head and squeezed her tightly.

Of course she hated that Sarah was upset, but it was a long time since she'd felt needed, and it was actually quite nice.

Eventually Sarah pulled away.

'You want to talk about it?' Tess asked. She crossed the room into the kitchen and filled the kettle. 'You don't have to. You can just stay here if you want; the sofa isn't the comfiest but it's good for a night or two.'

Sarah shook her head. 'No, thanks, I'm okay. I can't stay long, it's just fam— just stuff.'

Tess knew she'd stopped herself from saying 'family stuff'. Just another reminder that Tess wasn't a part of that life. That she never would be. Sarah cleared her throat.

'Have you found out who killed Richard Millington yet?'

'Rupert,' Tess corrected.

Sarah smiled weakly. 'Briliant! Have you arrested him?'

'Arrested who?'

Sarah waved her hand. 'The killer. Rupert.'

'No,' Tess said, her patience waning. 'Rupert is the victim, Sarah.'

Sarah pretended to look confused. 'So it was suicide?'

Tess sighed. 'Why does talking to you always feel like I'm in some kind of skit? Rupert Millington is the victim's name. We haven't found the killer and before you ask—' She held up her hand, anticipating her sister's next infuriating question. 'There is *no* Richard.'

Sarah sat back. 'You're no fun.' She smiled, letting Tess know that she'd understood the conversation all along. She was much easier to deal with when she was upset.

'Why did you come over, Sarah?' Tess asked. Sarah sighed.

'I came to ask a favour,' she said, and she looked like she

was going to cry again. Despite her sister's distress, Tess was immediately suspicious. She forgot sometimes that Sarah was an actress and con artist. However you felt towards her at any given moment was probably exactly how she wanted you to feel.

'Go on,' Tess said slowly. Sarah let out a sigh and threw herself back onto the sofa, tipping her head back over the arm rest.

'Aaargh.'

Despite her hesitation, Tess thought her sister's distress was genuine. She seemed torn over what she was about to ask. She didn't want to push her and scare her into retreat though. She poured a cup of coffee for Sarah and herself a tea and took them over, placing a mug in front of Sarah. She sat across from her and watched her expectantly.

'I want . . . I mean, I think I want . . . obviously I don't want but I think it's best . . .'

'Sarah,' Tess said.

'Fine.' Sarah let out another sigh. 'I want you to arrest Julia.'

Tess let her mouth fall open slightly but didn't say anything.

'Aren't you going to say something?' Sarah demanded.

Tess hesitated. It was what she had wanted, after all, so why didn't she feel elated? She could put Shaun Mitchell and Callum Rodgers' killer behind bars, claw back some of the respect she felt she'd lost in the last few months since Julia had escaped arrest. Their lives could go back to where they had been before she had stepped into Shaun Mitchell's flat back in February. Maybe she could request a transfer and get her career back on track without her family secret hanging over her. This was literally the moment she had been waiting for since she had knowingly let Julia go. So why didn't it feel like it? Maybe because she knew it wasn't ever going to be that easy – that she would always have to worry about Julia telling the world what Tess and Sarah had done in the past.

'Why?' she asked eventually. Sarah sighed again.

'Reasons,' she said. Then, seeing the look on Tess's face she nodded. 'Okay, you want more than that. Fine. I took Julia to meet the family.'

Tess sucked thorough her teeth. 'And that didn't go well?'

'What do you think? For a start – and don't act too pleased to hear this – but there's barely a crew left. Everyone who was so loyal to dad, I let them down when they needed me. I left them rudderless, a ship without a captain, Rick without Morty, Sooty without Sweep, Shaggy without—'

'Yeah, I get the metaphor,' Tess interrupted. 'Maybe it's time to think about retiring the crew altogether? Let them go their own ways?'

Sarah looked pained. 'What would I do, Tess? I can't imagine me ever taking up floristry, or driving a train, can you?'

Tess snorted. 'Absolutely not.'

Sarah tucked her feet underneath her bum and picked up her coffee. Taking a sip she screwed up her nose. 'Remind me to have a coffee machine sent over here,' she said. Tess scowled.

'So how does me arresting Julia fix everything for you?'

Sarah shook her head.

'It doesn't fix everything. Not even close,' she said. 'But it's a start. While Julia is free there's always going to be that cloud hanging over us. I feel torn in two directions: Julia thinks she can just join the crew and we'll all be one big happy family, and my crew think that now I know where Lily is I can just hand Julia over and she'll get what she deserves for killing Da— for what she did.'

'So you're sure about this? You think you can live with being part of the reason your sister is behind bars?'

Sarah made a pained sound in her throat. 'I don't know how I'll feel. But right now I don't feel like I have a choice. Not to mention the fact that I made a promise to you.'

'Well, I'm glad you remembered that eventually,' Tess remarked. Sarah frowned and put down her coffee.

'Don't be bitchy. Of course I remember that, and breaking my promise to you hasn't been easy. I know you don't like me but you're still my family too.'

Tess looked at her in shock. 'What do you mean I don't like you?'

'Well, you're always saying mean stuff about how annoying I am.'

Tess opened her mouth wide. 'I do not!' Sarah gave her a look. 'Okay, maybe I do but that's banter, right?' She stopped short of saying, *that's what sisters do*.

'Really?'

Tess threw a pillow at her. 'Stop trying to change the subject and make me be nice to you. You came here to ask me to arrest Julia and I'm asking you, is that really what you want?'

Sarah took a deep breath, paused, then nodded. 'Yes, that's really what I want. It's time. Julia has to face justice.'

Chapter Twenty-Two

They met again the next day, in an adorably kitsch café in Kemptown. Tess had discovered an empty back room, much to Sarah's consternation when she turned up. She preferred it busy, she told them, people were less likely to overhear. And as though to prove her point, the waitress walked in every ten minutes to wipe a table that hadn't been used, or refill the already overflowing sugar bowl. The look on Sarah's face made it clear immediately that she didn't want to discuss the conversation they had had last night, and Tess wondered if she'd already changed her mind about turning Julia in.

'So what do you have to report from the wake?' Tess asked, a small nod to acknowledge that they wouldn't discuss it there and then. 'And I don't want a list of everyone's favourite drinks,' she added.

Sarah produced a bottle of wine from her bag and presented it to them with a flourish.

'Bit early for that,' Jerome quipped. Sarah ignored him.

'It was Leodora who was the most illuminating,' she told

Tess. 'Turns out Rupert wasn't just a bit of a player, he was selling this dodgy wine to any idiot that would buy it. Including the idiot whose wife he was shagging.'

'Excuse me?' Tess put down her hot chocolate in shock. 'Are you saying that Rupert Millington was not only sleeping with Reg's wife but he was ripping him off at the same time? Sorry, but does anyone else hear *motive motive motive*?'

'I know, right?' Sarah said. 'But Leodora said Reg wasn't the only person who had bought wine from Rupert and ended up losing money. She wouldn't tell me who else he had sold it to but she implied something else had already gone wrong, and said it was only a matter of time before someone took the law into their own hands.'

'Well, someone definitely did that,' Jerome replied. He turned to Tess and she could see he was struggling to keep a straight face. 'How did your cow autopsy go?'

Tess scowled. 'God, I hate Geoff bloody Walker. You realize he's trying to make me into a laughing stock, right? Well, screw him. I actually did find something out. The cow overdosed.'

'Babette's cows are junkies?'

Tess shrugged. 'He's waiting for toxicology but it's looking like a cocaine overdose.'

'So someone gave Babette's cows *cocaine*? Who would have access to cocaine in a village like this? And why would they be feeding it to Babette's cows?'

'Maybe Babette had it and they got it accidentally,' Tess said.

'What, when they were going through her cupboards for baking powder?'

'Very funny,' Tess replied. 'Maybe we ask Lily if she knows anyone dealing in the village. I doubt a dealer is wasting their own product on poisoning cows but we might be able to find out who they sold it to. I'm not telling Walker yet. He doesn't think Babette's farm issues are relevant to Millington's murder and I'm not about to set myself up for any more stupid puns.'

'Good plan,' Sarah said. 'Oh' – she pulled a huge rolled up piece of paper out of her bag – 'sorry to change the subject but I got you this.'

Tess pulled a face. 'What exactly is that?'

'A map of the village. You said you wanted one,' Sarah replied.

'I didn't say I wanted you to steal one from the wall of the pub.' Tess rolled her eyes. 'Note to self: be more specific next time.'

'Well, we've got it now, we may as well use it.' Sarah used the salt and pepper shakers, the sugar pot and a bottle of tomato ketchup to weigh down the corners of the paper and smoothed it out flat. 'So this is Millington's house . . .' She took a blue biro out of her bag and circled Rupert Millington's house on the map. Tess inhaled sharply.

'We can't return that now,' she muttered.

'Well, let's hope Reg from the pub turns out to be our killer, then he'll have better things to do than have me arrested for criminal damage,' Sarah quipped. Jerome grinned and Tess sighed.

'You will literally be the death of me.'

'And this place belongs to a batshit crazy woman called Elma,' Sarah continued, ignoring her sister's complaints. She moved her finger across to another, smaller house. 'Her son Carl lives here. He's a no-good layabout who doesn't deserve his wife but there's no suggestion he's a killer.'

Tess gave Sarah a look. 'How do you know that?'

Sarah shrugged. 'Lily. She knows practically everyone in Kingston. Carl is the one who has been seeing strange lights flashing, coming from Rupert's house, remember? Even though Elma says Leodora has been staying with her family since Rupert's body was found – can't stand being in the place alone at night, apparently.'

'Strange lights?' Jerome asked. 'I hadn't heard about this.'

'Because it has nothing to do with Babette's cows or Rupert's murder,' Tess snapped. There was no way she could tell Walker they were investigating flashing lights and she didn't want Jerome getting his hooks into the idea.

'Okay, you're probably right, but it's weird still. Now, here's your friend Battering Ramsey's farm. See this building at the back? Incinerator. And here's where the bonfire society had their gathering, at the village hall.'

Tess looked at Jerome and he shrugged. 'I know you like her,' he said. 'But I'd say she's our number one suspect at the moment.'

Tess pictured Babette, and how devastated she had seemed over the loss of her lover. Could she have been a woman scorned turned murderer? One thing the experience with Julia had taught her was that you couldn't assume a killer had to look a certain way. But she just couldn't see it.

'We need to find out where Babette was on the night of the council meeting where Rupert was last seen, and where she went afterwards,' Tess said, her heart heavy. She refused to count Babette out just because she liked her.

'Okay, next steps,' she said, rolling up Sarah's map. 'Try to find out who else purchased dodgy wine from Rupert before he was killed. Find out where Babette and Reg were the night Rupert was last seen and try to locate a new framed map of Kingston to reimburse the pub. Sarah, you can come with me to Babette's where I can keep an eye on you.'

As they were leaving, and Tess was a few steps ahead, Jerome turned to Sarah, his voice low.

'You didn't really steal that map from the pub, did you?'

Sarah gave him her best wide-eyed innocent look and he raised his eyebrows.

'Fine, no.' She grinned and shrugged. 'I printed it off Google Maps then had my counterfeit friend blow it up on glossy paper and age it to look like it had been on the wall.'

'All that to wind Tess up?'

Sarah shrugged. 'It's what we do. Makes me feel all impish, like a little sister.'

Jerome chuckled and shook his head. 'You two are so fucked up.'

Chapter Twenty-Three

Sarah smoothed down the fitted black skirt and adjusted the hemline just above her knee. The bright red blouse matched her lipstick and a long black fringe fell into her eyes. With an irritated sigh she pushed the wig back into place so the fringe lifted almost to her eyebrows, and shoved another hairgrip in to fix it into place. She took a deep breath as the taxi pulled up at Queen's Road where Wes was waiting, leaning with one foot flat against the blue pillar of the community kitchen. He straightened up when he saw Sarah climb out, raised his eyebrows and let out a low whistle.

'Someone looks the part.'

'Don't get used to it. I'm back in jeans and trainers as soon as we're done. I don't know how women dress up like this every day. I can't even hitch my leg up over a low wall, let alone climb anything.'

Wes grinned. 'Normal women don't usually need to climb walls, Sarah.' He walked with her onto North Street, Sarah pulling along her small black trolley case behind her.

'You feeling okay about this?' Wes asked, giving her arm a nudge. It was the most physical contact they'd had since their fight about Julia. Things had never once been this awkward between them. Whenever they'd fought in the past they'd made up almost immediately. Being away from her family for so long had felt like having her arm cut off. When she'd called Wes after asking Tess to arrest Julia she'd been terrified he'd tell her to fuck off. Instead he'd asked her what she needed.

'Of course I'm not feeling okay about this,' she said. 'It's the first time I've pulled off a big money con without my dad. I miss him like crazy, Wes. And I feel guilty as hell about betraying Julia despite what she did. But it's got to happen sooner or later, and I'm a professional. I'll get the job done however I feel about it.'

Wes let out a whistle. 'Wow. I meant about those suspenders. They are suspenders, right? With a little belt and everything?'

Sarah felt her face flood with colour just like he had intended. The thought of Wes talking about her suspenders made her want to vomit. 'Oh, fuck off,' she muttered. Wes laughed.

'I know you're a professional, okay?' he said, as they approached the office building. 'And I know you can do this. Your dad would be proud.'

'Our dad,' she said, giving him what she hoped was an apologetic smile for giving him shit about it during their argument. He squeezed her arm and she hoped that meant she was forgiven.

Her heart thudded a little faster when she saw Julia waiting where she'd promised she would be, behind the desk of the office building. Sarah had to give her her dues, not many people would be able to find a way to get rid of the receptionist at exactly the right time. It broke Sarah's heart to think that if only Frank hadn't turned Julia away, he would be alive and Julia would be a member of the team. She was dressed to the nines and looked a hundred times more comfortable than Sarah did. She was stunning. Sarah felt Wes's body tense next to hers and could practically hear his teeth grinding. The hatred was pouring off him in waves. He wasn't taken in by a pretty face. Julia could be an actual Greek goddess and Sarah knew that Wes would still want her locked up and the key thrown away for what she'd done.

'You must be Wes.' Julia held out her hand, behaving in the coquettish way she usually did around men. Wes blinked and stared at it. Sarah nudged his arm and he took Julia's hand.

'Charmed,' he muttered. Sarah groaned inwardly. He was going to ruin this for them if he didn't shove his feelings aside. This was why he wasn't usually a front man.

'Everything set up?' Sarah asked.

'Like a well-oiled machine.'

'Right, let's go.' None of them said a word as they walked towards the offices where they knew their marks were based.

It had come to their attention that Deyton Kelly, an investment scammer that convinced innocent – mostly elderly – people to part with their money by investing in their children's future, rented an office in Brighton, and Sarah had been saving him for when the time was right. Conning a con artist who steals from OAPs was too good an opportunity to miss, especially to get them back into the game.

They walked into the office block at the exact moment Mr Kelly was leaving for lunch. Such a coincidence. Mac was already in the foyer, his phone in his hand. Sarah caught the eye of an attractive man in a suit and he winked at her.

'If you're not happy with the hundreds of thousands of pounds we've already made you, Mr Kertcher,' Mac was saying, and Sarah had to remind herself to concentrate, 'you are more than welcome to pull your stake. No, I don't appreciate a man whose annual earnings I have doubled' – Sarah glanced at Kelly who had slowed his pace practically to a stop – 'casting doubt on me. I'll give your place to someone who, no, I'm sure you weren't . . . I don't have anything else to say, my answer was the same yesterday as it will be tomorrow. Save yourself the phone bill. Have a pleasant afternoon.'

As Mac cancelled the call, Kelly crossed to the reception desk and Sarah watched him lean in to speak to the woman on the desk. *Julia*. She gave him their office number and Kelly nodded and left the reception as the lift doors closed behind them.

Wes let them into an office which was bare, save a desk in each corner and a flatscreen TV on the wall – nice touch, they didn't always have those – and immediately got to work, pulling a laptop from his briefcase and positioning it in the centre of one of the desks. Next, he started placing framed photographs and piles of paperwork around one of the desks. Mac did the same to the other and Sarah zipped open her pull-along trolley bag to dress her own desk. They had to work fast – Kelly would be back from collecting his lunch at any moment and he knew where they were. They moved quickly and Sarah couldn't help but look up every few minutes to take in the buzz of working with her family again.

The office door swung open and Gabe entered in a delivery

driver's outfit, wheeling in a filing cabinet and two potted plants. Mac was fixing frames to the walls and Wes had moved on to logging into the feed from the building security cameras. Sarah flicked on the TV and switched it to BBC News, muting the sound, for an extra touch of authenticity.

There was a knock at the door and Wes checked his screen. 'It's Kelly,' he said.

It was on.

'I'm sorry, Mr Kelly, but I can't offer a space to just anyone. We're at full capacity and our client list is vetted very comprehensively. There are certain, ah, aspects of the investment which makes it . . .'

'Illegal,' Rob Kelly finished for him. Mac looked embarrassed. 'Well, I can assure you I'm not concerned about that,' Kelly said. 'Your business is your business – I have the cash.'

'It isn't about having the cash,' Wes butted in. 'No one's questioning your legitimacy Mr . . .'

'Kelly. Of Deyton Kelly Associates. What exactly is it, then?' Sarah heard the irritation in his voice. Good, it was important *he* convinced *them* to let him get involved.

'We prefer to work with people on a small scale first, earn their trust as much as they are earning ours. Our start-up investments are full up at the moment but if we could take your name and number we would be happy to work with you at a later date – when a space becomes available.'

'I'm not interested in a start-up investment.' Kelly looked insulted and Sarah wondered if perhaps Mac had gone too far. The insistent banging on the door came at the perfect time and Sarah shot a look to where Wes stood. He gave her a nod – he'd summoned Gabe a few minutes early but it was the right call.

'I'll get rid of them,' Sarah said, approaching the door. As she opened it Gabe began to rant.

'Where is he? I want to see him!'

'Please, Mr Kertcher, calm down,' Sarah pleaded. 'He's busy right now but if I could get you to make an appointment—'

'I don't want an appointment!' Gabe sounded furious. It was sad knowing that this would have been Frank's role. Frank had been one of the best shills Sarah had ever seen – he knew when to ramp it up and when to dial it back; her father really had been the best. Gabe was good, though, and it felt nice to be working with them again. If it all went to plan, hopefully this would see her forgiven, and reunited with her family.

Sarah slipped out into the corridor and closed the door behind her, knowing everyone inside would still be able to hear his insistent shouting.

'How's it going?' he muttered, then raised his voice. 'Tell him if he doesn't see me now I'll wait here all day!'

'He wants in,' Sarah replied, her voice low. 'It's almost done.'

'He can't just boot me out – I need this spot!' Gabe yelled again.

'Is everything all right out here?'

'Yes, sir,' Sarah replied loudly, falling back into character. 'I was just explaining to Mr Kertcher . . .'

'Look, I said sorry,' Gabe said loudly. 'It was a misunderstanding. Completely my fault. Can't we just forget it?'

'I'll handle this,' Mac said, ushering Sarah inside where Kelly was listening intently to the two men.

'I'm so sorry about this.' Sarah stood a little too close, touched his arm and slid back behind her desk. 'This sort of thing doesn't happen often. Our clients can just get a little . . . passionate.'

'What's his problem?' Kelly asked. Sarah acted like she was about to speak and Wes butted in.

'We can't discuss other clients, I'm afraid. Confidentiality.'

Kelly ignored Wes and looked at Sarah. As far as he was concerned she was his weak link, his way in. Right on cue, Mac opened the door again.

'Daniel, could you escort Mr Kertcher downstairs, please? I need to make an urgent phone call. Mr Kelly, I'm so sorry, Wendy will take your details and we'll call you if anything comes up.'

Wes gave Sarah a warning look that Kelly was supposed to catch and left the room.

Sarah glanced out of the window at the street below where DCI Oswald and Geoff Walker were climbing out of an unmarked car. She knew there were several other vehicles in attendance. There was no sign of Tess. Julia was still downstairs waiting for them, thinking her brief stint on the front desk was over. This was it, then; they were going to take her. She would be gone by the time they left the building. Would she know Sarah had told the police where they were going to be? Or would she just assume she'd been spotted by chance?

'Is everything okay?' Kelly asked. Sarah looked at him blankly, then realized she was supposed to be doing something. She couldn't for the life of her think what.

'Sorry, yes,' she murmured, trying not to look back at the window. What was done was done. She'd handed Julia in, she'd ended it. Their dad's murderer would face justice, her sister would likely end up in prison. Lily might never speak to her again, who knew. 'Sorry, where were we?'

'You were supposed to be taking my details . . .' Kelly reminded her. *Jesus, Sarah*, she thought to herself. *Get a grip. You're losing him.*

'I'm so sorry,' Sarah said again, trying to look suitably embarrassed. 'Like I say, this is quite unusual. Mac will completely understand if you'd rather not get involved. It's all very embarrassing.'

She didn't even realize she had slipped up until Kelly said, 'Mac?'

Oh shit. 'Mr MacIntyre,' Sarah corrected quickly. 'Oh dear, I think this whole thing has shaken me. I'm not usually so unprofessional in front of potential investors.'

'Completely understandable, love.' Kelly wasn't wary of her in the slightest. It was a mistake a lot of men made. 'You tell me what that little floorshow was about and I'll make sure Mr MacIntyre knows what a good job you're doing.'

Sarah blushed. 'I shouldn't really. Like Dan said, it's confidential.'

'I won't tell if you don't.'

His wink made her want to barf. Instead she smiled coyly. 'Well.' Sarah lowered her voice to a whisper and glanced at the door, 'that man, Mr Kertcher – he's one of our biggest investors. He puts through hundreds of thousands. Then, last week he gets cold feet. It happens to a lot of them – they feel like it's too easy, like there must be some sort of catch. Heaven knows they wouldn't think it was easy if they saw the risks Mr MacIntyre had to take on their behalf, but still. Anyway, Mac, he's used to that. But Mr Kertcher out-and-out accuses him of being a con artist. When he's made half a million through us in the last eight months!'

Sarah glanced guiltily at the door again. 'So Mac gave him back his hundred grand and told him to stuff it. Said it wasn't worth a measly ten per cent to be called a crook. Kertcher wasn't expecting that – realized he'd lost out on four hundred and fifty thousand and he's been calling him every day to get his spot back. This is the first time he's turned up here, though. Got some brass neck, that one. If he knew Mr MacIntyre at all, he'd know not to bother. Once he's decided you're out, you're out. We're not running a creche, he said. Says that to me all the time.'

Kelly had been listening to all this intently. 'So who's filling his spot?' he asked.

Bingo. They had him. Thank God her slip of attention hadn't cost them the con. She was on thin ice with her crew as it was – she didn't need to mess this up and prove that she was too much of a hysterical female to take over. The legendary Frank Jacobs never let anything get in the way of a job.

Sarah shrugged. 'We'll get someone. Mr MacIntyre has a list as long as your arm of fully vetted candidates for the hundred grand slots. Look, I'm supposed to be taking your details – if Dan walks in I'll be in a heap of trouble. We can probably get you onto the 1k slot in a couple of months, maybe less if you take me for a drink.'

Sarah giggled and leaned forward to take a piece of note paper.

'I don't want a 1k slot,' he said, leaning forward to stroke her arm. 'You get me on to Kertcher's spot and I'll take you for more than a drink.'

By the time Mac arrived back at the office Kelly was ready to leave, smug in the knowledge that he had just flirted his way into a hundred k investment. Mac shook his hand.

'I'm so sorry about that, Mr Kelly. I trust Wendy has got your number?'

'She certainly has,' Kelly said, grinning at Sarah. *Eurgh.* 'And sorry, your name was?'

Fuck. Fuckity fuck fuck. Mac didn't have any idea that Sarah had used his real name – he was going to give him the fake name they agreed and it would all be over, just like that. He was going to be furious. She'd blown it.

'MacIntyre,' Mac said smoothly. 'Roger MacIntyre. Pleasure to have met you.'

'And you, Mr MacIntyre. And you.'

Sarah waited until she was certain that Kelly was safely in the lift before rounding on Mac.

'You were listening in,' she said, jabbing an accusing finger at him.

'Good job too. A day's work and a hundred grand blown by you calling me by my real name? You're better than that, Sarah.'

Sarah gestured in the direction of the window, where her sister was being led out to the police car. Mac looked over and his face fell.

'Oh, Sarah,' he said, putting his arm around her and pulling her in for a hug. 'I'm sorry.'

'It's what needed to happen.' Sarah sniffed and pulled away before she could get upset. 'Time to move forward. Nice work today.'

'And you,' Mac replied. The door opened and Wes appeared.

'You coming?'

As they stood waiting for the lift, Wes turned to face her.

'Listen, Sarah, I just wanted to apologise for the way I acted while you were away. You know, drinking too much and being so hard on you about Julia. Frank's death hasn't been easy on any of us but he was your dad.'

'He was our dad,' Sarah said as the lift doors opened. They stepped inside. 'You and Frank might not have shared a last name but he loved you, Wes, like a father loves a son. His only son, I might add. Sometimes I worried he wished you were his real child instead of me.'

Wes let out a snort. 'That would never be true. But I appreciate the sentiment. And I just want you to know . . .' The lift doors opened and they stepped out to the foyer. Wes was still talking but Sarah had stopped listening the minute the doors had opened. Tess was standing in the foyer.

'I heard she went without a fuss,' Tess said, reaching out to squeeze Sarah's arm. 'It's over.'

Sarah shook her head. 'I just turned in my sister, Tess. I'm not sure it will ever be over,' she said, her voice cracking slightly. 'Not for me.'

Chapter Twenty-Four

'You saw the news, then?' Lily opened the door to the cottage and walked back inside. Sarah presumed she was supposed to go in, so she did, following Lily into the large kitchen where she was moving bowls of herbs and pushing piles of string, trying to clear space. She handed Sarah the wrought-iron kettle and Sarah filled it from the tap.

'Was this Tess's doing?' Lily asked. She placed two mugs on the table and began filling the tea infuser with various herbs. 'The honey is on the windowsill.'

'Local?' Sarah asked, holding up the jar to the light.

'As local as it gets. Hives are in the back garden. Light that stove for me.'

Sarah shook her head. Nothing Lily did could surprise her anymore. Once a person has come back from the dead, they lose the capacity to shock.

'I told her where Julia was,' she said, in answer to Lily's previous question. 'It was me.'

She lit the stove and turned to Lily, who was inspecting

the herbs she was measuring out more intensely than she needed to. Sarah took the spoon from the woman's hand and dropped it back into the jar. 'It was me.'

Lily let out a sigh and looked Sarah in the eye.

'I don't blame you,' she said at last. 'It must have been a difficult decision for you to make.'

'She killed my dad,' Sarah said. Lily nodded.

'I suppose I always knew that something wasn't quite right with her,' Lily said, sitting down at the table. 'There was something missing, a connection that had misfired in her brain. Showmen have their own set of rules, but Julia didn't have limitations, she didn't know when to stop. She really does believe that she killed those men so that you would accept her into your family – for her, it makes complete sense.'

'And that's why I had to let Tess take her in,' Sarah said. 'You don't know what someone like her is capable of. Besides, Tess put her career on the line letting Julia go in the first place.'

'So you could find me.'

'Exactly. Tess let Julia go so she would lead me to you, and all she did was lead me on a wild goose chase. I take it she knew where you were all along?'

Lily nodded. 'I didn't always know where she was, but she always knew where to find me. I've been settled here for years now.'

Sarah had suspected as much but hearing that Julia had taken her completely for a ride was still like a punch in the stomach.

'And yet she acted as though we had just missed you every

place we went to,' Sarah seethed. 'She was so convincing! I made Tess a promise. When we found you, she would be able to arrest Julia, the way she should have been able to do on the day we first caught her. I don't break my promises.'

'I don't blame you,' Lily insisted. 'I just wish that you had met under different circumstances. As far as I know she's never done anything like that before.'

'Well, she really does believe in putting her all into a project,' Sarah said. She lifted the kettle off the stove and filled the mugs. Lily gestured for her to pass over the honey and busied herself preparing the tea.

'She said you taught her mentalism,' Sarah said, sitting down opposite her mother. 'Like Derren Brown mind control stuff.'

Lily shrugged. 'It's the power of suggestion, really. In the fair my family used to travel with, there was this guy, they called him the Great Merlini but that was a rip-off of some character in a book.'

'Clayton Rawson,' Sarah said. Lily gave her a quizzical look. 'He wrote the Great Merlini books.'

'Right. Well, this guy's real name was Neville. He'd spent years studying mentalism, had the best show I've ever seen, even all these years later. He used to teach me while we were travelling. It was him who taught me about bees, actually. He'd had to give his up to go on the road and he missed beekeeping terribly, he'd talk about it all the time.'

Lily looked wistful and Sarah couldn't bring herself to ask if Lily had been in love with the Great Merlini. Certainly, she didn't want to know about her loving anyone but her dad.

'It sounds interesting,' she said.

'I could teach you?' Lily's voice was small and hopeful. A mixture of emotions surged up in Sarah's chest.

'One day at a time,' she replied. 'You still might end up in a cell next to Julia.'

Chapter Twenty-Five

Oswald had asked Tess if she wanted to head the arrest team, despite not being a DI anymore. It was her case, he said, and she had more right than Walker to make the arrest. There was nothing Tess wanted less. She wanted to be free of the case, and she didn't want to be there when Julia was arrested. She couldn't look her half-sister in her eyes as she arrested her for the murder of their father. And much more than that, she didn't want to give Julia any more reason to implicate her in any of this mess.

But Tess knew that that was still a very real possibility. There was no telling whether Julia would use Tess to get herself out of the whole sorry situation, but that was a risk that Tess was willing to take. More than once over the last few months she had considered just letting Julia go – it was the only way to be absolutely sure that Tess's name stayed out of the investigation – but she knew, deep down, that she'd already compromised her morals and ethics far too many times. More than she would have liked to in her lifetime. She needed to try to claw back some sense of who she was. That was why she had joined the police force in the first place and now, even if it meant that everything she had done in the past came out, then so be it. The truth was, she was tired of lying and second guessing what might go wrong in her life next. If everything came out, at least she could stop looking over her shoulder.

Oswald had given Jerome the same option, and even PC Heath who had gone back to the beat after the investigation had dialled back its numbers. Heath had jumped at the chance to be part of a big arrest, and Tess was delighted for him. She was fond of the young ginger copper and hoped having his name and face front and centre would accelerate his promotion options. Jerome had declined, something she'd only learned when he had turned up at the Juggs ten minutes ago. The news of Julia's arrest played on a loop on Sky and BBC News, Walker getting out of the unmarked car, Oswald following. Pretending like he couldn't see the dozens of cameras or hear the shouted questions from the Associated Press, Walker opened the back door of the car and Julia Jacobs rose out gracefully wearing her tight black shift dress with huge sunglasses. And obviously handcuffs. She looked smaller than ever, her lithe frame appearing even more petite when surrounded by all those men. It was clear to anyone watching that this woman did not look like a killer.

'How many murders has she been arrested for?' one of the reporters called out.

'What will the charges be?'

It was all for show, a carefully choreographed dance, a circus act. The reporters knew that the officers were never going to answer their questions. They didn't bank on Julia Jacobs, though.

It was like a scene from *Chicago*. All at once, the beautiful young woman in handcuffs turned to face the cameras, throwing off-guard the officers who had been holding her arms to guide her towards the station. She reached up with both cuffed hands, her tiny wrists glinting with silver, and pulled off her sunglasses, giving the camera a full-frontal view of those huge, pleading eyes.

'I didn't kill anyone,' she said, her voice carrying up to where Tess and her team were standing as clearly as if she'd aimed the words at them. 'And they'll never prove I did.'

Walker, looking irritated, yanked Julia's arm backwards, which only added to the perfect performance she had just given. If Tess had been watching at home, she was fairly sure she would believe anything the young woman said, and she wouldn't be surprised if Julia Jacobs had her own range of merchandise and a TV show by the end of the month.

Sarah walked into the pub and scowled to see it playing on the TV.

'Can we get that turned off? They've been playing it over and over all day.'

Jerome stood up and switched off the TV. A woman two tables over tutted but after seeing Sarah's face she fell silent.

'How are you feeling?' Tess asked.

Sarah sighed. 'I don't know how I'm feeling,' she admitted. 'I don't know how I'm supposed to be feeling. I've never had so many goddamn emotions in my life. My sister is in prison and we still need to work on keeping my mother out of it. Do you have any good news on that score for me?'

'Yes, onto other limbs of your family tree,' Jerome commented. 'Do you have any thoughts on Millington's murder? How his body got inside Trump?'

'His body didn't get inside Trump,' Sarah said. She picked up a menu, pretending not to notice Jerome's mouth drop open slightly.

'What do you mean? Do you think it was the first person on the scene again? Amy something? Like maybe she had his skull in her handbag and she threw it onto the floor when the Trump head rolled off so it appeared that it had been inside there the whole time?'

'Maaaaybe,' Sarah said slowly, and Tess silently cursed her sister for toying with him. She knew full well that was a ridiculous idea.

'Amy Munroe didn't have a handbag with her,' Tess reminded Jerome. 'And she had no way of knowing that the Trump effigy head was going to fall directly at her feet for her to pretend the skull had rolled out of it. And she was surrounded by hundreds of people, one of them would have seen her throw the skull down.'

Jerome sat back, dejected. Tess looked at Sarah.

'Why don't you just tell us your theory instead of messing around?'

Sarah smiled at him and Tess was amused and bemused to see him blush. She didn't think she'd ever seen Jerome blush before. In fact, she distinctly remembered him telling her that black men don't blush. Liar.

'Ah, yes, well, it's obvious,' Sarah said, and Tess's jaw tightened. 'Have you watched the video?'

She leaned over to Tess's laptop and began clicking around.

When she turned the screen towards them, all three of them leaned in to watch.

'We've seen this,' Jerome said, as an image of the Trump effigy minus its head filled the screen. It was early evening, and a group of people were standing in a floodlit courtyard watching whilst three men positioned the body of the effigy onto the wheelbarrow. Three more men carried Trump's head to his body, while a fourth pumped Gorilla Glue onto the neck. The men with the head lifted it onto the squat neck and held it in place. Tess realized that one of the men was Harriet's husband, Reg.

'If Rupert Millington's body was inside that effigy, we'd see it, wouldn't we?' Sarah pointed out. 'On account of the effigy having no head. This was about twenty minutes before they wheeled him through the streets.'

Tess let out a moan of exasperation. 'Yes, well, we know it's bloody impossible – that's why we're asking you,' she said. 'By the time Trump got to the end of the high street and onto the bonfire, his body was very much in there. As seen by hundreds of traumatized bonfire watchers.'

'Not his body,' Jerome said slowly. He was looking at Sarah who was nodding as he spoke. 'His head. His head was inside Trump's head, but that doesn't necessarily mean his body was inside the effigy at all.'

Sarah whooped and clapped. 'Correct! Millington's head could have been put into that effigy at any point during the assembly process. Or rather, I'd guess, just his skull – already burned, it wouldn't have added as much weight and would be easier to hide.'

Tess raised her eyebrows. 'They found the rest of his body

on the bonfire. People would have noticed if someone had tossed a headless corpse into the fire, surely?'

Sarah shrugged. 'Not if the rest of it had already been burned as well. Remember, Millington had been missing for days by the time his body turned up on the bonfire. His killer would have had time to burn the body and place his bones on the fire when it was being built. Bones aren't difficult to hide when you've got barrows full of wood and a humongous bonfire.'

'So we're looking for whoever added fuel to that fire,' Tess concluded.

'So, anyone really?' Jerome said.

Sarah scowled. 'You could at least look a bit more pleased that I've solved your mystery for you. I feel like you just take me for granted these days.'

'Jerome solved the mystery,' Tess said, a sly smile on her face. 'I just watched him.'

It was Sarah's turn to raise a sardonic eyebrow. 'Touche. Congratulations, fact man. I look forward to reading the book on how you solved the case.'

Jerome grinned. 'I'll dedicate it to you.'

'Getting back to the point . . .' Tess sighed, her voice indicating that she was tired of the pair of them. She was scribbling down Sarah's theory in her notebook. 'How did they get the head, or the skull, in the effigy without anyone else noticing?'

'They use a mould for the paper mache,' Sarah explained. 'You can use a balloon, or a football. But this one would have been bigger, obviously. The killer only needed to hide the head inside whatever they used as the base. It could have been cut open and put in at any time between the council meeting and when they stuck the head on top. If they used a balloon our theory doesn't really stand up – you'd definitely see a skull bouncing around in a balloon – but if they used something sturdier . . .'

'So it still could have been anyone with access to the effigy?'

Sarah nodded. 'You know who the obvious suspect is when it comes to burning bodies and transporting them?'

'Babette,' Tess confirmed. 'Yes, I realize that. And I just don't see Babette being responsible. However, as we all know, we don't investigate based on feelings and first impressions of someone. She has a farm, she has the means to pull something like this off and, as his mistress or potentially woman scorned, she has the motive.'

'The unholy triad,' Jerome commented. 'And you know what they say about women scorned.'

'You know we wouldn't have to have a saying if men would just stop scorning us,' Sarah said, her voice scathing.

'Somehow I can't imagine a man ever scorning you,' Jerome said.

'And I can't figure out if you mean that as a compliment or an insult,' Sarah replied.

'You'll have to get used to that,' Tess said. 'Most of what Jerome says could be taken either way. That's why he has an equal number of women in his bed as those letting down his tyres.'

'Hmmm,' Sarah murmured. 'And I've always quite liked that car of yours.'

Tess saw Jerome blush for a second time. So she hadn't imagined it the first time. Oh dear, she hoped this wasn't going to become a problem.

Chapter Twenty-Six

'Babette?' Tess called. She banged on the sage-green farm-house door and stepped back to search the windows for movement. Sarah walked around to the side of the house and peered around the corner. Tess noticed the lack of noise from the machinery in the barns beyond; everything seemed remarkably still compared to the last time she had been there.

'We're not breaking in,' Tess called to Sarah, who appeared to be testing the sturdiness of the windowpane. 'So stop casing the joint.'

'You wanna know how I see things you don't see?' Sarah called back. She was peering through the window, her hands cupped around her face to block out the glare. 'Because I look in the places you don't.'

'You want to know why I don't get arrested?' Tess replied, pushing the doorbell again, a longer, more insistent ring this time. 'Because I don't go around breaking and entering.'

The door swung open and Tess stepped back, taken by surprise. Instead of Babette, a young man in his thirties was standing in the doorway. He was tall and sturdy, with muscular arms and the kind of permanent tan that came from working outdoors. He had short dark curls and eyes that Tess would call hazel. He was dressed in overalls and had a very distinct farm smell, to put it politely. He had one of those faces that didn't quite manage to be model good-looking but was easy enough on the eye. He looked from Tess to Sarah, who had appeared at her side, with an expectant expression.

'Is Babette in?' Tess asked. 'It's Tess,' she said, glancing down the hallway behind him. 'I met your mum the other day when she found out about the cows. She was so upset, I wanted to check on her.'

'So you're the woman she was telling me about.' He gave a nod. 'Thanks for listening to her, I know she really appreciated it, she was ready to kill that Lily Donovan. She'll be glad you came back today. I'm Martin, her son.'

He held out his hand and Tess took it. His handshake was firm, strong, a man used to manual labour.

Martin turned and called into the house.

'Mum?' He waited a beat but there was no reply and he turned back to them. 'Let me go and find her. She's been really spaced out since – the last few days. Now with the cows . . .' He lifted his shoulders in a shrug. 'I don't know what to do to snap her out of it.'

'Did she find out if it was foot and mouth?' Tess asked. He shook his head, his brow furrowed in anger.

'They don't think it was, thank God, but Paul thinks they were poisoned on purpose, which is still infuriating. Why would anyone do that? Bastards. We'll lose a few of them but at least the farm won't be shut down, which is something,

I suppose. Wait here. I'll go and find her.' Martin walked off into the house and Tess heard him calling his mother's name. She looked at Sarah, whose eyebrows were raised.

'Mum?' Sarah whispered. 'He's cute. Wonder if the farmer wants a wife?'

'Behave,' Tess mouthed as Martin appeared back in the hallway. His face looked distraught.

'She's in her bedroom,' he said, his tone urgent. 'It sounds like she's arguing with someone. The door's locked – can you help me?'

Tess looked at Sarah whose eyes were wide. They followed Martin into the house and up the stairs, passing dozens of framed photos of Babette, a child that she assumed was Martin and a man she assumed was Babette's late husband in traditional family shots, on a lake, on the beach, in front of a Christmas tree. Tess wondered briefly how many of these heart-warming family photos had been taken while Babette was having an affair. From halfway up the staircase Tess could hear Babette's voice, raised and angry as it had been in the pub the day before.

'I know what you did,' she was shouting. 'You're crazy. I'm going to call the police.'

'Babette?' Tess called. She ran down the hallway to a thick wooden door. 'Is she in this one?'

'That's Mum's room,' Martin confirmed. Tess hammered on the wood.

'Babette? Are you okay?' She turned back to Martin. 'Do you think she's on the phone?'

He shook his head. 'Her mobile is in the kitchen. There isn't a phone in the bedroom.'

Babette's scream cut through the air. 'Lily, Lily, no!'

Tess gasped. Martin shook the door handle furiously. 'Mum! Mum, let us in!'

'Lily, it's me, Tess!' Tess shouted. 'Babette? Lily? Let us in!'

There was the crack of a gunshot, and the voices stopped. 'Lily!' Tess screamed into the door. 'Babette! For God's sake, Babette, answer me!'

Martin began to hammer on the door next to her head again. There was a thick, ominous silence behind the heavy wood. Tess's heart hammered in time with Martin's fists, her chest tightening with every second Babette didn't answer. What the hell was happening behind that door?

'Mum! Let me in!' Martin backed up and ran at the door, hitting it with his shoulder. The door didn't move and he staggered back in pain, clutching his shoulder. On the other side of the door Babette and the intruder, presumably Lily Donovan, were silent.

'Babette!' Tess shouted again but there was still no answer from the woman inside. Martin started to back up but Tess grabbed his arm.

'You'll just break your shoulder. Hold on to the frame like this.' She demonstrated holding each side of the door frame. 'And slam the bottom of your foot into the door, next to the lock, as hard as you can.'

From the other side of the door there was a long, piercing scream. But it didn't sound like Babette, Tess thought. It sounded like—

She whipped around. Sarah was no longer with her in the hallway.

The lock on the door gave way with a splintering crash

and Martin stumbled halfway into the room. The first thing Tess saw when she ran in after him was Sarah's stricken face, floating in mid-air outside the window of the bedroom. The second thing she saw was the lifeless body of Babette Ramsey, lying in a pool of blood on the floor.

Chapter Twenty-Seven

'Mum!' Martin's scream drowned out the voice of the 999 operator who had answered Tess's emergency call. He was kneeling down by his mother's body, frantically feeling her wrist and neck for a pulse.

'This is Detective Sergeant Tess Fox. I need an ambulance and a police unit.' She recited the address of the farm and gave the operator a rundown of the details. She handed the phone to Sarah who had climbed down from the ladder she'd used to peer through Babette's window then sprinted up the stairs to meet them. 'Stay on the line until they get here,' she instructed her sister. 'And don't come all the way into the room. It's a crime scene.'

Sarah grabbed her arm. 'What happened to her?'

Tess had seen the bullet hole in Babette's chest and silently mimicked shooting a gun. Sarah raised her eyebrows and whispered to Tess. 'There was no one in there, Tess. No en suite, no hidey cupboards. No one got out of that window. So who shot her?'

Tess couldn't bring herself to look at Sarah. 'You heard her, Sarah, she shouted Lily's name.'

Sarah shook her head. 'That's impossible.' Her grip tightened on Tess's arm. 'Lily wasn't in there. There was no one in there . . .'

Tess shook herself out of Sarah's grasp. 'We'll worry about that later.'

She re-entered the room and knelt down next to Martin, putting a hand on his arm. 'Any sign of a pulse?'

Tears streamed down his cheeks. He shook his head. 'I can't feel one. There's so much blood . . .'

'Can you get me a towel, something to stop the bleeding?' She had a feeling it was already too late for that, but she needed to get him away from his mum's body. If there was even a tiny chance that Babette might be alive, she wouldn't be saved by someone sobbing over her.

Tess pressed her fingers to Babette's neck. Her skin was cool to the touch and there was no sign of even a weak pulse. The blood around the hole in her chest wasn't spreading – Babette was dead.

A sob came from the doorway and Tess looked up to see Martin clutching the towels to his chest. 'She's . . . she's dead, isn't she?'

'Martin, I'm so sorry.'

He wailed and moved to fling himself onto his mother's body. Tess caught him in her arms and held him as he sobbed into her shoulder. The sound of the paramedics flooded the stairway and Tess manoeuvred Martin, his head still buried in her shoulder, out into the hallway to let them pass.

'This is a crime scene,' she called to remind them but none

of them gave any indication they'd heard her. 'The police are on their way.' She heard them trying to find any sign of life and then silence. They walked back out of the room and Martin looked up as the first one gave a small shake of his head.

'I'm so sorry,' the paramedic said. 'There's nothing we can do.' Martin backed up, shaking his head and muttering, 'Nonononono,' until his back hit the wall opposite and he stopped, staring at the doorway to the room that held his mother's dead body.

Sarah passed Tess her phone and Tess looked at it stupidly.

'I should call Walker,' she said, the weight of everything that had just happened beginning to sink in.

'I already know, Fox.' The voice came from the stairs. Both Sarah and Tess turned around to see DI Walker and one of his detective sergeants making their way down the hallway towards them.

'Sir,' Tess said. 'This is Martin Ramsey, the deceased's son. I was here when he found the body. Victim is Babette Ramsey. She owns the farm.'

Walker nodded at Martin Ramsey, who was still staring at the door to his mother's bedroom. 'Take him downstairs and make him a drink,' he instructed the DS with him. The man nodded and took Martin's arm.

'Come with me, sir. Is there anyone I can call for you?' Martin didn't answer, just allowed himself to be led slowly down the stairs.

Walker rounded on Tess. 'The second murder in Kingston in less than a fortnight and *you're* the one who discovers the body? What the fuck are you doing here?'

Tess held up her hands. 'I came to talk to Babette about the autopsy of her cow. The one you told me to attend.'

Walker looked as though he'd been punched in the face. Tess was momentarily overjoyed at the irony – she was slap bang in the middle of the murder scene because he had her chasing stupid leads about poisoned cows. Then she remembered that Babette was dead – there was no joy in this situation.

'And Ms Jacobs . . .' Walker gestured to Sarah who was, to her credit, trying to stay as quiet as possible for once. 'She's a friend of Ramsey's, I suppose? Second cousin twice removed?'

'Oh no, sir,' Sarah said quickly. 'I never met her.' Walker gestured for her to go on. 'I saw Te— um, DS Fox coming up here and I followed her. I wanted to ask her about my dad's case. I was just being a pain in the ass.'

They say the best lies are ninety per cent truth, and Sarah's 'pain in the ass' story must have been believable enough for Walker because he turned his attention back to Tess. 'So what happened here?'

Tess faltered. There was no way of keeping Lily's name out of this; Martin had heard Babette scream it, clear as day. Besides, Tess couldn't cover up for any more of Sarah's family members – especially one who had only recently returned from the dead. Whatever she said, Lily was tied up in this somehow. She relayed exactly what had happened to Walker, noticing Sarah cringe when she got to the part about Lily's name.

'So you heard this argument?'

'We all did.'

'And she definitely said "Lily"?'

Tess nodded. Walker scowled. 'But the door was locked?'

'It wouldn't open so it seems that way, yes. Mr Ramsey kicked it in and broke the lock.'

'And surprise, surprise, no Lily Donovan.'

'No, sir.'

Walker glared at her. 'Go back to the station, Fox, and give your statement. Take your shadow over there and make sure neither of you leave anything out.'

'But, sir—'

'This is my crime scene, Fox. The Millington case is my case, and I'm not going to let you get your sticky fingers on it. Back to the station. And at some point I'm going to want to know' – he held up a finger – 'one, why the daughter of a murdered businessman always seems to be hanging around with you. Two, why Lily Donovan asked for you specifically to visit her at the station, and three' – here he thrust three fingers in Tess's face – 'why the phone downstairs on the kitchen table has a text message from Lily Donovan saying she'll be here in five minutes.'

Tess tried to hide the shock on her face. She heard Sarah gasp.

'Sir—'

'Station, Fox,' Walker snapped. 'And don't leave until I get there.'

Tess nodded and tilted her head for Sarah to follow her. She passed the kitchen where Martin was sitting at the table with the DS, staring at a mug of tea. It wasn't until they were out of the house, down the driveway and Tess was sliding into the driver's seat of her car that Sarah said, 'Are you okay?'

'What?' Tess asked absently. Sarah lifted up a hand and brushed Tess's cheek. Her fingers came away wet.

'You're crying,' Sarah pointed out. Tess looked up at the mirror and saw tears trickling down her cheeks.

'Poor Babette,' Tess whispered. 'She lost her husband, then Rupert. She was just so sad. And now she's gone.'

'Shot to death in a locked room,' Sarah murmured. 'With a member of my family under suspicion. Ever feel like you've been here before?'

'So she couldn't have climbed out of the window?' Jerome asked, pointing his pen at the drawing of Babette's bedroom that Sarah had done on a piece of A3 paper tacked to the wall. Sarah nudged Tess's arm out of the way to draw a stick figure of herself on a ladder at the window. They were squeezed into the stationery cupboard in Lewes Police Station, Sarah and Tess desperately trying to fill Jerome in on what had happened at the farm before Walker came back. There was huge racking either side of them filled with notepads, pens of every colour and description, magazine files and brown cardboard sleeves.

'Can we stop saying "she" as if we're certain it was Lily?' Sarah asked. 'And the window was one of those ones that opens at the top but not the bottom, and it was closed when I got up there,' she said. 'If anyone had opened it, it would still have been open when I got to it – you couldn't close it from the outside. Besides, I had to drag the ladder from over by those sheds. Why would a killer fleeing a scene take time to return the ladder?'

'So not the window.' Tess turned the paper, as though a new angle might open up a secret door in the bedroom wall Sarah had drawn. 'Then how? And if not Lily, then who? Why would she scream "Lily, no" if Lily wasn't in there?'

'Maybe whoever it was told her Lily had slept with Rupert?' Sarah suggested. 'And she was all like, "Not Lily! Nooooo!"' Sarah faked clutching at her pearls.

Tess shook her head. 'Can you imagine the look on Walker's face if I went to him with that theory? He's going to laugh in my face and Lily will be suspect number one.'

'Okay, let's say it was Lily, just for a second. What's her motive?'

'Babette accused her of cursing her cows,' Jerome pointed out.

'So Lily would be stupid to kill her, right? After she's just had a fight with her in public. And what would be the point in someone poisoning the cows if she was just going to kill Babette anyway?'

Tess's phone buzzed and she glanced at the screen. 'Oh Lord. Walker's on his way up. I'll go and head him off. Jerome, go back to your desk. Sarah, stay here – I'll tell Walker you've been waiting to give a statement this whole time.'

'Can't I just leave and we'll pretend I disappeared from a locked room? Might push him over the edge.' Sarah grinned and Tess laughed.

'I'm actually quite glad it's Walker's case,' Tess said. 'Let him be the butt of the invisible man jokes.'

'I've been working on my invisible man jokes, as a matter of fact,' Sarah said. 'He'll never see them coming.'

Chapter Twenty-Eight

Walker had had surprisingly little to say about Tess being at Babette's house, given that she had the perfect excuse – after all, he'd tasked her with the 'mysterious case of the cow poisoning'. Both she and Sarah had stuck to the story of her being a pest about her dad's murder, so he'd taken both of their statements and told Tess to return a stack of documents to Arnold Page. She'd wanted to ask more about the text message – was it definitely from Lily, was it definitely on Babette's phone and not Martin's . . . but Walker's face was still like thunder from finding her at his crime scene and she was not about to push her luck. He had half the force out looking for Lily Donovan; Babette's murder had tipped the scales against her and Tess had no doubt she'd be arrested and brought in for questioning as soon as they found her. They hadn't issued a media statement yet but it was only a matter of time.

Arnold Page was an eccentric little man, no bigger than five foot two. He was bald on top of his head, but had thick grey hair around the sides that had been carefully smoothed down.

He wore a rich scarlet velvet waistcoat and a blue checked shirt underneath. There was a gold watch pinned to the front of his waistcoat which bounced as he walked. Tess noticed he was wearing a watch on each wrist, yet despite this, he was five minutes late for their arranged meeting at his own home.

'Sorry!' He shuffled down the path towards her, keys jangling in his hand. 'Just had to pop out to pick up some worming tablets for the cat.'

Tess gave him an uneasy smile as he unlocked the front door. She hoped she wasn't going to be expected to be part of any de-worming procedure.

'Come in, come in!' He led her down a small, cramped hallway, made more so by the bookshelves bursting with battered old paperbacks that lined the walls. He opened a door to the left and presented his office to her with a big flourish of his arms, as though it was supposed to be impressive. And it certainly made an impression . . .

Tess walked in and momentarily panicked. The office walls were covered with huge pictures of what she assumed were Lewes bonfires from over the years and at first glance it looked as though the room was on fire. It was quite disconcerting.

'Terrible business this year,' he said, gesturing for Tess to take a seat behind the desk. 'I only have one chair in here. It's usually only me. Would you be more comfortable in the living room, or the kitchen perhaps?'

Tess just wanted to get this over with and get out of the suffocating little house.

'No, it's fine, thank you,' she said. 'I've got to get back to the station. I just came to return . . .'

'You can't leave so soon!' he said, as offended as if she'd

suggested she would sit on the main road. He perched himself on a stack of books that wobbled precariously and immediately stood back up again. Tess imagined what Sarah's reaction would have been and stifled a laugh.

'Do you have any leads so far? As I told your colleague, any information I can give you I shall endeavour to provide.'

Tess smiled at the unusual man. 'Thank you. How long have you been the chair of Cliffe Bonfire Society?'

'Ten years this year. I've been a Bonfire Boy since I was eleven, though. Used to march with my grandad and my dad, then just my dad, now my son. That's why the procession is so important to everyone – it's not just a bit of fun. It's an honour. A tradition. It's wood and smoke and sparks and memories. It's the tossing of the magistrate in the Oust and the playing of the band.'

'And is it something people would kill to keep going?' Tess asked. Arnold's eyes widened.

'Good Lord, no. If we burned every person who wanted the bonfire procession banned . . . well, we wouldn't need wood for the fires.'

'Where does the wood for the bonfires come from?' Tess asked, thinking about Sarah's theory of how Rupert Millington's body ended up in the fire. He gave a wide sweep of his arm.

'Everywhere!' he proclaimed. 'We take wood donations for weeks before the actual night.'

Tess held out her phone.

'This video shows the effigy being assembled on the night of the bonfire by some members of the society. We've already identified the people in the video, but the effigy itself was being

169

built for weeks. Could you give me the names of the people involved in its construction?'

'Like I told the other officer,' he said, his face grim all of a sudden, 'the Trump effigy was made by some of our most trusted and well-known members. Whoever put poor Mr Millington inside that yellow-haired buffoon had nothing to do with them.'

'I'd still appreciate a list of their names, so we can double check it against the one we have.'

'Oh yes, check and double check!' He opened the top drawer of his desk and pulled out a battered red notebook. 'I made a list of all those I could remember. There were more than six layers of paper mache, then there were the painters – a lot of people had a hand in the making.'

He handed her the list and Tess scanned it.

Samuel Kent
Laurel Parr
Harriet Ellis
Reg Ellis
Betsy Holliday
Truly Fletcher
Emma Bartez
Andrea Seddon
Babette Ramsey
Jackie Doyle
Gary Harris
Tom Wooloff
Leodora Millington

'What about just the head?' Tess asked. 'Did anyone in particular work on that?'

Arnold grinned. 'The crowning glory. That hair itself took a week to get right. Thank goodness for Harriet Ellis – she did a brilliant job. But I think most of the people on that list had a hand in the head. Ha! A hand in the head. Sorry, not the time for jokes, I know. Terrible business. Truly terrible.'

Chapter Twenty-Nine

Sarah glanced down at her ringing mobile phone. It was a number she didn't know, but she was used to that in her line of business. She changed phones every couple of months anyway.

'Hello?'

'Sarah, it's me. Your . . . um, your Lily.'

Oh great, Sarah thought. *Why must I always be caught between my family and my sister?* 'Lily, where are you? The police are looking for you. Do you know what happened to Babette?'

'Of course I do. And I'm calling to tell you that I wasn't there.'

'She screamed your name, Lily. And the police found a text on her phone from you saying that you would be five minutes.'

'Babette asked me to meet her at the farm, but the place was already crawling with police when I got to the top of the lane, so I legged it.'

'That wasn't five minutes.'

'It's a figure of speech,' Lily snapped. 'I have no idea why she'd scream my name, I wasn't anywhere near that farmhouse.'

'Why would you run away at the sight of police if you didn't do anything?'

'Force of habit. Surely you don't think I killed old Battering Ramsey?'

It was a question Sarah had been asking herself ever since they'd heard Babette scream at Lily, minutes before the gunshot rang out. 'I don't even know you,' she said, her voice quiet. There was a pause at the end of the phone and Sarah wondered if the other woman had hung up.

'Well, that's my fault, isn't it?' Lily said eventually, her voice heavy with regret. 'If I'd been a real mum then you'd know that I wasn't capable of murder. Hopefully I'll get the chance to prove that to you.'

'Not capable of murder is a pretty low bar to want to hit,' Sarah managed to joke. She heard Lily chuckle.

'It's a start, though. Anyway, I was also calling because I need your help.'

Sarah's stomach turned. 'What with?'

'I thought you might be up for a little nocturnal snooping,' Lily said. 'I saw Leodora go out fifteen minutes ago. And then the lights started.'

'You want to go and break into Rupert Millington's house whilst on the run from the police to investigate lights?'

'Yes.'

Sarah thought about what the letter from Rupert in Babette's bedroom had said about an 'amusing discovery about our resident witch'. He'd said it required further investigation. Was Lily trying to find out what Rupert knew about her?

'Where are you?' Sarah asked. 'I should tell you to go to the police.'

'But you won't,' Lily replied. 'I'm at the end of the lane leading up to Millington's house, hiding behind a tree. I saw the police turn up my drive and thought better of going home.'

'I can't believe I'm being the responsible one, Lily, but I don't think you should be doing this.'

'I want to find out what the hell is going on with those lights,' she said. 'And I thought you'd be the one to help me get through the locks.'

'I didn't think you believed in ghosts. And I didn't think this was the kind of place you worried about locking your doors.'

'I would never presume to think I know everything about this life and the next,' Lily said. 'But one thing I do know is that people can't be trusted.'

Sarah snorted at the irony of the fact her mother had called her there to help her break into a house. She supposed she was right – you just couldn't trust people these days.

Sarah didn't believe for one second that Lily just wanted to investigate the lights in Rupert's house. She had an ulterior motive, and Sarah wanted to find out what it was.

'Where shall I meet you?'

'You think you can get us in?' Lily asked, when Sarah met her at the end of The Street, or Street Street as Sarah liked to call it.

'I've been breaking into buildings since I was a little kid,' Sarah said. Lily winced.

'Do you ever wish you'd left the family and gone with Tess when she went to join the police?'

Sarah gave her a quizzical look. Lily didn't know that Tess

had left the family because she'd had to kill a man to get Sarah out of a horrific situation. That her sister had been trying to atone for a murder for fifteen years. 'Do *you* wish I'd gone with Tess? Are you ashamed of who I've become?'

Lily shook her head quickly. 'Of course not,' she said. 'I never really saw another path for you, given who your father and I were. But seeing Tess make a life without the threat of prison hanging over her head every day . . .'

'Boooring,' Sarah said. Lily smiled but Sarah knew that she wasn't going to be satisfied with her answer. She'd probably let it go for now. Lily had been absent from her life for too long to start playing concerned mummy, but sooner or later she was going to want to know more about Sarah's life, and Sarah was going to have to decide how much she was going to let her in.

But not tonight. Tonight they were on a fact-finding, house-breaking mission. Everyone has to have a hobby.

'Have you spoken to Julia?' Lily asked. Sarah's chest tightened at her sister's name.

'How can I?' Sarah asked. 'She's accused of murdering my dad. No one knows that we even know each other. I saw in the news that she's still being questioned under caution, they haven't charged her yet.'

'She's quite the story in the nationals,' Lily commented. 'Suspected murderer who won't tell the police her name. Her face is all over the papers, it's only a matter of time before they find out who she is.'

'As soon as they run her DNA they'll know she's Frank's daughter. And my sister. We're all going to be dragged through it, except maybe Tess. They don't have any reason to link Tess to any of us unless Julia talks.'

'She might, you know.'

'I know.' Sarah sighed. 'Why did Babette want to see you?' she asked, changing the subject. Lily shrugged.

'I don't suppose I'll find out, now. She's gone and I'm going to be clapped in irons.'

'Nah. Tess will crack the case, don't you worry. Then when the real killer is found you can go back to being the local witch.'

'Maybe that time is over now,' Lily looked doleful. 'I've always leaned into my reputation as the local witch. Encouraged it, given that people pay quite a bit of cash in hand for a potion, a cup of tea and some advice. Maybe a glimpse into the future, some reassurance from the tarot cards. Now the very thing people around here valued me for is the thing that has them hoping I'm a murderer.'

'Hoping?'

Lily nodded. 'Of course. I'm the easy choice. I have no family here, I'm not the local church warden or the licensee at the pub. While it's me, it's not one of them. That's what they're really scared of, that it could be any of them.'

Sarah tripped on a tree branch and stumbled. Lily caught her arm.

'Careful. We're nearly there. Look, can you see that house there? That's Rupert and Leodora's.'

The lane gave way to a field. Lily was pointing across the field to where a thick, grand hedgerow guarded a large house. Six bedrooms at least, Sarah thought. In the dark she could only make out the size, and the modern outdoor lighting that spread shafts of light up the wall giving it a chilling, ominous glow.

'We can't get through that hedge and I doubt we'll be able to go through the front gates. I'm assuming they have security gates for a house like that.'

'They do. But the hedge doesn't go all the way around – there's a wall at the back with another gate. It's code locked.'

'And you know the code, I suppose? Or was Rupert not a fan of the back—'

Lily poked a finger at her. 'Do not finish that sentence,' she warned. 'I've said it a million times, Rupert and I were *not* having an affair. But that's why I called you, my dear. Because if I know Rupert, the old cheapskate will have done the cheapest job possible. Nothing my little girl can't handle.'

Any worries Sarah had about not making her mother proud began to dissipate when she saw the smile on Lily's face. Sarah sighed and shifted the backpack into a more comfortable position.

'Come on, then,' she said. 'Let's go and break in to a murder victim's house.'

Chapter Thirty

Sarah shone the torch at the security lock. Lily had been right – Rupert had installed the cheapest code lock you could get. It might deter your local scrotes and scallies but anyone a sight more determined wouldn't have to try too hard. Sarah herself was going to have no problem getting it open. She pulled a couple of tools from her bag and handed Lily the torch.

'They've got a basic Amazon Ring system up there as well,' Sarah said, indicating the camera attached to the wall of the house. 'Which, given the size of the garden, doesn't have enough range to quite meet the outside of this wall. Once we're inside, however, our motions will probably be picked up within feet. Sound too. Put this on.'

She pulled a balaclava from her bag and tossed it to Lily whose eyes widened.

'How are we supposed to explain this away?' she hissed. 'If someone catches us?'

'If someone catches us we're already screwed,' Sarah explained. 'What were you going to say, that you got lost in the field and accidentally broke through the coded lock? Once we break in, we're committing the crime. There are about fifty other ways we can get in if you'd like – I can deliver her some flowers and you can hide in the van, we can pretend to be from the funeral directors, the bank. I can sell her a new security system . . .'

Lily considered these options, then shook her head. 'We're here now. Do you think the cameras will set off an alarm?'

'Not those ones,' Sarah said. 'People rarely have all the bells and whistles on regular houses like this. Maybe if you're a celebrity or some kind of target. And even then, most of the time people don't bother setting the alarms. You would be surprised how lax people really are about securing their belongings. They rely on these cheap Ring doorbells, false sense of security. It's how we do what we do. You can get devices that literally turn off these cameras, you know? We've got some at the . . . at work. Just remember the audio on those cameras while we're outside. Don't say names.'

'Got it.' Lily nodded. Sarah gave her a stern look and Lily held her hands up. 'Honestly, I've got it. I won't get us caught.'

'Good.' Sarah pulled on her balaclava and adjusted it over her face, and Lily did the same, mimicking Sarah's action of tucking her hair underneath. Then she handed her some latex gloves and Lily slipped those on too. Sarah felt around the sides of the security lock and slipped one of her tools into the groove on the left. She gave it a wiggle. It opened with a click, and even with the balaclava on Sarah could see her mother's eyebrows rise.

'Maybe leave that detail out of the family newsletter,' Sarah whispered. Lily snorted. As Sarah prepared to step forwards into the garden she motioned for Lily to be quiet and follow her. They slipped inside, backs close to the wall. Sarah handed Lily a rock and made a throwing motion. Lily tossed the rock into the middle of the garden and the security light came on. They stayed, frozen against the wall until the light went off, then Sarah repeated the action. The light came on again. Three more repetitions and Lily was giving Sarah a quizzical look. Sarah grabbed her arm and pulled her around the perimeter until they were at the closest point to the house. She pulled Lily to the house, then stopped against the wall as the light came on. Lily froze in fear. Sarah waited for the light to go off again, then inched closer to the patio doors, her back against the house. The light didn't come on.

When they reached the patio doors, Sarah indicated that Lily should stay flat against the wall. She pulled a long, flat tool out of her bag, and slid it under the door. On the other side it sprang back up and Sarah manoeuvred her side over the door handle. With a slight hand movement the other side hooked over the handle and Sarah pulled downwards. The door swung open.

She motioned wildly for Lily to follow her inside, then slammed the patio door shut.

Lily bent over, hands on her knees, gasping for breath. Sarah knew why – the adrenaline rush of breaking and entering, especially your first time, was immense.

'If she's going to call the police, she will have done it by now,' Sarah said. 'They will likely be on their way, given who she is and what's happened recently. If anyone pulls up, just leg it for that back gate. They probably won't even bother chasing us.'

'What was the rock tossing all about?' Lily asked, straightening up at last.

Sarah smiled. 'Psychological warfare. The first time Leodora gets a notification that there's motion detected in her garden, she checks the camera. Nothing. Probably a spider in front of the sensor. The next time, nothing again. It's irritating – especially if she's with a man as we suspect she might be. The third time maybe she doesn't even check, by the fourth or fifth false alarm she's snoozed the notifications for an hour, guaranteed. Now, we're still on that camera – there's nothing we can do to stop that. But if Leodora hasn't seen us break in, and we leave the place exactly how we found it, she might never even check the cameras. She never needs to know anyone has been here.'

'You're a genius!' Lily beamed. 'Come on, then, let's get to it.' She started to move, then stopped and looked at Sarah. 'What are we getting to?'

Sarah laughed. What Lily lacked in housebreaking skills she made up for in enthusiasm.

'I thought you wanted to find out about the lights?'

Lily looked suitably ashamed. 'I thought . . . I was wondering . . .'

'You were wondering what evidence in this house might make you look guilty of murder.'

'I didn't kill either of them, Sarah, you've got to believe me. But there were things going on . . .'

Sarah held up a hand to stop her. 'We don't have time now. I'm guessing we're looking for papers.' She held up a finger. 'Everyone has a junk drawer, or a bureau or something where they keep their recent post. Find that.' Second finger. 'Men like Rupert always have an office, we find that.' Third finger. 'Bedroom. Bedside drawers are often a treasure trove.' Last finger. 'Calendars or diaries. Touch as little as possible, take nothing. Photograph anything you find. I'll do the office, you look for post and calendars. Bedside tables if no one has busted us by then. Half an hour, Lily – anything longer is pushing our luck.'

Lily nodded like she were an army cadet and her superior had spoken. 'Understood.'

'If someone comes, just run for that back door and keep running. Don't wait for me, don't look back, just go.'

'Understood.'

Sarah nodded. 'Let's go.'

They split up, Sarah heading off to find Rupert's study, leaving Lily alone in the spacious kitchen–diner. Possibly not the best idea to leave her mother on her own when she was as giddy as a schoolgirl from her first break-in, but they didn't have enough time to stick together. Especially because neither of them knew exactly what they were looking for. Sarah silently cursed Lily for not telling the truth before they got inside. It could have been helpful to know.

The entryway to the house was large and minimalist, with just one small, stylish console against the wall, a large round mirror above it, and a painting on the opposite wall. That meant the door to the left was most likely a coat room, as there was nowhere in this empty hallway to hang coats or kick off shoes. The house was equally proportioned on either side of the front door, so one way would be the living area, and the other way would usually be the spare downstairs room – sometimes an office, sometimes a second living space, smaller but cosier.

Sarah wasn't a housebreaker – she wasn't a thief at all, not really. The money that her team made was always given to them willingly, usually by greedy people who wanted to make more of it and didn't care if it was illegal. Her breaking and entering skills had been useful for recon, though, and the odd blackmail or bribery. She mainly kept up with the latest lock-breaking techniques because she found it interesting – and you never knew when you were going to have to get yourself into – or out of – a locked room. It was rare she didn't have some kind of door entry device in her handbag, and she had an entire kit in one of them.

The first room she came to was a living room, which made it likely that Rupert's study was the other side of the giant hallway. Wrong. So it must be upstairs, which meant getting further away from her emergency exit, which she didn't like the idea of. She took the stairs two at a time, and, ignoring the first door which was almost definitely a bathroom, started trying the others. She found the office on the third try.

Rupert had exactly the kind of 'look at me I'm very important' office she would have expected. She was only surprised, really, that he hadn't taken up the trend of having a summerhouse built in the garden – the ultimate 'home office' to brag about to friends. Perhaps it hadn't been tax deductible.

The bottom of the walls were panelled despite the house being a new build, and painted a rich mahogany colour. The top was a deep scarlet, with gold-framed paintings hung on two walls, windows on one and a row of expensive mahogany bookcases lining the other. There was not a single book on the shelves that wasn't part of a gold-lettered, leather- or fabric-bound set. No tattered Stephen King paperbacks or the latest by Richard Osman. They were props, for show. Sarah doubted Rupert had ever read a single one.

A completely empty, obscenely large antique desk, complete with a protective leather rectangle, sat at the far end of the room, a black filing cabinet next to it. Sarah crossed to the desk immediately and began opening drawers, feeling under the rims, checking the bottom of each one. These gorgeous old desks were fairly common in antique shops – not even as expensive as they looked, and sometimes even came with the infamous secret drawer inserts. She found no such drawer inserts, and the drawers were all empty. The police had probably been through them already. She was turning to leave when she noticed something about the book on the shelf. There was one book that wasn't part of the leather-bound set. It was slightly larger, thicker, and the gold-leaf lettering wasn't cracked in the same way the others were. Sarah slipped it off the shelf – it was hollow. Hollow, but not empty.

Sarah slid the papers out, trying not to touch them too much, despite wearing gloves. Complete caution. They were bank statements by the looks of it. Nothing stood out too much until she got to January of that year, when two thousand pounds was transferred to an external account. There were also transactions in March and May for similar amounts. Sarah took some photographs on her phone. Was Rupert being blackmailed? He'd had his fingers in so many dodgy pies that it was very possible. But if he was paying blackmail, why would that person kill him and have their cash flow stop?

Underneath the bank statements was a small red book. Sarah flipped it open and saw a list of names, and what looked like quantities and prices. These must be the people Rupert had been flogging his dodgy wine to. Sure enough, Reg Ellis was on there. And . . . well, well, well . . . Walter Ramsey, Babette's now-deceased husband.

Sarah took photos of the pages and put them back exactly as she found them. The last thing in the book was a thin, folded brown A4 envelope. Sarah slipped out the sheets of paper and scanned over them. Oh no. Oh no . . .

She was trying to figure out just how much damage this could do when Lily appeared in the doorway, out of breath and frantic. Sarah heard the slamming of a car door. Shit. She shoved the envelope inside her hoodie and the book back on the shelf. 'What's going on?'

'She's back!' Lily gasped. 'Leodora's back!'

Chapter Thirty-One

Sarah grabbed Lily's arm and pulled her along the upstairs hallway, just as they heard the sound of keys in the front door. She took a gamble, rushing to where the corridor took a small turn, and pushed open the door she found there. As she expected, a storage room. As far as she knew, Leodora and Rupert had lived alone, so even if Leodora had been unable to face the marital bedroom after her husband's death, there were still four other spare rooms. One was Rupert's office, the other three were either guest rooms or storage. Odds on.

'In here,' Sarah hissed, pulling Lily behind a stack of cardboard boxes. 'Did you leave anything out of place?'

Lily cringed. 'I don't think so . . . I'm not sure! I panicked and ran to you.'

'That's fine. I closed the patio doors behind us so she won't be able to tell that anyone has broken in. Hopefully she won't notice anything untoward, and hopefully she doesn't need anything out of these boxes.'

There was banging from the other side of the wall, as though someone was moving around in the room parallel to them. They heard a shower switch on.

'En suite,' Sarah whispered.

'Listen,' Leodora's voice came through the wall as clear as if she were standing next to them, 'I'm sorry about tonight. I know you're all over the place with what's happened, and I am too but we really need to talk about this. I do love you, Reggie. Call me when you get this.'

Lily raised her eyebrows in shock.

'Did she say Reggie?' she mouthed.

Sarah thought back to Rupert's wake, and the gruff-faced man behind the bar. He was untidy, unkempt – a world apart from Rupert Millington and his well-pressed suits and Just for Men hair. As unlikely as it seemed, they had both heard it. Leodora Millington was having an affair with Reg Ellis.

Tess was going through her notes and trying to organise herself when the text from Sarah came.

Stuck in Millington's house. Leodora has been seeing Reg Ellis. Need you to get us out. DO NOT RING ME

Tess stared at the text message for a few minutes, reading and rereading the information. What did she mean she was stuck? Had she gone to talk to Leodora and not been able to get away? But Leodora didn't seem the overly chatty type, and if Sarah needed a rescue call why would she explicitly say not to call?

Unless . . . Tess groaned. There was, of course, another way that Sarah could be stuck in Leodora's house. If she'd broken in.

'Oh, for the love of God,' she muttered. What exactly was

she supposed to do? Sarah had said don't call but she hadn't said not to text back.

Get you out how?

DISTRACTION

Tess wished she was with her little sister right now, so she could wring her neck. She lived over an hour away from Kingston – how on earth was she going to distract Leodora from here?

Think, what would Sarah do? Well, Tess mused, Sarah would probably call in some kind of bomb scare to Leodora's house, then change into her bomb squad uniform that she conveniently kept in her left pocket and slip out undetected whilst getting a lift home with the squad. But Tess wasn't Sarah.

Where are you?

Spare room.

Need to go through the front door?

No but need to pass it inside to get to the back door

That made things considerably more difficult. Her first thought had been pizza delivery – then Sarah could have snuck out while Leodora was arguing about unordered pizzas. But that would put Leodora at the front door . . .

Okay, trying something

She sifted through her notes to find the Millingtons' telephone number and dialled.

She's not answering phone

She's in the shower

Is the shower in the hallway?????Why can't you sneak out now?

Funny. Don't know how long

yeah she's out now
Fine

Tess dialled again. It took a few minutes for Leodora to answer. Tess imagined her cursing at the ringing as she stepped out of her shower.

'Hello?'

'Hello, is this the occupant of . . .' Tess glanced at her notes and reeled off the Millingtons' address.

'Yes, who is this?'

Tess didn't blame her for sounding suspicious. After Rupert's very public and very odd death, she'd probably had journalists on the phone at all hours.

'I'm from the gas board. I'm sorry to be calling so late. We've had a call about a potential gas leak in the area and we're trying to work out how many properties it's affecting.'

'Oh dear. I can't smell any gas.'

'I don't think at this stage it's on a large enough scale to smell, and please don't worry about explosions yet.'

'Yet?' Leodora's voice sounded panicked and Tess felt terrible.

'Yes, well, it's just best to get these things dealt with quickly. Where is your gas meter?'

Tess crossed her fingers that the meter would be outside.

'It's just outside the front door.'

She tried to hold in her sigh of relief. This con business had her adrenaline pumping as much as an arrest. 'Right, I just need you to take a look at it for me – is that okay?'

Leodora sighed. 'Okay, just let me get my coat on, and I've got to find the key and a torch.'

'No problem. You'll need to turn the electrics off until we're done – just in case there's a problem.'

'What? Okay, fine. I really could do without this. Are you okay to hold?'

'Of course, madam, take your time.'

The line went quiet and Tess fired off a text to Sarah.

She'll be out the front in a few minutes. Hurry up and I'll keep her talking

You're so good at this. Must be a Jacobs

Tess couldn't help but smile. Leodora came back on the line and Tess talked her through the numbers she needed from the gas meter, hoping that it would buy Sarah enough time to leave. After ten minutes of made-up checks, Tess said, 'It sounds like you're not one of the houses affected, Mrs Millington. Have a good evening.'

She thanked her and hung up, and Tess hoped to hell that Leodora didn't realize that she'd never given the helpful gas woman her name.

It was two hours later, nearly midnight, when Tess heard the downstairs buzzer go. Knowing it could only really be one person, she buzzed her in, then went to her own front door and peered through the peephole. Sure enough, Sarah was there, dressed all in black and waving at her.

Tess opened the door and silently stood aside for her sister to come in.

'Were you asleep?' Sarah asked. Tess shook her head.

'Actually, I was up trying to sort out these notes. I spoke to the head of the bonfire society earlier today and all five of our suspects had access to the Trump head, but Harriet Ellis did a lot of work on it alone, apparently. I presume, seeing as you haven't asked me to post bail, that you weren't arrested getting out of the Millingtons'?'

'Thanks to you, big sis.' Sarah held her hand up for a high five, then saw Tess's glare and dropped it.

'What were you doing breaking into Leodora's house? That wasn't part of the plan. And do you know where your mother is? They have a warrant issued for her arrest – Jerome called me before to tell me.'

'I've got no idea where she is.' Sarah walked past Tess and dropped down onto the sofa, moving aside a set of papers. 'And the break-in was spur of the moment. You were brilliant, though – turning off the electricity – genius! Knocked out all the cameras.'

'Yeah, well, I won't be doing anything like that again,' Tess warned. 'Makes me worry for women living alone; how easy it is to get them to disable their security systems.'

'Maybe we should go into the security consultancy business. Jacobs and Fox.'

'Sounds like a biscuit company.'

Sarah laughed.

'Now that I've saved your ass,' Tess said, putting the kettle on, 'and made my feelings clear about you breaking and enter-ing into victims' houses, tell me what that message was about? Reg Ellis?'

Sarah explained what she'd heard Leodora saying on the phone.

'Do you think she started the affair to get back at Rupert for sleeping with Harriet?'

Tess let out a breath. 'From the amount of rumours flying around this village, Leodora would have had a full-time job starting revenge affairs for everyone Rupert was sleeping with. There's Babette, Harriet, Lily—'

'And I think someone was blackmailing him,' Sarah said. She explained what she'd found in the hollow book in Rupert's office. 'Regular sums going out – that sounds like blackmail, doesn't it?'

'I thought Walker's team searched Rupert's house?'

Sarah raised her eyebrows. 'And now your team have.'

Tess smiled. 'Anything else?'

She saw Sarah hesitate. 'Nothing,' she said. 'Nothing else.'

Chapter Thirty-Two

Tess pushed open the door of the incident room they had allocated to Rupert's – and now Babette's – murder. Walker was inside, leaning over a young female PC close enough to count the hairs on her arms. Tess cleared her throat, wishing she could punch Geoff Walker in his. There was no way the PC was comfortable with him being that close, and no way she would feel able to say anything. Tess made a mental note to speak to Oswald about it. Men like Walker should have gone when the dinosaurs did.

He stood up straight, not even looking guilty at being caught invading the PC's personal space. 'What can I do for you, Fox? More mysterious cattle crimes? Don't tell me, alien probes?' He made the usual jokes but Tess could see the signs of stress on his face. His eyes were ringed purple and he rubbed at them as if he was struggling to keep them open.

'No, sir.' Tess said the word like it tasted of cow pat. 'Any news on tracking down Lily Donovan?'

Walker looked like he wanted to tell her to mind her own business. Actually, he looked like he'd tell her to eff off if they'd been alone. He glanced at the young PC and back at Tess then sighed.

'We had officers outside her house all of last night but she didn't go home. I trust that you'd tell me if you knew where she was? I haven't forgotten that Donovan asked for you by name the night we took her statement.'

'Of course I'd tell you, sir. I only met Mrs Donovan very recently, I barely know her at all. She was friends with my father, that's how she knew to ask for me.'

'And have you asked your father about her known contacts, where she might be?'

'He's dead, sir.'

Walker didn't even have the good grace to look embarrassed. 'No help there, then,' he said. 'Was there anything else? Unless you've forgotten, I have two dead bodies and only a batty old medium as a suspect.'

Tess cleared her throat. Perhaps he'd have more information if he stopped chasing down political conspiracy theories and looked at the people around Millington. 'Actually, there is. It's about Rupert Millington's finances. Before she died, Babette mentioned that Rupert might have been blackmailed. She said to look for any regular transactions going out to a Fletcher.'

Walker's face reddened now. 'She did, did she? Babette Ramsey was murdered three days ago. Why are you only telling me this now?'

Tess cleared her throat. 'Sorry, sir, given what happened, with being present at the murder scene and everything, it slipped my mind.'

'Slipped your mind?' Walker repeated, theatrically loud. She knew he was doing it for the benefit of the young PC and Tess wished she'd excuse herself so she could cut the 'yes, sir, no, sir' bullshit. 'Well, it's a good job we already looked at Millington's bank accounts and spoke to his wife about those transactions. Charity donations, Fox. For a young woman whose son tragically passed away from SIDS.'

Tess frowned. 'And you believed the wife?'

It was Walker's turn to frown. 'Why wouldn't I?' Tess looked at the young PC. She did not want to question Walker's judgement in front of her – men like Walker didn't take kindly to things like that. But she didn't have much choice.

'Because her husband was killed and he had large amounts of money being paid regularly to a young woman.'

Walker's face coloured. 'I don't know what you're trying to insinuate,' he said. Tess wanted desperately to point out that she wasn't insinuating anything – she was saying it outright. To her mind, Millington was either being blackmailed or paying child support to one of the many other women in his life. 'But you'll do well to remember that Rupert Millington was a respected public figure. I personally followed this lead up myself and it went nowhere. So I don't think there's any need for raking a man's name over the coals any further.'

Tess understood. Anything that was a bad look for Lewes Council was a bad look for the hand that fed their budgets. DI Walker was thinking about his future in the force. Well, although Tess had been fairly certain for a while now that her chances of a future on the force were getting slimmer with each new family member accused of murder, she was still a police officer, and a better one than Walker. While he tried to go for the angle that didn't jeopardise his career, she was going to find out why Rupert Millington was being blackmailed, and whether it was why he'd been murdered.

Chapter Thirty-Three

Sarah fanned the papers out on her bed and leafed through them once more. Rupert had certainly been thorough in his investigation into the real Lily Donovan – or, as he had found out – Lily Dowse. She supposed it had probably started with him trying to prove that Lily had never been related to the previously long-standing secretary of Cliffe Bonfire Society, Aubrey Taylor, and therefore undeserving of membership. A simple safeguard against her blackmail. But then he'd hit on a goldmine. Obviously Lily wasn't related to Aubrey Taylor, she was from a Showman family, working the fairs up and down the country for most of her life. She'd been married to Frank Jacobs, millionaire businessman, and she had been running one of the biggest long cons Sarah had ever heard of.

The papers in front of her were proof of Lily's involvement in a pyramid of 'gifting tables', a scheme that started between middle-aged housewives and played on the concept of sisterhood to get women to join. Each 'table' was comprised of four levels, Appetizers, Soups and Salads, Entrees and Dessert. To join, a woman must be 'invited' in. Once she was, she would join at the Appetizer level and make a £5,000 'gift' to the woman at Dessert level. Members would move up as they recruited more women. When the woman at the top had been 'gifted' £40,000 she would move on, probably to start a new pyramid with herself at the top. The con relied on more and more women being brought on board, but of course very few women ever made it to Dessert level. When the table failed to recruit enough new members the pyramid collapsed, leaving the newest members with nothing and down five thousand pounds.

Just knowing that Lily had been lying about her name, her family connection to Cliffe and her connection to the worst killing spree to hit Brighton in the last few decades would have caused Lily problems in the village, at least. But what these sheets of paper on the bed in front of her did was implicate Lily in tax evasion at the very least, along with probably three counts of fraud. From what Sarah could see here, Lily had been Dessert level at least six times. What this did was give Lily a major motive to see Rupert Millington out of the way. Add that to the threats on his life, and Babette screaming Lily's name moments before she was shot . . . it was bad. And now Sarah had to decide whether to tell Tess, and put Tess in the middle of her family's criminal enterprise once again.

She gathered up the papers and shoved them back in the envelope. It would have to be a future Sarah problem; she'd decided that she'd follow Leodora today, trying to find evidence of her affair with Reg Ellis, like Joey Greco from that show *Cheaters*. It might come to nothing, but it was information that Walker didn't have. If Reg and Leodora were sleeping together, perhaps he wanted Rupert out of the way – especially after Rupert's dodgy wine had almost bankrupted him.

Cheaters was actually a great show, Sarah thought an hour later as she watched Leodora climbing out of her late husband's blood-red Jag. She had been on the phone inside the Jag for ten minutes while Sarah had spied on her from the café opposite, trying not to think about what she'd found in Rupert Millington's papers. It wasn't that she was judging Lily – how on earth could she? Lily was one of them, a grifter, and a pretty good one if what she'd read was just the tip of the iceberg. No, her issue was the motive for murder it gave Lily, and having to decide whether to keep it from Tess.

She took a sip of her coffee, wishing again that she'd had access to the car to get a listening device into it. This was why her jobs usually took so long to set up – people didn't just let you walk up to their car and bug it, everything had to be facilitated. For now she was going to have to settle for following Leodora and when she'd found out where she was going and who she was meeting she would come back and at least fix a tracker to the wheel arch.

Sarah finished her drink and left the café to follow Leodora at a reasonable distance. She didn't think the woman would recognize her from their drunken encounter at Rupert's wake, especially without the wig and prosthetics, but there was no point in taking chances.

It was as she glanced in the reflection of the window on the other side of the street that she saw him. She was being followed too. She crossed the road to be sure. The guy stayed on his side of the street until Sarah turned left down a side street. The streets in Brighton were in grids, so Sarah was confident she would come out by Leodora again, unless she turned right. The guy appeared behind her again. It was no coincidence. Sarah thought back to what Becky had told her the day she'd come back – Wes, Mac and Gabe had been to the warehouse to talk about someone following the crew on a pigeon drop. Was this the guy? They'd been so mad at her she hadn't had chance to ask them about it.

She slowed down until he was right behind her, and without thinking she swung around to face him. His eyes widened and he took a couple of steps back. Sarah stopped short of actually knocking him over. Or walking into him, to be more accurate, because up close she wouldn't have stood a chance at knocking him over, even caught off-guard. He was lean, but solid, the kind of physique that said he worked out but he didn't need the world to know about it. He was at least six foot two, nearly a full foot taller than Sarah. That didn't stop her glaring up at him.

'What is your game?' she demanded, pointing a finger up at him. He looked shocked for a second then his face broke into a grin. For the first time, Sarah realized he was incredibly attractive.

'I don't know what you mean?' His faux innocence angered her even more.

'You know exactly what I mean. You're following me. And I want to know why. Are you a cop?'

He laughed again, and this time Sarah noticed his dimples, how his eyes lit up when he smiled. *Oh good lord, get a grip,* she thought to herself. *You're going soft.* Maybe it was time for a casual hook-up before she started spending her days reading romance novels and watching *Bridgerton*.

'I'm not a cop,' he said, and for some reason she believed him. Maybe because she wanted to believe him.

'A grifter, then. Lone wolf, or do you have a crew?' The guy shook his head. Man, they needed someone this good-looking on her crew – the kind of face that made even the best con artist forget herself. Wes was boy-band cute but he wasn't a front man. And he didn't have it in him to charm people. To do that you had to be a real—

'Oh!' Sarah slapped herself on the forehead. 'I know what you are. You're a – what do you call yourselves? A social engineer?'

His smile didn't falter but she knew she was right. A social engineer – she'd never met one of those in the flesh. Social engineers were hired by businesses and rich people to test their security, to help keep out people like her. Legal grifters were more dangerous than the police to Sarah and her family. The police could only take away their freedom if they got caught. Loophole closers like this guy could take away their entire business.

'Look,' he said, holding out his hands. 'We've both got a job to do. It just so happens that watching you do yours helps me to do mine.'

'You mean you follow me to see how I get around the security, then you report back how I did it and you get paid?'

He shrugged. 'When you say it that way it sounds an awful lot like I'm using your skills to make money.'

'Almost like a grifter,' Sarah said. He raised his eyebrows.

'I'm nothing like a grifter,' he argued. 'I find ways to get into these places to make them safer, not to use their offices to trick people into investing in fake schemes, or hack into their systems. I'm on the side of good.'

'All right, Batman,' Sarah retorted. 'Well, you're not good enough. You've been made – and that's rule number one.'

'Except I spotted you first,' he pointed out. 'I saw you using the offices at the Brinell Building when I knew they weren't in use. I saw your team move furniture in under the noses of everyone who worked there, I saw you hook in that idiot with the fake ruckus in the foyer. It was . . .'

He paused, taking a moment to look Sarah in the eyes. Her belly did a weird flipping thing. 'It was beautiful.'

Sarah opened her mouth to say something witty but nothing came out. That had never happened to her before. She tried again.

'Holy lactose, Batman, that was cheesy,' she managed at last. He didn't laugh, just kept staring at her in that weird way. 'What?'

'Who are you?' he asked.

Sarah beckoned for him to lean in closer. He did, and he smelled of sandalwood and soap. When he was close enough to kiss, she whispered in his ear, 'Fuck off.'

He did laugh this time, and the sound made her want to track down every joke book ever written so he would never stop. Sarah had never been so desperate to impress anyone in her life.

He stepped back. 'Are you at least going to tell me what you're doing following that woman?'

'Solving a murder,' Sarah replied. 'You?'

'Solving a murder? You're a private detective as well as a con artist?'

Sarah scowled. 'How are you making both of those sound like an insult?'

He gave an amused smile and raised dark eyebrows. 'Practice, I suppose. Whose murder?'

'Join my team,' Sarah said, without thinking. His eyes widened, then he shook his head.

'I'm not a thief,' he said.

Sarah lowered her voice to a seductive tone. 'I don't just have thieves,' she said, moving closer. 'I have forgers.' She lifted her hand and brushed imaginary lint from the front of his suit jacket. She was close enough now for him to bow his head and they would be kissing. 'I have ringers and badgers . . .'

'Go on,' he murmured.

'I have a tech guy whose hacking skills would make you bark like a sealion.'

He gave a low whistle. 'Doesn't sound like you need me, really.'

Sarah looked up into his dark blue eyes and her heart was pounding so hard she was certain he would be able to hear it. She'd been around plenty of attractive men before, had her share of one-night stands and meet cutes but she'd never felt like this. A million stupid, cheesy one-liners ran through her head but she couldn't bring herself to use any of them. For the first time for as long as she could remember she felt really, stupidly nervous.

There was an excruciating, agonising pause that they both seemed to know could go either way. Then Sarah stepped back, breaking the silence.

'You're probably right,' she said, trying not to let the disappointment come through in her voice. She knew that getting involved with this guy would be a mistake, and she tried not to make too many of those if she could help it.

Chapter Thirty-Four

Sunlight sneaked through the cracks in the unfamiliar dark grey curtains, spilling light over the unfamiliar bedroom as Sarah opened her eyes and focused on the unfamiliar navy-blue king-sized duvet. The room was large with light-grey painted walls and a huge TV opposite the bed. At least there were no mirrors on the ceiling. Flashbacks to the night before reminded her where she was . . . and who she was with.

'Oh God,' she muttered. 'That was a mistake. That was a huge mistake.' She pulled the covers up over her head. The man next to her gave an all-too-familiar laugh and yanked them back down again.

'Do you mean the first time?' he asked, good-naturedly. 'Or all three?'

Sarah groaned. 'All of them,' she said, covering her face with her hands.

'Not quite the reaction I'm used to, if I'm honest,' Jerome said, still smiling. 'But while we're both here, fancy making another mistake?'

'Oh God,' Sarah said, still from behind her hands. 'Oh God.'

'I hadn't realized until last night how religious you were,' Jerome said, his face straight. Sarah put down her hands and couldn't help laughing despite her dismay. Last night might have been the stupidest thing she'd done in her life – she'd had sex with her sister's work partner, what had she been thinking? Then Jerome got up out of bed, still fully naked, and she knew exactly what she'd been thinking. She hadn't been able to get that guy – she'd never even managed to get his name – off her mind, and so she'd called DS Morgan through sheer frustration. She'd known he had the hots for her, and Tess wasn't the slightest bit interested in him. What harm could it do? she'd thought. Now, in the cold light of day, she could think of a million reasons why last night had been so ill-judged.

'Tea or coffee?' Jerome asked her, and she realized she'd been staring. He really was incredibly good-looking. A body to die for. And the sex had been great. But it had been just that – great sex and nothing more. Sarah just hoped he felt the same, otherwise it would be very awkward.

'Coffee would be good, thanks,' she replied. Weirdly, it didn't feel awkward. Maybe it was the fact that there would be no uncomfortable promises to call or expectations that this would ever be more than a one-night stand. She sat up and grabbed for her phone. Three messages from Tess. Christ, it was 11 a.m. Sarah hadn't slept in that late for years.

How did it go with L? the first message read. Shit, Tess didn't know yet that her recon had been foiled by a handsome stranger. At least she didn't seem to know about Jerome either. Sarah doubted the tone would be so polite.

Got some news re Babette house. Text me when you're up, said the second one. Then the third, *u ok?*

'I think we overslept.' Jerome came back into the room with two mugs of coffee and placed one next to her. He'd put on a pair of grey jogging bottoms that did nothing to hide what was underneath. Or maybe Sarah was just more aware of it now. 'I've got two missed calls from your sister.'

'Three texts,' Sarah said, holding up her phone. 'Did you call her back yet? We should leave some time between, otherwise she'll think it's weird if we both reply at once.'

'I've got another hour at least before she suspects anything weird of me,' Jerome said. 'I make a point of not texting people back too quickly – makes them think they can rely on you.'

'An hour?' Sarah said, raising her eyebrows. She took a sip of her coffee; it was too strong and bitter. 'I wonder how many mistakes we could make in an hour? Unless you've learned from your mistake already?'

Jerome gave a surprised smile and pulled back the covers to climb back into bed. 'I'm a slow learner,' he said, moving closer. 'I could make the same mistake all day.'

Chapter Thirty-Five

Sarah swung her legs out of bed. Jerome tried to grab her arm but she was up before he could catch her.

'Why don't you take a day off?' he grumbled. 'You're not a police officer, it's not your job to visit crime scenes.'

'No, it's yours.' Sarah grinned. She picked up the T-shirt she had been wearing last night and pulled it over her head. She could feel his eyes on her as she dressed.

'Come back to bed,' he entreated. Sarah shook her head.

'Big sister's orders. Besides, this' – she indicated the two of them – 'is not a thing. Cannot be a thing.'

'Who said I wanted it to be a thing?' Jerome asked. 'Wait there, I'll get dressed and drive.'

'Oh yeah, that's all I need, for Tess to know we're having sex.'

Jerome grinned. 'Is that future tense "having sex"? Because I know you enjoyed last night as much as I did. More than once.'

Before she could answer, Jerome's phone rang. He rolled his eyes and answered with a pointed, 'Hello, Tess.'

He went on, 'Yeah, sorry, but it's actually my day off, so I don't have to ans— sorry. No, you're right.' Sarah walked around the bed to Jerome's side and dipped her head to his neck, running a series of light kisses over his collarbone. He made a funny sound in his throat and coughed to cover it up. Sarah smiled and wandered over to the mirror to fix her hair.

'Great, that's great. I'll meet you there. About an hour? Yeah, I haven't showered yet. Okay.' He sighed as Sarah bent over to put on her jeans. 'Fine. See you in a bit.'

He ended the call and jumped out of bed, pulling Sarah to him by the belt hooks on her jeans. She squealed and put her arms between them, blocking his attempt to kiss her. 'Are you trying to get me into trouble?' he murmured. She stopped squirming and looked up into his dark eyes.

'It would, you know,' she said, her face and voice serious now. 'Get us into trouble. That's why this can't be a thing.' She didn't mention that the whole reason she'd called him last night was because she was trying to get someone else out of her mind. She didn't regret that they'd slept together – they were both adults who found one another attractive – but she would regret if what they had done negatively impacted on Jerome's career in any way. Tess seemed resigned to the fact that one day it would come out that she was Frank Jacobs's daughter, and that would be that for her job. Sarah couldn't help being Tess's sister, and Tess had gone into the police force knowing she was going to lie about her family ties. But that didn't mean that Sarah had to drag Jerome into their mess. When the truth came out, he could pretend to be as stunned as anyone else, and his hands could stay clean. If it came out the two of them had been sleeping together, he might not be able to bounce back as easily.

'Even if it's just sex?' Jerome asked. He was still inches away from her, so close she could feel the heat from his muscular body. Still, she managed to shake her head.

'Tess would be furious. Your job would be at stake. All for something you can get from pretty much any woman you fancy,' she reminded him. She pulled away from him and picked the brush back up, securing her hair into a ponytail. She heard him sigh.

'I'd better jump in the shower,' he said, which seemed to Sarah to be a sign that he knew she was right. 'Your sister's already uptight about something. If we both turn up smelling of sex . . . she's a detective, after all.'

'I'll let myself out,' Sarah said, catching a glimpse of the regret on his face as he headed for the bathroom. She sighed. Complicated men were like buses. Not a one in sight for years, then two of them turned up at once.

Tess cradled her take-out coffee, the heat warming her hands. She'd left her gloves at home in her rush to get to Lewes that morning, waiting for the call from Martin to say she could go back to the farm. She was being made a laughing stock by Walker, she'd barely slept a wink thinking about Babette and her frustration at not being able to get hold of her sister or Jerome had been mounting all morning, so by the time Sarah actually answered her phone, Tess was in an utterly foul mood.

'Where have you been?' Tess snapped. 'I haven't been able to get hold of anybody.'

'I don't actually work for you, Tess,' Sarah said, and Tess scowled, mentally flipping her sister the 'V'.

'Your text said you had some new information?' Sarah said.

'You first. Where have you been? You were supposed to be following Leodora yesterday.'

'Yeah, well, I ran into a bit of a problem,' Sarah said. She sounded thoroughly pissed off.

'Anything I should be worried about?' Tess asked.

'Nope,' Sarah said. 'It concerns the other side of the family.'

'Lily? Is she going to hand herself in? She's doing herself no favours on the run.'

'I told you, I don't know where Lily is,' Sarah replied. 'I mean the family business.'

Tess felt a pang of what – disappointment? Sadness? She couldn't help feeling something about the fact that there was a big part of her sister's life that she could never be part of. Of course she could have been, she still could be, at any moment. She knew Sarah would gladly welcome her into the family business. The caveat being, of course, that she couldn't be a Jacobs and a police officer.

After losing out on the promotion to DI Walker, Tess had seriously considered leaving the police force and taking her place alongside Sarah in the crew. She'd pictured herself on a badger con or a melon drop, but the truth was, although Frank Jacobs's blood ran in her veins, and although she knew she could think like a grifter, whether she could act like one, well, that was a different question. Anyone could pass the theory test but taking the practical – she'd been out of the game too long, dealt with too many victims of crime, developed too much of a conscience. It just wasn't her reality.

'Nothing I can help with then?' she asked. There was a moment of silence at the other end of the phone. Then Sarah said, 'Suppose it wouldn't hurt you to know. We've been made. Some guy, calls himself a social engineer, he's been picking us out on jobs. He's a threat to our business, if I'm honest.'

Tess got the impression there was something her sister wasn't saying.

'What's a social engineer?'

Sarah sighed. 'Basically the opposite of me, but with the same skill set. He's a grifter, a con artist. Specializes in breaking in to businesses so he can tell them where their weak spots are. That's why he's such a threat, if he closes all of our loopholes we have to find new weaknesses in order to get information. They can also be hired to check out a person's personal security – maybe a politician wanting to know if he can be hacked, or how much information can be found on them.'

'You don't think it's anything to do with Rupert Millington?'

'Unlikely. If it was someone trying to find out what we were doing, he wouldn't have made himself known to me. This arrogant idiot wanted me to know he'd rumbled me. That he's one step ahead.'

'Sounds like a job your crew would be quite good at,' Tess remarked.

'Don't tell them that,' Sarah said quickly. 'The last thing I need is for my employees to start growing consciences. Besides, it's supply and demand. Without us, that jumped-up idiot wouldn't have a job. It would be like if all the criminals in the country downed tools tomorrow – you lot would all be out of a job. You'd be singing on cruise ships within a year.'

'Yes, yes, on behalf of the police, and people on cruises everywhere, we're very grateful,' Tess said dryly.

'Have you seen Julia?' Sarah asked. Tess swallowed. She'd been waiting every minute since Julia's arrest for the call to come from Oswald, to tell her she had some questions to answer, but so far her half-sister had been strictly 'no comment'.

'She's not talking, not a word so far. Oswald is frustrated as hell but he's relying on forensics before he charges her with murder.'

'So she might get out? If all he has is her being at the crime scene . . .'

'We've got her on a host of fraud charges relating to pretending to be Callum Rodgers' girlfriend, false statements, deliberately misleading a police investigation, et cetera, but I honestly don't know where it's going to go at the moment.'

'What a mess.' Sarah sighed. 'Maybe we should have just let her go.'

Tess shook her head, knowing that Sarah couldn't see her over the phone. 'No. Whatever happens, we did the right thing. Anyway, I was trying to get hold of you to tell you that the SOCOs have released Babette's crime scene and I've spoken to Martin, he said we can go around and take a look.'

'Okay,' Sarah replied. 'Shall I meet you there in an hour?'

Tess frowned. 'Can't you get here any quicker? I've been waiting all morning. You live twenty minutes away.'

'Go ahead without me,' Sarah said. 'I've got something urgent I need to do. I'll get to you as quick as I can, I promise.'

Chapter Thirty-Six

Martin Ramsey sat at the table of the farmhouse kitchen, staring into his cold mug of coffee. It happened every now and then, Tess had noticed. He'd be talking away, then suddenly his words would tail off and he'd go into a kind of trance. Obviously he was still in shock. The house beyond was silent, no one had come to take care of him or keep him company. Tess reasoned he was in his thirties and, of course, capable of looking after himself, but still, he shouldn't have to be alone in the house where his mother had been shot to death five days earlier.

'Is there somewhere else you can stay for a bit?' Tess asked, her voice gentle. 'A relative's or friend's?'

She didn't think he'd heard her for a minute, he didn't make any move to reply, or look at her to acknowledge her question. Then, after a long silence he shook his head.

'Not really,' he said. 'Not when I've got the farm to look after. Mum has a sister, but she lives in Cornwall. She said she'll come up and help with the funeral arrangements, which is good, I suppose . . .' He tailed off again. Tess looked around for signs that he'd eaten but saw no dirty plates or leftovers.

'I had some toast,' he said when she asked him. 'Last night, I think. Or maybe it was this morning. I didn't sleep much,' he added, by way of explanation.

'It was such a shocking thing to have happen,' Tess said, placing a hand over his on the table. 'And it happened so fast.'

'But what happened?' Martin asked. He looked at her. 'Do you know? Because I can't for a minute figure it out. She was arguing with Lily Donovan, and she'd locked the door – or Lily had – but that doesn't make any sense. Why didn't she respond to our shouts at all? And how the hell did Lily get out? Have the police arrested her yet?'

Tess wished she had a positive answer to even one of his questions. Lily still hadn't surfaced and Tess had an awful feeling that Sarah had lied to her about not knowing where her mother was. Not that she wanted to have to shop Lily as well as Julia, so maybe it was best she didn't know for sure.

'We're looking for Lily, I promise you we'll find her. Look, I have to ask you, did your mum talk about Rupert Millington's murder with you at all? Did she have any theories as to who might have wanted to kill him?' Martin shook his head.

'Every time I brought it up she looked as though she might have a breakdown, so I never wanted to push it. Don't worry, detective, I know about their affair. Don't look at me like that, I'm a grown man, I can handle it.' He gazed out of the kitchen window, pausing once again.

'Do you know how long it went on?' Tess asked. He looked at her sharply.

'Are you asking if it was going on before my dad died?

Because it was.' There was bitterness in his voice. 'Everyone knew about it, as well. Not that she realized, of course.'

'And your dad?'

Martin scoffed. 'Of course my dad. Why do you think he killed himself?'

Tess must have looked shocked because a look of dawning comprehension that he'd slipped up came across Martin's face.

'Babette told me your dad had a terminal illness.'

'Yes, that's right.' He looked miserable. 'My lovely mother told everyone he had cancer. That way, even if people did get wind that he'd taken his own life, they would put it down to finding out about the illness.' He suddenly looked very sick, and Tess wasn't sure if it was the realization of how horrible he'd been about a woman who had just been murdered, or remembering what she had done to his dad.

'So he was never ill?'

'Not in the physical sense,' Martin replied, his voice quieter, less harsh. 'He went mad with grief, you could say. He loved Mum so much, couldn't bear it that she was genuinely in love with that prick Millington. Part of me is glad he's already dead – this would kill him. He thought she was going to leave him for Millington, so he took a rifle from the cabinet and shot himself.'

Tess shuddered. This poor man, to lose both of his parents to guns, one self-inflicted, but both as shocking and violent an end as you could meet.

They both jumped at a banging on the front door. Martin looked at Tess in alarm, but she put up a hand. 'Don't worry, it's just my colleagues. They're coming to have a look at your mum's bedroom, remember?' She realized she was talking in soothing tones – treating him like he was fragile as a bomb. Like he was a suspect capable of violence, not the family member of a victim. 'I'll get the door, you wait there,' she said, getting slowly to her feet.

At the door she sighed with relief to see Sarah.

'Jerome not here too?' she asked, looking over her sister's shoulder. Sarah frowned.

'Why would Jerome be with me?' she asked. Tess shook her head.

'He said he'd be here around now,' she said. 'He sounded a bit weird on the phone, though. I think he was with a woman.'

'Be weird if he wasn't, wouldn't it?'

Tess gave a small smile. 'Touche. Will you text him and ask him to get a move on? He's ignoring me. Martin's through here.'

Sarah followed her back into the kitchen with her phone in her hand. Martin was still catatonic at the table.

'Martin, this is Sarah, she was here with me the other day,' Tess reminded him. No response.

'Martin, how are you holding up?' Sarah asked, shoving her phone into her pocket and crossing the kitchen to pull the man at the table into an embrace. Martin looked surprised at the sudden physical interaction, but Tess saw him relax into Sarah's arms. He turned his head into her stomach and Tess realized that he was sobbing.

'There, there,' Sarah said, stroking his hair. Tess looked at her in alarm and Sarah raised her eyebrows in a *what can I do?* expression. Martin continued to cry, not looking up when there was another knock at the door. Sarah shooed her with a hand.

'Get that,' she hissed. Tess shot out of the kitchen to the

front door and yanked a bemused Jerome inside. She was back in the kitchen in seconds, but neither Martin nor Sarah had moved. Jerome walked in behind her and she saw a stunned look cross his face at the scene in front of him. She didn't blame him. It's not every day you walk into a victim's house to find them sobbing like a baby in the arms of a notorious con woman.

'Everything okay, Sarah?' he asked, an edge to his voice. Sarah rolled her eyes.

'All under control, Superman,' she remarked. Tess frowned.

'Um . . . why don't I make us a cup of coffee, let these ladies do their job?' Jerome asked. Sarah peeled Martin off her waist and sat him at the table like a marionette.

'Good idea, we'll be upstairs,' Tess said, grabbing her sister's arm and leading her out of the kitchen.

'All under control, Superman?' Tess repeated as Sarah followed her up the stairs. She turned to look at her with raised eyebrows. 'And how did you have Jerome's number to text him?'

Sarah looked incredulous. 'You asked me to text him!'

'True,' Tess conceded. 'But I didn't think until afterwards that there was no reason for you to have his phone number. Where did you get it? Is something going on that I should know about?'

Sarah rolled her eyes and gave her sister's shoulder a shove. 'You don't have to detective everything,' she admonished. 'He gave me his number so I could send him a meme I made.'

'What meme?' Tess challenged.

Sarah looked sheepish. 'I don't think you want to know.'

'What meme?'

Sarah pulled her phone out of her pocket and scrolled through. She held it up to show Tess a picture of a woman and a man walking, the man looking back at another woman. The man was labelled Tess, the woman he was with was labelled 'regular police work' and the woman he was looking at was labelled 'other people's cases'. Tess growled.

'Told you you didn't want to know,' Sarah said. She stopped short opposite Babette's bedroom. 'Eurgh. Hard to believe it was only five days ago that we were here while she was being murdered,' she said. 'Poor Babette.'

Tess thought of Martin downstairs, the man who had lost his father because of Rupert and 'poor Babette'. She'd been so shocked to find out that Babette had lied about her husband's illness. How could someone do that to cover for themselves? She filled Sarah in on what Martin had told her about his father downstairs.

'You're pissed off at her, aren't you?' Sarah asked. 'You met her twice, why has it bothered you so much?'

'I don't like being wrong about someone,' Tess admitted. 'I feel like I've been duped.'

'There's no one alive who is all good,' Sarah said. 'So Babette and Rupert are in love. Babette's husband finds out and kills himself. Meanwhile, Rupert's wife is sleeping with the man whose business he nearly ruined. Oh, and Rupert is also sleeping with said man's wife. Did I get it all?'

Tess shook her head. 'We don't know for certain that Leodora is seeing Reg Ellis. And we only have Lily's word for it that Harriet was sleeping with Rupert.'

'She definitely didn't seem head over heels with him when I spoke to her at the wake,' Sarah remembered. 'She said she'd rather shove a rotten cucumber up her you-know-what. Sounded like she meant it, too. But then she also said that Leodora didn't have a clue what Rupert was really like.'

'Maybe she meant the wine,' Tess suggested.

'Leodora definitely knew about the wine,' Sarah said. 'And it sounds like she probably knew about the affairs, too, from everything we've been told. The wife is looking better and better for these murders.'

Sarah, standing in the doorway of Babette's room, was just about to reach up to feel the architrave around the door when Tess stopped her.

'Here,' she said. 'Put these on.' She tossed Sarah a pair of rubber gloves. 'Forensics are finished but better safe than sorry.'

Sarah slipped the gloves on in a theatrical manner and ran a finger down the door frame. She pulled and tapped, but everything stayed firm.

'Maybe she lied about her husband killing himself because she had to live here afterwards,' Sarah continued. She knelt down on the floor and felt around the bottom of the frame. 'Oh, lookie here.' She scratched at the carpet with her finger, and peeled a strip away from under where the door would be had it been closed. 'Someone cut a strip out of this carpet.'

Tess frowned. 'Why would anyone do that?'

Sarah shrugged. 'Maybe it was an accident when they laid it. Could be nothing.'

She rubbed her finger across the carpet and lifted it away. 'Does that look like ash to you?'

Tess pulled a swab from her bag and gestured to Sarah to move out of her way so she could get a sample. 'The carpet isn't burned. Maybe that's the bit that was cut away.'

Sarah stood up and studied the lock. The door and frame were splintered where Martin had kicked it in, but the heavy iron lock was still intact, just dislodged slightly. 'Can I get one of those swabs?' she asked. Tess pulled another swab from her bag.

'I'll have to do it – if it turns out to be important it's not exactly going to stand up in court if you took the evidence.'

Sarah looked as though she was going to laugh or make a smartass remark but thought better of it. Instead she stepped back and pointed to the lock. 'Inside there, please.'

Tess poked the swab inside the lock and pulled it out. She looked at the end. 'Ash?' she asked. Sarah nodded.

'You knew that was going to be in there?'

'Of course I did.'

Tess bagged the sample. 'If forensics haven't had a sample analysed already I'll convince someone in the lab to put it in with the others.'

'Where's the key?'

'It was on the inside when we broke in,' Tess said, her eyes scanning the room. 'Look, it's on the cabinet now.'

Sarah looked carefully at the key. 'Wish I'd felt the temperature of it at the time.'

Tess frowned. 'Well, I'm pretty glad you didn't. We call that tampering with a crime scene.'

'You and your cute rules,' Sarah teased. 'Can I look around? If I don't touch anything? I think I'm getting there with the how, feel free to concentrate on the why.'

Tess looked at her sister with incredulity, then shook her head. 'Fine.'

As Sarah busied herself poking at walls and window frames,

Tess began looking in Babette's bedside drawers. Despite it being something she'd had to do at plenty of crime scenes before, this was the first time she'd gone through the drawers of someone she'd sat and had tea with so recently. It felt oddly intrusive.

In Babette's top drawer were various face creams and lavender room sprays, an old alarm clock that had clearly been replaced by the Alexa dot on the nightstand, and a small pile of envelopes, secured by an elastic band. Tess lifted these out of the drawer and pulled off the band, spreading the envelopes out onto the bed.

She picked one up and slid the paper out from inside. It was creased to the point of falling apart, like it had been unfolded and refolded many times.

Flowery drivel. Rupert Millington clearly saw himself as Mr Darcy. One by one, she skimmed through the letters, hoping to find some big clue that pointed to anyone else who had it in for Rupert, but they were full of over-sentimental rot rather than anything useful. There was a mention of going to see one of his constituents after 'their terrible loss', but the rest was stilted poetry and fluff. If Tess had been a more cynical person she'd have suspected that Millington had got half of what he'd written from ChatGPT, with awkward phrases like 'your flashing eyes can pick me up when I feel down'. The last one she read, though, made reference to an 'interesting discovery about our resident witch that I must look further into'. Surely he must be talking about Lily? What had Rupert found out? Could this be what Lily had been alluding to when she'd asked Tess that first day about if they found 'other motives' for her to kill Rupert?

'Look at this,' she said to Sarah, showing her the reference. Sarah whistled through her teeth.

'I wonder if Walker found these?' she asked. 'He must have done. God, Tess, if we don't find who killed Millington and Babette, she might actually end up being charged with this.'

Sarah shook her head and handed Tess the piece of paper back. Tess took a photo of it, gathered up the rest of the letters and put them back in the drawer. The second one down held pyjamas and a small teddy bear. Strange, Tess thought, but then she'd seen so many strange things at crime scenes, this was hardly the oddest. The bottom drawer contained nothing but a hairdryer and some hair products.

'Anything?' she asked Sarah, who had pulled out a tape measure and was measuring the distance from the bedside table to the far wall. 'What on earth are you doing?'

'Testing something.' She pulled out her mobile phone and looked to be searching for information. 'Interesting . . .' She put the phone back in her pocket and left the room without another word.

Chapter Thirty-Seven

Jerome stood up as soon as they re-entered the kitchen, looking as though he had been waiting for them to get back almost from the minute they had left. Martin was staring straight ahead at the wall and Tess wondered if they had exchanged a single word.

'Will you be okay, Martin?' Tess asked. He looked at her and gave a small smile.

'I think I just need some sleep,' he said, and sighed. 'It's a lot to take in. First Dad, now this. And the farm . . .'

'What will you do with the farm?'

'Probably sell it,' he said, although his face said he wanted to do anything but. 'Move away. The farm was Mum and Dad's life but there's nothing for me here now but bad memories.'

'I'm so sorry for your loss,' Tess told him. She watched his face for a reaction to her next words. 'We're going to find who did this. They won't get away with it.'

Martin nodded, his eyes glistening with tears. If he was acting, he was good at it.

'The man is broken,' Jerome said, as they walked down the lane to where they had parked separately. 'If he's acting I'm nominating him for an Oscar. I know he lost his dad, but that doesn't turn people into serial killers.'

'Needs one more,' Sarah and Tess said simultaneously. They looked at one another and grinned.

'Obviously I know that,' Jerome grumbled, kicking a stone along the ground.

'The joker's right about one thing,' Sarah said. Jerome raised his eyebrows at the insult. 'I didn't see any tells that Martin was making anything up. I don't think he killed Rupert and I don't think he could have killed Babette, not the way it happened. He didn't know that we were going to be there. Why go to such an elaborate set-up if there wasn't going to be witnesses? I mean, he could have done the locked-room thing easily, obviously. But he wouldn't have been able to do the disappearing-Lily thing without a bit of advance set-up . . .'

Jerome looked at Tess. 'Does she always speak like a Sphinx?'

Tess nodded. 'Mostly. If you can understand what she's saying, be careful – she's trying to con you.'

'I can understand *you* perfectly, by the way,' Sarah said. 'And I'll explain later. I have one more test to do.'

'Great, do take your time, won't you?'

'Am I the only one investigating this murder?'

'Actually,' Tess said, opening the car door, 'unfortunately, Walker is too. And he'd already looked into those transactions you found in Rupert's bank statements. They were charity donations to a woman called Truly Fletcher. Lost her son to SIDS.'

'Oh, how sad,' Sarah said, walking around to the passenger

side. 'Why was Rupert involved in the fundraiser? Is that normal for a local councillor?'

'It usually is,' Tess said. 'But not for Millington. I couldn't find another single incidence of when he was involved in any other fundraising events. He seems to have taken a personal interest in this one, though.'

'Personal enough to have the money go through his bank account,' Sarah mused. 'I can't imagine his accountant would love that.'

'Pretty woman,' Tess said, holding up the phone for them to see. 'Makes you wonder, given Rupert's, um . . . reputation.'

'Oh wait!' Sarah snapped her fingers. 'I saw her the other day. She runs the shop in the high street.'

'Truly Yours,' Tess confirmed. 'Yeah, says that here.'

'She doesn't look like that anymore,' Sarah said. 'She looks kind of . . . broken.'

'I'm not surprised,' Tess said. 'If she lost her son just a year ago. I can't imagine the pain.'

'You think Rupert could have been the baby's father?' Jerome asked.

'Am I driving you home?' Tess asked Sarah. 'How did you get here?'

'Taxi,' Sarah said. 'Stop changing the subject. Are we thinking Rupert was baby daddy?'

'I don't think we can go around assuming Rupert has fathered every child in Sussex just yet,' Tess said. 'SIDS might be a topic close to his heart, or Truly could be a friend of the family. We should reserve judgement until we can get proof of anything untoward.'

'There's another possibility, looking at this picture,' Jerome said. He paused dramatically. 'Rupert could have been Truly Fletcher's father.'

'Either option gives his wife one more motive to get rid of him,' Sarah said. 'Then again, I don't think the five circles of hell combined have enough fury to counter the amount of women Rupert Millington has scorned.'

Chapter Thirty-Eight

It took forty minutes of being passed around and put on hold before Tess could get the information she needed, but a lovely nurse called Carmen eventually agreed to email the details over to Tess's police email. Given that Walker had made it more than clear that he didn't expect to see Tess and Sarah hanging out like sixth formers – his words – Tess had dropped her at home while she went back to the station to make the calls. Now she and Jerome gathered around a laptop in an interview room and FaceTimed Sarah.

'Got the birth certificate which only shows the mother's name. Truly Fletcher.'

'Not surprising,' Sarah said. 'Rupert wouldn't have allowed his name to be on there. Proper scandal.' She picked up a cheeseburger and took a bite. Jerome practically salivated.

'God, I'm starving,' he said.

'This tastes amazing,' Sarah replied, waving the burger in front of the screen.

'Right,' said Tess. 'Now for the trickier bit. I got the medical records, cause of death listed as SIDS, like the paper reported. But here's the weird part. This says there was no post-mortem done.'

Sarah frowned. 'Would there usually be a post-mortem done on a child who died from SIDS?'

Tess nodded. 'SIDS is only usually confirmed as cause of death if there are no signs of anything else. And to find that out you'd need a post-mortem, or at the very least blood tests, etc. There was none of that done here. Nothing. *Nada*. Just a cause of death listed as SIDS.'

'Wouldn't an inquest ask why no post-mortem was done?'

Jerome frowned. 'You only have an inquest if a coroner requests one. There's only a post-mortem if the coroner deems it necessary.'

'Which they do, in most infant deaths. And this boy was nearly a year old, most SIDS deaths are below six months. Jerome, FaceTime Sarah from your phone, I'm about to take a call.' She disconnected her sister and Jerome pulled out his phone. Tess could have sworn she saw him press 'recently dialled'. When would he have been calling Sarah? Her face popped up again, complete with cheeseburger.

She shook her head, telling herself not to be so paranoid. She pressed 'forward' on the email and within minutes her phone rang.

'This is neither an interesting meme nor a dinner party invite,' the voice on the other end said.

'Kay,' Tess said, smiling. 'How are you?'

'I'm good,' the pathologist replied. 'I keep meaning to call you, actually. Since you refuse to join the world of social media, you probably don't know.'

'Know what?'

'Beth's pregnant.'

Tess beamed. 'That's fantastic! Congratulations! When's she due?'

'End of April.'

'How's she doing?'

'She's whiny and permanently tired, so about normal.'

Tess heard the thud of a pillow and Kay grunted. 'She says hi.'

'Send her my love. Wait—' Tess froze. She didn't know how to ask the next question without being horrifically intrusive. It wasn't really any of her business, anyway . . .

'It's not Chris's sperm.' Thank God for Kay and her bluntness. Chris Hart, Tess's ex-fiancé was Kay's best friend, after her partner, Beth. The four of them had been a permanent fixture in one another's lives, homes . . . it made her sad to think that once upon a time, Tess would have been one of the first people Kay would have called. That was then. Chris had got custody of them, given that Tess was the one who had walked out on him weeks before they were due to get married.

'Right, I, um . . .'

'He offered, obviously, being Chris. But Beth thought it would be weird and I didn't want the baby to risk getting his nose.'

Tess laughed. 'Good call.' She'd always loved his nose, actually. She'd loved everything about him, and yet the idea of marrying him had terrified her.

'Anyway, this photo you sent me. What's with that?'

Tess cleared her throat. 'SIDS case, from a year ago. There's no post-mortem attached – does that seem weird to you?'

229

'I would expect a post-mortem, especially on an eleven-month-old. SIDS usually occurs under six months, and we generally only rule it when all other options have been exhausted. We'd look for natural causes such as undiagnosed illness, then things like shaking, poisoning, neglect. If I'd been the coroner we definitely would have carried out a PM.'

'The baby died in Sussex,' Tess said. 'Why weren't you the coroner?'

Kay hesitated. 'Looking at the dates, I'd say it was when Beth's mum passed away. I took some time off, we had to go to New Zealand to arrange the funeral.'

Tess sighed. 'I'm sorry, Kay, I had no idea that Sylvia had passed.'

'It was quick,' Kay said, 'which was a blessing,' and Tess could tell she was trying not to talk about it in front of her pregnant wife. 'So anyway, this would have fallen to Richard Johnson-Wells. He's from Bexhill.'

'What's he like?'

'Bit of a smarmy prick,' Kay said. 'But usually thorough. I've been asked for a second opinion on his cases before and I've never found anything I haven't backed up with confidence. It seems really strange that he'd drop the ball on this one. But I presume that's why you're asking.'

'Well, yes,' Tess admitted. 'It seemed strange to me, too, and it's come up in the Millington case.'

'I thought that was Walker's case?'

Tess cleared her throat.

'I see,' Kay said, a smile in her voice. 'Well, anything I can help with, let me know.'

'Thanks, Kay,' Tess said, with feeling. Things had been so

awkward between them since the break-up, but her voice still felt like home. She ended the call and looked at Jerome.

'Did you get the gist of that?'

Jerome held up his fingers. 'Beth is pregnant, Chris not baby daddy, Kay didn't sign off on the SIDS ruling, there should have been a post-mortem.' He took a theatrical breath. 'Guess I know where we're going tomorrow,' he said. 'Eastbourne General Hospital.'

Chapter Thirty-Nine

Richard Johnson-Wells put his coffee down on the desk in front of him and crossed his arms in what Tess thought to be a defensive stance. 'Yes, I remember this case, of course I do. Tragic. Is the mother pregnant again?'

Tess frowned. 'No – why would you ask that, Mr Johnson-Wells?'

He smiled, and Tess realized that she did not like this man. He was tall, with a full head of dark hair that was beginning to turn silver at the sides, and a slight tan, like he might have just come back from somewhere exotic. His dark eyes were too close together for his face to be strikingly attractive, nevertheless, he wasn't totally unfortunate-looking, and what his symmetry lacked, his grooming made up for. He smelled incredible.

Tess and Jerome were sitting in his office, where they had barely had to wait ten minutes to see him. They had been treated with courtesy, reverence by the reception staff, even, who were obviously used to police officers dropping in without appointments. He had greeted them like old friends, offered them hot drinks, been pleasant and welcoming. And yet Tess still didn't like him. There was something about him that was smarmy and false. There was also something about him that she thought was incredibly familiar. Like she'd been served by him in a shop somewhere, which was likely ridiculous because although coroners often had other jobs, they were rarely in the local Spar.

'Please, call me Richard,' he said. 'And I'm assuming she's pregnant again because usually the police only turn up asking about previous child deaths if there's a chance that someone in the home is a danger to another child. Truly didn't have other children, that I can remember, so I thought she might be pregnant again.'

'No, she's not pregnant again, as far as we're aware.'

'So why are you looking into her son's death, if you don't mind me asking?'

Tess did mind, very much, actually, but she also knew that Sussex Police enjoyed a good working relationship with the coroner's office and she wasn't about to sabotage it.

'Truly's name has come up, in a general sense, in a murder investigation,' Tess said. Jerome gave her a sharp look and she gave him a small shake of the head. 'Rupert Millington.'

She saw it then, the sudden and uncontrollable dilation of his pupils. Why had Rupert's name elicited that response?

'I see,' he said, putting down his coffee cup. 'And how can I help?'

'Did you know Mr Millington, Richard?'

Richard looked shocked. 'I thought this was about Truly Fletcher. Am I being interviewed in relation to a murder now?'

'No.' Tess shook her head emphatically and gave her warmest smile. 'Certainly not. I'm sorry, I thought I saw you react to his name and assumed he might have been a friend of yours. I didn't mean to be insensitive if he was.'

Richard looked both mollified and relieved. He let out a breath. 'No, I didn't know Mr Millington. I saw on the news that he was a councillor. He wasn't even my councillor, I don't live in Sussex. If I reacted, it was just because it's quite a hot topic at the moment, obviously, the body in the bonfire.'

'Why didn't you do his autopsy?' Tess asked. 'Just out of interest.'

'I'd had a few days off last week so I wasn't the on-call. But I was the coroner in charge of poor William Fletcher. So any help I can give you, of course I will.'

'Why wasn't there a post-mortem?' Tess asked, without missing a beat. Richard frowned.

'There *was* a post-mortem.'

It was Tess's turn to frown. 'I couldn't find one. Would you mind?' She motioned to his computer and watched as he loaded it up. After five minutes of tapping he looked up.

'Sorry, it's being a bit slow.'

'No problem.'

'Here it is, the file is loading now. Well, that is odd.'

'Odd?' Tess asked, knowing what he was about to say.

'Yes. You're right, it's not there. It's not anywhere. I can't see the boy's post-mortem on the system at all.'

'But you definitely did it?'

Richard raised his eyebrows. 'Have you ever autopsied an eleven-month-old child, Ms Fox?'

Tess's cheeks coloured. 'Not personally. But I have attended one.'

'And do you think it was something you could ever forget?'

Tess knew it was something she would definitely never forget.

'Does this happen often?' Jerome asked.

Richard scowled. 'No, officer, it doesn't. Although, obviously we only come back to the post-mortem years later if there's a trial. If the death is ruled natural like this one was, then there would be no reason to check other cases.' He picked up a pen then put it back down, took a tube of moisturiser from the desk and put some on his hands. He rubbed it in as he continued to talk, the pace of his voice quicker now, he sounded nervous. 'I can have our admin assistant, Becky, run a script to check how many deaths don't have post-mortems attached in the system – she's very good at that sort of thing, she can tell us by type, if needs be—'

'Let's not get ahead of ourselves,' Tess said, putting out a hand as if to slow him down. 'Would you have a paper record of the post-mortem anywhere?'

He shook his head. 'When we had paper versions they were all scanned and attached to digital files. We had a company come in and digitise everything. Now we barely touch paper in this office. I know other parts of the hospital still cart around thick paper files but we deal in after-death records in here. It's all computerised.'

'So if it's not here, it's not anywhere?'

He nodded, his face glum. 'Afraid not. I've never come across it before, though. The system automatically saves them to the file. The only thing I can think of is that if the file number was inputted incorrectly then it might have been attached to another file. I can have Becky do a more thorough, back-end search, no problem.' He pushed his hair absently away from his forehead and Tess realized in an instant where she had seen the man before.

'That would be great, thank you,' she said. She pulled out her phone and scrolled though her photographs. 'Mr Johnson-Wells, sorry, *Richard*, you say you didn't know Rupert Millington?' She handed him the phone. 'So I'm wondering what you were doing at his funeral, with your arm around his wife?'

Chapter Forty

'*No way.*'

Tess nodded and Sarah could tell that she was proud of herself. She put down four aces. Tess scowled and threw her cards down on the table and Sarah collected her matchsticks. Her pile was significantly bigger than Tess's. She took in the cards and shuffled again. They were in the small room underneath the Black Dove. Sarah's family had been using it to plan their schemes for as long as she could remember, way before they got the warehouse. It felt nice having Tess here with her.

'Way,' Tess said. 'I knew I'd seen him somewhere before, but we were at a distance at the funeral and everyone looks different in a black suit. Besides, I hadn't expected to see him sitting right in front of me.'

'So how did he explain being there?' Sarah asked, dealing another hand. 'Bit of a blatant lie, if you ask me.'

'I suppose he's not from Sussex, he wouldn't expect people here to know him. Leodora was telling people in the village he was Rupert's cousin, remember?'

'But he's not?'

Tess shook her head and took a sip of her drink. 'No relation. That was just a cover to have him there to support her. She told Rupert's family that he was *her* cousin.'

'Bet they weren't still cousins by the time he got her home.'

Tess shuddered. The thought of that smarmy coroner and uptight Leodora having sex just seemed too weird. 'It was him she was staying with when she went away after Rupert was found. And probably who she was with the night he was killed. Her official alibi was her friend, Rita Hamer. They allegedly got a bottle of wine from Waitrose then stayed in watching films. But if that's a lie she'll be easily caught out.'

'So what did he say, when you confronted him all like,' Sarah put on a dramatic movie voice, '"Well, if you don't know Rupert Millington . . ."'

Tess laughed. 'He admitted that he was "friends" with Leodora. It took him a little while longer to admit that they had been sleeping together for almost six years. That's probably why Leodora turned a blind eye to Rupert's indiscretions – while he was out sleeping around he wasn't questioning where she was.'

'So Leodora was saying Richie, not Reggie, when we heard her on the phone,' Sarah said. 'God, good job we didn't convict on my testimony. So does that make the coroner suspect number one now? Get the husband out of the way, get to keep the wife?'

'I suppose it does,' Tess mused. 'But I don't think it was him. On paper, yes he's the perfect suspect. I couldn't ask him too much . . .'

'Because you haven't told Walker you were even talking to Richard Johnson-Wells in the first place, have you?'

Tess grimaced. 'No. And if the good doctor ends up a suspect I can't use anything he said in that discussion in evidence – he wasn't under PACE. But Walker has the same bank statements we have, he knows about the charitable donations from Rupert's account to Truly Fletcher, and he knows her son died. He expressly said he wasn't looking into it.'

'Did you ask Richard Johnson-Wells if he thought that there was any connection between Rupert and Truly's son?'

'In a roundabout way. He was already clamming up once he realized he'd put himself front and centre in a murder investigation, so he wasn't exactly forthcoming, but he did say that if there was any connection between Rupert and William Fletcher, Leodora hadn't mentioned it to him. He said it had been a tragic case of SIDS and Rupert Millington's name had never come up.'

'Hmmmm,' Sarah said. 'Hmmmmmmmm.'

'What?' Tess demanded. Sarah looked at her, wide eyes and innocent.

'What?'

'You're doing that thing where you have a theory and you're not telling me.'

Sarah laughed. 'If I told you every time I have a theory in my head, your head would explode. And most of them turn out to be so ridiculously off-base that it's embarrassing.'

Tess picked up the hand Sarah had dealt her. 'Four.'

Sarah wiggled her eyebrows. 'Go fish.'

Chapter Forty-One

Tess had just lost her fourth hand and was beginning to suspect she was being conned when her phone rang.

'We don't usually get a signal down here,' Sarah remarked. 'Sam must have put wifi boosters in.'

'DS Fox.'

'Fox, it's Oswald. I just thought I'd better give you the heads-up before anyone else does.'

They've caught Lily.

'We've got the DNA results back on our Jane Doe.'

'Jane Doe?' Tess asked, confused. They didn't have anyone currently unidentified that she was awaiting DNA on. Unless . . . oh. Tess felt her face drain of colour and her legs go weak. Julia was currently in the system as a Jane Doe. The only fingerprints on file for her had been under a false name and she had refused to tell Walker her real identity.

'Our suspect in the Mitchell, Rodgers and Jacobs killings,' Oswald said, his voice impatient.

'Of course, sorry.' She'd obviously known it would happen

but she'd managed to put it out of her mind somehow. So this was it, they would know that Julia was Sarah's sister. Would they dig further into Frank's background? Would they find out about Tess? Surely there was no reason for it all to link back to her, but the tightrope she felt like she'd been walking ever since the evening she first saw Shaun Mitchell's body seemed thinner than ever now.

'And?' Tess asked, trying not to let her voice betray how nervous she was. 'Does it match anything at the crime scenes?'

'Nothing,' Oswald said. Tess froze. Nothing? She didn't know whether to feel relief or disappointment. Or confusion.

'Did you test it against the victim's DNA?' she asked. She saw Sarah's eyebrows rise. 'To see if she has any link to them?'

'Of course we bloody did,' Oswald snapped. 'What do you think – we're incompetent? There was nothing matching our suspect to any of the crimes, or any of the victims. Basically we have nothing forensically on her whatsoever.'

Sarah stared at Tess, unable to take in exactly what she had just been told.

'How is that even possible?' she demanded. Her eyes filled with tears, emotion raged through her. Was she angry? Upset? Had Julia been lying to them all along?

Tess looked as confused and hurt as Sarah felt.

'So Julia isn't my sister?' she asked. 'Or your half-sister?'

'She's not Frank's daughter,' Tess said. 'But Lily would surely know if she wasn't her daughter. So even if she's not related to me, she's still your half-sister.'

'What if—' She stood up straight as a horrifying thought

dawned on her. She dropped her voice to a whisper, unable to say the words too loudly. 'What if Frank wasn't *my* dad?'

Tess was at her side in an instant. 'Oh no, don't you start thinking like that. You are one hundred per cent Jacobs, I'm certain of it. And Frank was certain of it.' She pulled her sister in for a hug, and Sarah put her head on Tess's shoulder.

'Do you think the police will tell her?' Sarah asked.

'Her lawyer will tell her that her DNA wasn't at any of the crime scenes,' Tess surmised. 'And I'm guessing Julia – who has been expecting the news that she's Frank's daughter to come out any day now – will want to know what's going on. Her lawyer will tell her she's not related to Frank.'

'We can't let that happen,' Sarah said, pulling a string of duplicate cards from out of her sleeve and putting them down on the table. 'We're going to have to tell her first. She should hear this from me.'

Chapter Forty-Two

Tess stood outside Brighton Custody Suite, contemplating her next move. The news she'd had from Oswald had bothered her all the way there – was Julia really not Frank's daughter? This couldn't be like the fingerprint situation – Julia had been arrested in the past and given her name as Sarah Jacobs, thereby recording her fingerprints in CODIS under Sarah's name. DNA didn't work like that. The swab had been taken from Julia and compared to the DNA from the body of Frank Jacobs. Not faked, not manipulated. Julia wasn't Frank's daughter, and Tess had no idea how she was going to react to the news. Never mind that, Tess had no idea how she was going to explain the fact that Sarah needed to be the one to tell Julia that she wasn't related to Frank. What was Oswald going to think when Sarah – the daughter of Julia's last victim - asked to break the news gently to her that her DNA didn't match the crime scene?

Where the hell was she? Tess checked her watch – they had set off at the same time and yet Tess had been waiting here for a good fifteen minutes already. And Sarah drove faster than her.

A short, stocky woman with long black hair and wearing a light-green suit walked towards her. She was holding a briefcase in one hand and a Starbucks coffee in the other. Tess moved out of her way. The woman hesitated in the doorway and looked at Tess.

'Are you coming in?' the woman asked, in her half-sister's voice.

Tess did a double take and gaped at Sarah. How had she not realized it was her? Okay, so the thick black fringe and glasses obscured a lot of her face, but how on earth was she at least thirty pounds heavier?

'Padding,' Sarah said with a smile. 'Good to see it works.'

Tess followed her into the custody suite, stunned into silence. Of course she'd known that Sarah and her crew were good, but she'd never really appreciated how much skill it took to perform a makeover so complete that a person who had been with you just thirty minutes before could no longer recognize you.

'Catherine Harris,' Sarah was saying to the woman at the desk, holding up an ID card. 'Here to see your Jane Doe on behalf of Watson Little Solicitors to have these forms signed.'

The woman barely glanced at the ID. 'Do you have an appointment?'

'I do, yes,' Tess heard Sarah lie. 'Made by Caroline yesterday.'

The woman scrolled on her computer and frowned. 'I don't see it in here.'

'I confirmed the appointment on my end' – Sarah checked the woman's badge – 'Mary. There's really nothing I can do to ensure the person on your end enters it properly now, is there?'

'Look, Mary,' Tess said, holding up her warrant card. 'All Ms Harris needs to do is get some signatures on a few forms. I'll even escort her myself if that helps you out.'

'It does, thank you, DS Fox.' Mary looked as though Tess had offered her her firstborn. 'Are you sure you don't mind?'

'Not at all,' Tess said, her voice warm. 'I'm sure Ms Harris can promise to behave herself.'

Tess followed Sarah down the hallway. 'We make a good team,' Sarah said, looking back. 'Admit it, that was way funner than getting in through the normal channels.'

'Be quiet and keep walking,' Tess hissed. 'If she contacts Walker, or looks up your imaginary solicitors, we're done for.'

'They're not imaginary,' Sarah said. 'And there really is a Catherine Harris working for them. I googled them.'

'Impressive.'

Tess walked Sarah to an interview room that Mary on the desk had promised to bring Julia to. They sat in silence at the grey plastic table, Tess tapping her foot, Sarah picking at the skin beside her nail. Both of them looked up when the door opened and Julia was led in by a uniformed officer.

'Just knock on the door when you need to leave, or if you feel threatened in any way. I'm right outside.'

'Thanks,' Tess said, and the officer nodded. 'She's not given us any trouble so far.'

He left the room but Tess could see his bald head through the glass panel in the door.

Julia sat opposite the pair of them and looked each one of them over in turn. She looked disturbingly well. Her hair was clean and hung in a sleek sheet around her face. She was even wearing some make-up and didn't look like she'd lost a moment's sleep. It was as though she'd been put up in a five-star hotel rather than a custody suite.

'Sarah,' she said, and Tess felt a stab of annoyance that Julia had recognized her immediately. 'Tess. Isn't this a rather lovely family reunion? To what do I owe the pleasure? Are you here to break me out?'

'Not today, Julia,' Sarah said. Julia pretended to pout.

'Lost your sense of adventure, little sis? Let me guess, hanging out with the Old Bill has dampened your spirit. I don't blame you. Get me out of here and we can go on that trip we talked about.'

Tess gave Sarah a look and Sarah shrugged. She didn't know what was more annoying – that Julia knew exactly what to say to push her buttons, or that it had worked. That protective, jealous feeling she'd had when Sarah and Julia had been off hunting for Lily had begun to prickle at her again, that taunting voice telling her that she would never be like them, that they would always have a bond that she didn't share, as long as they were on opposite sides of the law.

'You look like you've swallowed a wasp,' Julia teased. Tess pushed her chair back and stood up.

'Come on, Sarah,' she said, giving Julia a look of defiance. 'Let's go. Let her lawyer tell her, you don't owe her anything.'

'Tell me what?' For the first time ever, Tess thought she saw a flicker of uncertainty cross Julia's pretty face. Sarah remained seated but raised her eyebrows at Julia.

'Say sorry and play nice, or we'll leave and you won't play at all.'

Julia scowled like a petulant child. 'You want me to say sorry to her? She's the one who had me arrested. What happened to family loyalty?'

Sarah snorted back a laugh. 'I'd say as far as families go, we're on the less conventional end of the scale,' she said. Tess watched her half-sister carefully. She clearly wasn't going to own up to being the one who had told Tess where Julia was at the time of her arrest, and that was fine. Tess was happy to keep her secret.

'Fine,' Julia said. 'I'm sorry, Tess. Please do take a seat and I'll be nice from now on.'

Tess sat back down.

'You came here to tell me something?' Julia repeated. 'Are you coming to my hearing on Monday? It's at Lewes Magistrates' Court.'

'I'll ask Castro what he thinks,' Sarah replied. Wayne Castro was Sarah's family lawyer. He had declined to represent Julia, on the grounds that the murder she was accused of was his favourite client, but on Sarah's request he had found her a good lawyer. 'I'm supposed to know you only as my father's killer, remember?'

Julia nodded. 'I haven't told them who I am yet. I suppose they'll find out soon.'

'Well,' Sarah looked at Tess. Tess nodded in support. Julia looked between the two of them.

'What?' she said. 'What is it? Just tell me, this cloak and dagger stuff is so annoying.'

Sarah took a deep breath. 'The police got the DNA back from the crime scene.'

Julia put her head in her hands. 'Oh Lord,' she muttered. 'I thought I'd been so careful. What did I mess up? Was it the horseradish? No, I used gloves for that. Urgh, the knife in the lift shaft? I mean, I wiped it clean but I'm no Mrs Hinch . . .'

'There was none of your DNA at the scene whatsoever,' Sarah interrupted. Julia let out a sigh of relief. Then she looked at the pair of them in turn again.

'That's a good thing, right? I don't really see the problem. Or why you both look like someone ripped apart your favourite stuffed toy.'

'There was no DNA at the crime scene, and no match to any of the victims,' Sarah said. Tess watched the confusion on Julia's face, watched her frown and then comprehension dawn.

'It didn't show up that I was related to Frank?' she asked. She gave a little laugh. 'Well, they probably didn't do that test. They wouldn't do that test, would they?'

She looked uncertainly between the two women. 'Tess?'

'The police have been using familial searching in murder cases since 2003,' Tess explained. 'They would have put your DNA in the system as a suspect, and Frank's in as a control – to rule out his own DNA at the crime scene. If there had been a familial match the system would have thrown it up immediately.'

'But it didn't,' Julia said, her voice barely above a whisper.

'Which means, Frank wasn't your father, Julia,' Sarah said quietly. 'I'm so sorry.' She reached across the table to take the other woman's hand but Julia yanked her hand away, folding her arms.

'There's some mistake, then,' she said, her voice defiant. 'Their testing must be wrong, or they're using imbeciles to run the tests. Frank was my dad. Mum told me so. She told me that Frank was my father, and that you were my sister. She would know better than some stupid test, wouldn't she?'

Tess wished she could throttle Lily Dowse for what she'd

done to her daughters. For giving Julia up, for leaving Sarah when she was just three, but most of all, for coming back and continuing to lie. Surely she had known there was a chance that Frank wasn't Julia's father? Granted, she probably hadn't anticipated that Julia would accidentally kill him, leading her to be charged with his murder and their DNA both be entered into NDNAD, but still, her lies had caused the situation they were in now.

Tears began to roll down Julia's face and she sucked in a sob. It struck Tess that she hadn't seen Julia cry once since the day they told her that they knew she'd killed Frank. It had meant so much to her, to belong to something. If there was one single thing Tess could empathise about with Julia it was that. Tess had never felt like she really belonged somewhere either, not since she left Frank and his crew fifteen years ago.

'Julia, I'm sorry. Look, it doesn't really matter. Maybe it's a good thing,' Sarah said, her voice soothing. 'Maybe once you get out of here you'll be able to find your real dad and—'

'Frank was my real dad!' Julia shrieked. She stood up so abruptly that her chair was flung away from the table. Her eyes looked wild and she slammed both hands onto the table, her face close to Sarah's now. 'Do you hear me? Do you hear me?'

Tess jumped up to bang on the door but it was already being flung open and the officer outside was grabbing Julia by the arms, cuffing them behind her back and she was pulled into the corridor, still screaming, 'It's wrong! The test is wrong!'

Sarah let out a long breath.

'Well, that went better than I expected,' she said.

Chapter Forty-Three

They left the custody suite with a stark warning that if they required any further visits the usual procedures would have to be followed. Julia's outburst had caused quite a stir with the other detainees and Sarah and Tess weren't the most popular of people by the time they got back out onto the street.

'I could hardly take you seriously, looking like that,' Tess complained. Sarah grinned.

'It's not the job Gabe would have done.' She bit her lip at the mention of her friend. Tess rushed to change the subject – slightly, at least.

'Who do you think Julia's father is? I guess we could ask—'

'Reg Ellis,' Sarah blurted out. Tess frowned.

'What does Reg Ellis have to do wit—'

Sarah grabbed her arm and yanked her behind a large white van. 'No, Reg Ellis is over there,' she hissed, pointing across the street. Tess peered around the side of the van. Sarah was right, Reg from the Juggs pub was walking quickly away from them down the street. He was pushing a crate trolley stacked with boxes, like he was making a delivery.

'Come on,' Sarah said, motioning for Tess to follow. They crossed the road and followed Reg, who was glancing around furtively, but thankfully he didn't look behind.

When eventually they saw him stop, Sarah motioned for Tess to duck into the entryway of a shop opposite. Sure enough, before entering, Reg gave a good look around, then pushed his boxes inside.

'We're going up there,' Sarah said, motioning to a set of fire escape steps at the side of the building entrance.

'You can't open fire doors from the outside,' Tess argued.

Sarah opened her eyes wide. 'Are you fucking kidding me?' she hissed. 'It actually really hurts my feelings that you would say something like that to me.'

She dashed up the fire escape steps and Tess followed, shaking her head. Sarah opened her Michael Kors handbag and pulled out a piece of wire that had been wound around in a circle to fit neatly down one side. She unlooped it and handed Tess the bag. Sarah got to her knees and fed the wire under the door, pulling her hand back in a quick gesture. Tess heard a thump from the other side of the fire door and it moved outwards ever so slightly. Sarah put her fingers into the crack and pulled it open. She gave Tess a *told you so* look and unwound her wire from where it was hooked over the pull bar on the fire exit.

'I mean, I've seen it done on YouTube,' Tess said, 'but I'll admit, that's the first time I've ever been on this end of a break and entry.'

'Technically not,' Sarah said, her voice a whisper as they

moved through the darkness. They were in a long corridor with what looked like office doors every few feet. All of the lights were off and there wasn't a person in sight. The entire place looked abandoned.

'What do you mean, technically not?' Tess hissed.

'I mean,' Sarah said, 'the offices we used back in February to set up Julia. Do you think we rented those?'

'I assumed you did,' Tess said, stifling a groan.

'You assumed wrong, big sis.'

They came to a staircase at the end of the corridor. Sarah pointed down and made a quizzical face. Tess nodded. They made their way downstairs. When they got to the stairwell, Sarah held up a finger. Reg Ellis's voice carried through the air, echoing from the room beyond as if the whole floor was empty.

'Shall I just offload these here?'

They didn't hear the reply. Sarah stood on her tiptoes and looked through the glass panel at the top of the door.

'White guy, six two, six three-ish. Light brown hair, looks a bit like a lumberjack.'

'What's in the crates?'

'They're still closed,' Sarah reported. 'Reg is just unloading them. Shit! Duck!'

She dropped to the floor, and Tess did the same. 'Did he see you?'

Sarah shook her head. 'I don't think so. He turned around but I think I was too fast.'

Tess sighed with relief, just as the door to the stairwell opened and Reg stood in the doorway.

'Out,' he commanded. Sarah sighed and followed him into the dusty, gloomy warehouse along with Tess.

The space obviously hadn't been used in quite a while. Cobwebs were strung between roof beams and rust dribbled down the walls. The whole place had a musty, mouldy, damp smell that reminded Tess of the basement at her mother's old house.

Reg turned on them both and they jumped.

'Okay, what are you doing here?' he demanded. 'Are you police?'

Sarah paused. How hadn't he recognized her from Rupert's wake? Then she realized she was still wearing her prosthetics. 'Do I look like police?' she said, her voice full of scorn.

Reg looked her up and down. 'A bit, yeah.'

He grabbed the expensive handbag from her shoulder and opened it. He began pulling things out, the likes of which Tess hadn't even come across in her fifteen years of policing. And she thought she'd seen every way a person could think of to break into somewhere. Reg looked outraged.

'You're a thief!'

'Well, you're a . . . a . . . what exactly are you doing here?'

'I'm delivering some booze for a function,' Reg said, without missing a beat.

'In here?' Tess looked around incredulously. 'It's completely bare. And dusty.' She wrinkled up her nose. 'Who would be having a function here?'

'I'd say the same kind of people who would be paying cash for the alcohol,' Reg said. 'Anyway, what business is it of yours? Why did you follow me here?'

'We didn't follow you in here,' Sarah said. 'We were in here first.'

'Oh yeah?' Reg looked suspicious. 'Doing what?'

Tess knew better than to try to come up with a lie. Whatever she could think of to say right now, Sarah would have something better. And she did.

'This.' Sarah pulled a small, clear packet out of her pocket. It was filled with white powder. Reg's eyes opened wider. He reached out to take it but Sarah pulled it back.

'I don't think so. And if you tell anyone you saw us here we'll tell the police about the illegal party you're supplying alcohol with. No reason for any of us to get into trouble, is there?' She stuck her chin out defiantly and Reg shrugged.

'Suppose not,' he said, turning back to unload his boxes.

'Fine, we'll go then, shall we?' Sarah asked. 'Just like that?'

Reg snorted. 'I'm not the mafia, love. I'm not going to shoot you for being in the same place as me. I'm not even doing anything particularly wrong, just helping a mate out with some booze. You're the ones acting like we're in a *Goodfellas* movie.'

He turned back to his unloading and Sarah looked at Tess who inclined her head to the door.

'Do you think he's shifting his dodgy wine supplies onto students?' Sarah asked when they were outside.

'I could put in a call to someone who deals with licensing at the council,' Tess said. 'But it's certainly not an MIT matter. And I don't think this is getting us anywhere. Also, what the hell are you doing with cocaine in your handbag?'

Sarah laughed. 'As if.' She pulled it out again and waved it in front of Tess. 'It's the packet the spare buttons for my jacket were in and some sugar packets I carry around in case I need some for my tea.'

'You did that in your pocket?'

'While he was going through my bag.'

Tess looked impressed. 'You are basically a genius.'

'Basically,' Sarah said. 'Now let's go before he realizes I dropped two of the empty sugar packets on the warehouse floor.'

Chapter Forty-Four

Sarah waited until she'd rounded the corner before beginning to peel away bits of her face.

'God, that looks disgusting,' Tess complained. She opened her bag and pulled out a pack of wet wipes. 'Here, let me sort it out.'

Sarah stood patiently and let her sister remove the silicone from her face. When she was done, Sarah pulled her dress containing her extra twenty pounds in weight over her head to reveal a vest top and some cycling shorts underneath. She popped open the pull-along crate that had appeared to be full of paperwork. Underneath, in a hidden compartment, was a pair of jeans and a jumper. Sarah pulled those on and stuffed her dress back into the crate.

'You guys really have it all down to a tee, don't you?' Tess mused.

'Hey, we're good at what we do.' Sarah shrugged.

'Aren't you going to make some quip about me joining you?' Tess asked. 'You wouldn't usually miss such an opportunity.'

Sarah pulled a face. Without make-up she looked even younger than she usually did – and with her slight build and small stature she usually looked early twenties at most. 'Maybe I'm starting to think that you're exactly where you belong,' Sarah said. Tess raised her eyebrows.

'Well, well,' she said. 'Can't say I saw that coming. To what do I owe this sudden change of heart?'

'I've got one half-sister in jail and an undead mother who might be joining her in the cell by the end of the month. Maybe it would be nice to keep a family member on this side of the bars.'

'I don't have a clue whether to say thank you or screw you,' Tess said. 'But I've got to get back to the station – I need to talk to Oswald about Walker and this Truly Fletcher stuff.'

'What, you're not going to make some quip about me joining the police?'

'And have you behind bars for murdering Walker in your first week?'

Walker emerged from Oswald's office and Tess got a glimpse of his sweaty, stressed-out face. It gave her a childish satisfaction. She hadn't been able to argue with Walker getting the promotion they had both been working for – she'd let a killer get away from right under her nose, after all – but that didn't mean she had to be happy about it. For a start, she knew she was the better detective, the harder working definitely. But there would be other promotions, and now that Julia was behind bars – thanks to Walker, according to the rest of the world – and there was no chance of her hurting anyone else because of Tess's actions, well, her career and her promotion just felt less important now. The force was still her calling, just lately she felt as though she was being called in a different direction and it was getting harder to resist.

Walker disappeared down the corridor without even noticing her. Tess dashed forwards to Oswald's still open door. 'Sir,' she said, lingering in the doorway. DCI Oswald turned and gestured for her to come in.

'Tess. You've been interfering in Walker's investigation. Again. And you've come to either apologise or to hand in your resignation.'

'Um, not exactly, sir.'

'Not exactly to which one, Fox?'

'Well . . .' Tess hesitated. Oswald wasn't stupid. He was pretty grumpy, increasingly so these days, a little old-fashioned, but also intolerant to bullshit. Which he had a pretty good nose for. It was probably best just to be as upfront as possible. What was it that Sarah always said about the most convincing lies being ninety per cent truth?

'I was just doing what my DI told me to, sir,' she began. *True.* 'But I've been acquainted with Lily Donovan before.' *Almost true.* 'So when she came to talk to me at the Juggs in Kingston, she was telling me some information about the people involved in Rupert Millington's life.' *Also completely true.* She was getting quite good at this. 'And Babette Ramsey, she'd been upset about her cows being poisoned, and when I mentioned it to Walker he put me on that case, to get me out of the way and take the mick a bit, I suppose. So I was going round to take her statement – about the cows – and she was killed while I was there. Just outside the room.'

Wow, Tess thought. She was very good at this. Every

statement she'd made was basically the truth, and yet none of it made it seem as though she'd been going behind Walker's back at every opportunity she got.

'And you were at Rupert Millington's funeral because . . . ?'

Ah. Tess faltered. 'That was just me being a bit nosy.'

'And the ever-present Sarah Jacobs was working the bar at his wake because the millions her father left her aren't stretching far enough?'

Oh crap. Leave it to Walker to start being observant at exactly the wrong time. Sarah hadn't mentioned seeing him there but obviously he'd seen her, and held on to the information, too. As far as anyone in the force could prove, Frank Jacobs was a millionaire businessman, but there had been talk about his real criminal activities for years. Tess had dreaded the day that she would be put onto a team to investigate her father, but he'd got himself killed by his other daughter before that had ever happened. Funny, that the police officer should turn out to be the least threatening of his children.

'And the call that Walker took personally from a nurse at Eastbourne District Hospital regarding the SIDS death of a child that Walker expressly told you to leave alone?'

'Ah.'

'Stop trying to play down your involvement, Tess,' Oswald said with a sigh. 'I actually don't give a toss anymore, I just want people to stop getting murdered in Sussex. Especially business owners and MPs. I don't need to tell you how high-profile Rupert Millington's murder has been in Sussex. And thanks to the, um, the manner of his death, I've got journalists calling me every day. That's not to mention the fan club I'm fighting off for the suspect for the last three murders.'

Tess's jaw nearly hit the ground. 'Her what?'

Oswald tutted and shook his head. He had actually begun to look really old this last year, and he'd had his hair cut too short. Tess didn't think it was the best time to mention it.

'Honestly, Tess, it's like we've arrested Velma Kelly.'

Tess almost laughed at the thought of Oswald googling '*Chicago* the musical' so he could make that reference. She wondered how many times he'd used it already.

'I suppose she's got that innocent young woman look about her,' Tess said. 'She hardly looks like a serial killer.'

'Well, you've seen the headlines,' he said, and she had. The papers were full of speculation, and, of course, pictures from the arrest of Julia looking like little orphan Annie. Not to mention the added fact that the police still didn't know who she was – that was like catnip for the red tops. And surprisingly, not one person had come forwards to identify her. In a case like this it wasn't unusual for the papers to find out her identity before the police – they were the ones paying mega-bucks for the story after all. But nothing. Either Julia had managed to float through life without ever being identifiable, which was possible, or the people who could identify her hated the police and the papers more than they loved cash. And given the circles Tess knew Julia had been in, she'd bet on the second.

'She gets fan mail every day,' he continued. 'I swear to God, if she's found not guilty she'll be running a cult by this time next year.'

'She won't be found not guilty, will she, sir?' Tess asked. 'All the evidence suggests that she was at the crime scenes, and lying to us about who she was and pretending to be the victim's girlfriend . . .'

'We just have to hope it's enough,' Oswald replied, but the look on his face didn't fill her with confidence. 'That's for the CPS now. What we need to deal with now is this Millington case.'

Tess sighed. 'I'll stay away from it, guv.'

'Actually, you won't.'

Tess froze. Of all the things she'd been expecting, this wasn't one of them. 'I won't?'

'If you think there's something to the SIDS case, then I trust your instincts.' Oswald shook his head. 'You are a better detective than Walker. Don't look at me like that, we both know it. The promotion thing was above my head, and Walker has made friends in higher places than I can overrule. Of course not being able to get a suspect in custody for the triple homicide, that was the nail they used to close your coffin. But I still have faith in you. I know you are a good detective, and I suspect – although I'm not going to try to prove it – that you have some kind of link to this case that would be better undisclosed. I want Millington's murderer behind bars and I don't care who brings me the smoking gun.'

'But Walker . . .'

'Will remain officially the SIO. But I'm not taking you off the case. I will turn a blind eye to you ignoring Walker's direct instructions as long as – *and I mean as long as* – official police procedure is followed. I'll deal with the whinging Walker as long as the evidence is tight, beyond reproach. Anything you find comes back to me to be put through the official channels: search warrants, the lot. Am I clear?'

Tess was stunned. She had been expecting to be told to stay away from her superior's investigation, let the big boys deal with the murders and go back to writing up reports of drug deals and city centre fights. Perhaps when Oswald had told her that he believed in her last February, he had actually meant it. And maybe, just maybe, her place was in the police force after all.

'Yes, sir,' she replied. 'As crystal.'

Chapter Forty-Five

'Mrs Hamer!'

The woman turned around at the sound of her name. She gave them a polite smile. 'Hello?'

'Mrs Hamer, I'm DS Fox, Murder Investigation Team. Might I just ask you a quick couple of questions?'

Rita instantly looked nervous. People who lied to the police often did.

'Of course, come in.' She indicated for them to follow her down the long, winding driveway and punched in a code to disable a security system. Sarah was impressed. Unlike the Millingtons, Rita Hamer had forked out for a full alarm system – and not one of the cheap ones, either. The last time she tested one of those it had taken her six attempts to bypass the automatic alarm service callout.

'Can I get you anything to drink?' Rita took them through to a spacious kitchen with a huge living area attached, and full bifold doors. Expensive, secure ones, Sarah noted. They were the kind that spanned the full length of the wall, so you were basically outdoors by the time they were fully open.

'I'll take a coffee,' Sarah said. Rita seemed pleased. Nervous people liked having a job to do. 'Thank you.'

'I'm fine, thank you,' Tess said. 'You have a beautiful home.'

Rita smiled. 'Thanks. I designed it all myself.'

'You have a keen eye.' She wasn't just flattering Mrs Hamer, the house was impeccably decorated. Tasteful art hung on walls painted in Farrow & Ball pastels. It was minimalist, but the ornaments she had chosen fit beautifully. A headless ceramic torso-and-legs on a stand next to a vase of autumn-coloured flowers and a small Jo Malone candle that cost a week of Tess's salary. There were no signs of children or teens, other than a small teddy bear on the arm of the grey suede sofa, next to a pristine log burner. Sarah wondered if it had ever even been used, it looked so clean.

'How can I help you, ladies?' The mundane act of putting on the kettle had allowed Rita to compose herself slightly, and Sarah and Tess both smiled warmly in unison. It was no good for them, Sarah thought, to have poor Rita on the back foot, all stressed out and defensive. She may have lied to the police about Leodora being with her the night of Rupert's murder, but she had almost certainly done it to protect her best friend from the scandal of an affair on top of her husband's death. Rita Hamer probably never imagined in a million years that her lie could be protecting a killer. If they were going to get more information on Leodora and Richard Johnson-Wells, first they would need confirmation that Leodora's alibi was a lie, and Rita seemed more likely to crack than Leodora herself.

'Just a little follow-up,' Tess said, 'on the information you gave my colleague about the night your friend Rupert was killed.'

Rita nodded, biting her bottom lip. Tess pressed on. 'You said that Rupert's wife, Leodora, was with you the night Rupert was last seen alive,' she said. 'Is that correct?'

Rita nodded, but said nothing. She turned back to the kettle and poured hot water into two mugs. 'It's instant, I'm afraid.'

Sarah smiled. 'That's fine, thank you. I'll take it black.'

She stirred Sarah's coffee and placed it on the coaster in front of her. She didn't finish making her own.

'According to your statement, you bought a bottle of wine, and came back here to watch a movie?'

Another nod.

'Which movie?'

'Um . . . it was *Halloween*.'

'On DVD?'

Rita shook her head quickly. 'No, on Sky.'

Tess jotted something down in her notebook and Sarah watched Rita's eyes widen slightly. Right now, she was wondering if the movie *Halloween* was available on Sky, and if Tess was going to ask to see her Sky box, and the recordings on it, or if she was going to ask her how it ended or what her favourite part was – and a million other things people thought about when they were lying. It was a very stressful job, trying to keep your lies straight. Sarah should know.

'It's just that, we've checked the CCTV from Waitrose in Lewes the night of Rupert's murder – Leodora isn't on there. There's a woman who I believe might have been you . . .'

'Oh, yes,' Rita said. 'I went in for the wine. Leodora met me here.'

Tess smiled, as though relieved to have that confirmed. Sarah had to admit, her sister was very good at this, all the micro expressions needed to put someone at ease, to make them talk. The same skills, in fact, that she employed as a grifter.

'Brilliant, thank you for clearing that up. So if we could just see the cameras, we'll be out of your way.'

Rita's jaw seemed to drop slightly. 'Cameras?' she repeated. 'Of course, we have cameras.'

Tess nodded. 'I noticed outside that you have a great camera system. Very sensible, by the way. Keeps footage for thirty days, too. So Leodora will be on that footage, from the night Rupert went missing, won't she?'

Rita let out a breath.

'She wasn't here, was she, Rita?'

She shook her head. Sarah could see the strain of all those little lies just flowing out of her as she shook her head. Her face was miserable, yet relieved.

'No, she wasn't here. I'm sorry, I'm really sorry.'

Sarah reached out and put a hand on Rita's arm. 'You were just trying to do the right thing by a friend who had a horrific tragedy befall her. You don't believe for one minute that Leodora had anything to do with Rupert's murder, do you?'

Rita sniffed. She pulled a tissue from a floral box on the counter and dabbed at her eyes. 'Of course not. I suppose you know where she was already?'

'She was with Richard Johnson-Wells.'

Rita didn't even looked surprised, she just nodded. 'That's why I said she was here. I know she couldn't have killed Rupert, so it wasn't like I was perverting the course of justice. Having the whole country judging you for where you were when your husband was being murdered isn't justice. Not after what Rupert put her through! She loves Richard, he never loved any of the little slappers he messed around with.'

'But how do you know she was definitely with Richard that particular night?'

'She called me from his place. She always calls me to check in when I'm her alibi. That night, her phone battery had run out – it was always doing that, actually – so she just called from Richard's place. It's not unusual. I think she likes that someone knows, that she can be real and honest with me. Anyway, it was his landline, and I heard him in the background saying to tell me hello. Richard lives in Bexhill – miles away from where Rupert was last seen.' She looked at them both in turn, her expression imploring. 'I wouldn't have lied for her if I wasn't sure she hadn't done it.'

Sarah believed her. Evidently so did Tess, because she gave the woman a serious look and said, 'I understand, Mrs Hamer. Let me tell you what's going to happen now. You're going to get in your car and drive to Lewes Police Station, and ask to speak to a man called Detective Inspector Walker. Then you're going to tell him that you have realized that you made a mistake about your dates, and that on the night Rupert Millington died, you were not with Leodora. You won't mention that you are only there because one of his officers caught you in a lie – you never lied, you made a mistake. We never came here. That's the best I can do for you to keep you out of any trouble. Upstanding woman like you? You won't even be cautioned. People make mistakes all the time.'

Rita nodded. 'Thank you. I can't thank you enough. I'm so sorry.'

As they got back into Tess's car, Sarah looked at her sister. 'You could have got the credit for figuring that out, you know?'

Tess said nothing. Sarah grinned. 'You are such a big softie, DS Fox.'

Chapter Forty-Six

Sarah pretended to peruse the spreadsheet in front of her and put on her most apologetic face at the man in front of the desk he thought was hers. She hadn't told Tess why she had asked her to drop her off in the middle of Brighton after they'd been to Rita Hamer's house, but Mac had found another 'investor' and she'd been the only one available to be their ringer.

'I can get you in early next year?' . 'I mean, it sounds like a long time but it's only about eight or nine weeks . . .'

'Nine weeks is not acceptable,' Richards insisted, as she'd known he would. He was a short man but puffed himself out when he spoke as though trying to make himself bigger, more imposing. He wore an expensive suit but cheap aftershave that made Sarah want to sneeze.

'I could, ummmm . . .' Sarah pretended to look on her laptop for available 'dates'. The man tapped his foot impatiently and she wanted to smack him in the face.

'Listen, what if I made it worth your while?' he asked. He took his wallet out – of course he was the kind of man who carried a wad of cash around Brighton. He peeled off three twenty-pound notes and placed them on Sarah's desk. She raised her eyebrows and looked bored. He sighed. 'Fine.' He peeled off another few notes, then two more and slammed them on the desk. Sarah picked them up, folded them and slid them into her back pocket.

'Look, Mr Garrick genuinely doesn't have anything free until January,' Sarah said. Before the man could speak she held up a finger. 'But. He's meeting his lawyer tomorrow at a restaurant in town and they never run too long. He goes to the gym straight afterwards but I can get him to see you for fifteen minutes in between. Fifteen minutes, that's all I can get you. Do you think that will be enough?'

The man's face was a picture of relief. Sarah knew she had him on the hook. He had no idea that this wasn't her desk, or that the man he was arranging to meet – a well-known and respected investor for real estate development – would not be the person he met in the restaurant tomorrow. In fact, he would be meeting Mac, who he would proceed to beg to be allowed to invest in a scheme Mac had been setting up for months, the same scheme they had used for the Kelly con.

'Heather!'

Just as the man was thanking her for her help, someone burst through the office doors. Sarah glanced quickly at the clock – Garrick and his secretary were supposed to be locked in a passionate embrace for another hour yet. At least they had been at this time for the past few weeks that she'd followed them.

But the man who had burst into the office wasn't Henry Garrick. Fury swept over her when she realized who had interrupted her con, and why he was there. Her stomach flipped at the sight of him, and she wasn't sure it was the knowledge that he was about to ruin her con. She waited to see what he was going to say. He was wearing black jeans and a black short-sleeved shirt, some kind of Celtic tattoo showing on his tanned, slightly muscular arms.

'Heather, how many times?' he said in his Irish lilt. He walked over to where she was sitting and took her arm. She allowed him to ease her up out of the chair.

John Richards looked between the man and Sarah in confusion. 'Do you mind?' he snapped. 'We were in the middle of arranging an important meeting.'

'Oh, I'm sure you were,' the man said, giving Richards a look of pure sympathy. 'This is the fourth time this week. Only Heather here, she doesn't work in this office. She delivers the sandwiches from the canteen.' He lowered his voice. 'She likes to play pretend, ever since the head injury. We've had to start putting a minder on her, but they snuck out for a cigarette and let her loose.'

Sarah's mouth dropped open. There was nothing she could do to defend herself – if she started protesting, Richards might demand proof that she really worked there, or call in security. This was it. Months of planning and surveillance, not to mention the hundred grand Mac was sure he could get this guy on the hook for – all down the drain.

'Sorry,' she said, trying to sound as pitiful as possible. If this was going south, she was going to have to get out of there without being arrested at least. Tess would have a field day with that. 'You said that if I was good I could play up here sometimes.'

'That was the office at the facility, Heather,' the man said kindly. His hazel eyes twinkled with utter amusement as he turned his back on Richards and gave her a triumphant smile that only she could see. Damn him! 'You can play on the spinny chairs later.'

'This has got to be some kind of piss take,' Richards snapped. His face was bright red, a bead of sweat forming above his brows. He wanted this deal more than Sarah had realized. 'Are you telling me that the meeting we just arranged doesn't exist?'

'You were never going to be meeting Mr Garrick,' the man said truthfully. 'Heather here has only ever met him long enough to give him his sandwich. Egg and cress, is it, Heather?'

'Tuna and sweetcorn,' Sarah responded, her voice flat. In her mind she was running through all of the ways she was going to try to explain this to Mac.

'This is ridiculous,' Richards snapped. 'You'll be lucky if I don't have your job!'

He turned and stormed out of the office, slamming the door behind him.

'Shame,' Sarah said. 'I was beginning to warm to being a sandwich delivery person.'

The man burst out laughing and she punched him in the chest.

'Ow!' He clutched his chest. 'There was no need for that!'

'No need?' Sarah's voice was mutinous. 'No need? Are you aware that you've just cost me a hundred thousand pounds? If one of my team had been here instead of me, you'd be needing hospital treatment right now.'

He smiled. 'A hundred grand?'

Sarah was struck with the urge to punch him in the face, but if Richards came back with security she would be in even more trouble.

'I need to get out of here,' she snapped.

'I'll come with you,' he said. Sarah turned on him.

'Maybe as far as the front door you will,' she said. 'Then you'd better run. Far away, where my family can never find you.'

Chapter Forty-Seven

Sarah was dreading going back into the warehouse. She'd had to tell her family that she'd lost them a hundred grand thanks to their social engineer friend; it was the first time that someone had managed to track her and block a con so effectively, and she was worried the family would think it was because she was losing her touch. Mac had, unsurprisingly, wanted to 'hunt him down and kill him' – and for the first time, Sarah had believed her uncle might actually be being serious. Gabe had had what amounted to a tantrum, flouncing and declaring that if things carried on getting worse he'd be homeless, despite the fact that Sarah's lawyer handled all of their investments and she knew that Gabe had plenty of money saved up and invested. Wes had remained silent, barely saying a word. When she'd finished talking he'd shrugged, got up from his seat and said he was taking the rest of the day off.

Sarah didn't believe for a minute that it was the money that had upset everyone so much. It was the fact that they had been bettered by someone. And before Julia had shown up in their lives and proceeded to ruin everything no one had ever got the upper hand on them.

Sarah was terrified she couldn't fix things. Not least because the one thing that needed fixing was their grief over losing Frank, and she would never get over that herself. Frank, who had been killed by a woman who was trying to make him proud, trying to show off that she was good enough at scheming and plotting and ruthless enough to be his flesh and blood. And now even that wasn't true.

Sarah sighed as she let herself into the warehouse and listened to her footsteps echo across the empty upper floor. She'd thought having Julia arrested would be a step towards healing the cracks that were widening between them, but if that had been one step forward, this new drama was two steps back.

The main room downstairs was silent, and for a minute Sarah thought that everyone had quit and gone home. Instead, as she stepped out of the lift, she could see that they were all gathered around a huge box in the centre of the room. Desks and chairs had been moved aside to make way for the object, and over thirty people were crouched down in front of it. As she got closer, she could see that it wasn't a box, it was a safe.

'Sarah!' The woman who had been kneeling in front of the lock jumped up. 'I was just showing the others how to use this—' She held up a safe-cracking tool. 'I hope you don't mind? Mac approved the purchase . . . you weren't here.'

Sarah raised her eyebrows. 'Are you planning on pulling off a bank job anytime soon?' she asked. 'Or was this just a bit of fun?'

The woman's face fell. 'I, um . . .'

Sarah instantly felt terrible. There was a time when her team would have known that that was a joke. 'I'm kidding,' she said, and there were a few nervous laughs from the congregation. 'Knock yourself out. I haven't done one of those myself for a while, might come and have a go in a bit.'

The woman smiled, relieved. 'Of course, yeah, that would be great.'

Sarah carried on to the office, her chest feeling weary. She felt as though she were walking under water, absolutely nothing felt right. She pushed open the door to see Gabe and Mac in the middle of what looked to be a heated debate. Wes sat in the corner, at his computer, headphones on and either didn't notice her entrance or had no desire to acknowledge her. Great. Just when they were making headway again. Mac and Gabe stopped talking as soon as she walked through the door and looked at her. Both looked guilty – they had been discussing her.

'What?' she asked. 'What's going on?'

'Nothing,' Mac said. 'How are you?'

'Shit. I feel terrible about what happened, and—'

'The rest of us felt great about it,' Wes's voice came from the corner. So he had noticed her coming in, and there was nothing playing on those headphones.

'Say again?' Sarah said, her voice sharp. She felt her anger close to the surface now, the anger she always felt when she was here, in this place, around these people.

'I was talking,' Wes said, spinning around in his chair and taking off his headphones, 'about the rest of us. You know, people who aren't you? People who are here every day, thinking of ways we can carry on making a living rather than off playing police officers? People who are keeping the business afloat?'

Sarah scoffed. 'By spending their time playing with safes?' she asked. 'When was the last time we pulled off a bank job? In fact, Wes, you and I have never pulled off a bank job, not in our time here.'

'They needed something to take their mind off things,' Mac said, his voice gruff. 'They're worried.'

'What are they worried about? It's me who has a bloody stalker now.'

Mac walked over to Sarah and put his hands on her shoulders. She resisted the urge to melt into his arms, like she would have done her dad's. She had to be strong. Things here were too volatile for her to look weak now.

'We've put a stop to all activities until we know who this guy is, and the depth of his operation,' Mac said. Sarah stepped back.

'You did *what*?'

Mac held up a hand. 'I tried calling you. Multiple times. We discussed it between ourselves and most people thought it was too risky, while this guy is out there two steps ahead of us. He blocked your con the other day but he could've shopped you. You could be looking at a stretch now. We can't ask people to risk themselves, not at the moment. So until we know more about this mystery man, we're on a break.'

Sarah sighed. It was the right decision to make, the one she would have made if she'd been around.

'You're right,' she admitted. 'Thank you for stepping up.'

Chapter Forty-Eight

Tess had been waiting in the secret room in the Black Dove for twenty-five minutes when Sarah and Jerome eventually walked in. Together.

Not together, Tess told herself. *Just at the same time.* There was a difference.

'So Oswald basically told you to ignore that prick Walker and do your own investigation?' Sarah asked as Tess shuffled through the papers on the table and tried to hold her tongue about them being late. And together. She knew she would just come off sounding paranoid.

'Not in so many words,' Tess said. 'But he did agree to me following up the Truly Fletcher angle.'

'I was thinking about that,' Jerome said. 'And if she was blackmailing him it's unlikely she'd kill him, surely? I mean, she kills him and the money stops.'

'My thoughts exactly,' Tess said. 'And I looked up her company accounts. Except there aren't any. Her business hasn't been running long enough to file accounts yet. So I did a records search for Truly Fletcher.' She paused for dramatic effect.

'And?' Sarah prompted.

'And Truly Fletcher has a rap sheet for drugs from ten years ago. Cocaine, mainly.'

'Cocaine,' Sarah muttered. 'Like Babette's cows were poisoned with?'

Tess nodded. 'Like that.'

'Cocaine is hardly rare, though,' Jerome said. Sarah fanned through the sheets of evidence they had collected, the lists of people involved in the effigy, the blown-up pictures of Rupert's accounts, the ledger of his dodgy wine customers.

Sarah's phone beeped and she picked it up, grinned, and placed it back down.

'So I know how Babette was killed,' Sarah said, her voice as casual as if she'd just told them what day of the week it was.

'Excuse me?' Tess said, putting down her drink so hard it slopped over the side of the mug. 'How? When did you figure it out? Why didn't you—'

'Woah, Hold your horses. I had to check some things before I said anything, and Wes has just text me with the answers. He's made this adorable paper mache thing that he's very proud of. He's going to bring it over then I'll explain—' She stopped talking and frowned.

'What?' Tess asked.

'Have you seen this?' Sarah held up the print of the Facebook charity fundraiser. Truly Fletcher's little boy stared up at her, a huge smile on his face.

'Seen what?' Tess scanned the text and the photo. 'I've read that a dozen times, I – oh, I see.'

'Right?' Sarah's eyes widened and she passed the photo to Jerome. 'That teddy bear on the floor behind him,' she said. 'We saw one of those in Rita Hamer's house. The exact one. No other children's toys, nothing to suggest a stuffed toy collection. Just that exact teddy.'

'I've seen it somewhere else, too,' Tess said. Sarah scanned her memory then snapped her fingers.

'Babette's. There was one there.'

Tess frowned. 'I don't understand what this means,' she murmured. 'We should get back to Rita, ask where she got it.'

'Wait,' Sarah said. 'Lily has one of those bears.'

She picked up her phone from the small table and dialled Lily's number. She'd only just got used to being able to make a call downstairs – she'd preferred it when the secluded little room felt more cut off from the world, but at least it meant they didn't have to go into the street to make a phone call anymore. It rang and rang. 'Shit,' Sarah muttered. She rang again.

'Hello?' Lily sounded worried. 'Sarah? Is everything okay?'

'Yes, don't panic, no one is hurt. I need to know about that teddy bear you have in your downstairs cloakroom.'

'The what?' Sarah could hear the wind whipping around Lily in the background – she was outside. 'Sarah, look, I've got to go and sort something out, I've had this weird message . . . Can we talk about this later?'

'No! Lily, don't hang up! I know it sounds odd but it's really important. Where did you get that bear?'

Sarah heard Lily harrumph. 'Sarah, you've seen how much stuff is in my house. I don't remember where I got every little thing from.'

'Think!' Sarah insisted. 'It's to do with Rupert's murder.'

'Oh, that's it!' Lily exclaimed. 'That's where I got that stupid bear.' Sarah put her mother onto speaker phone and they all leaned in to hear her properly. 'Rupert. God knows why but he had a box of them in his garage when I was there. When I, um, when we . . .'

'Yes, okay, we get it. Was he giving them out as souvenirs?'

Lily made a choking sound. 'What?'

'Well, you had one, Babette had one . . . Truly Fletcher had one. Perhaps the whole bloody village has one of Rupert's post-coital party favours in their house.'

'Oh, behave,' Lily tutted. 'Rupert didn't give me the bear, I stole it. I assumed they were for some teddy tombola or something. I stole two of them, actually. I needed a gift for someone that afternoon, but the baby shower was cancelled and I ended up keeping it, and I gave Truly the other one for her son. Rupert went nuts when he saw a photo of William with it on Facebook. He stormed round to mine to demand that I get it back but I told him to piss off. Then that awful tragedy with her son happened. I offered to pay him for them. I'd forgotten all about that.'

Sarah looked at Tess. She had an idea forming, and she was wondering if her sister was getting the same one.

'Where are you now, Lily?' Sarah asked. 'Can we go and look at the bear?'

'I told you, I'm sorting something out.' Sarah heard the ding of a bell. 'There's a key in the third plant pot by the pond, it's a yellow pot with a blue rim, if you want to let yourselves in. You know I can't go back there.'

'Thank you.' Sarah hung up the phone. 'We need to go and take a look at that bear.'

They went in Sarah's car, but much to Tess's surprise, she let Jerome drive. As a result of this, they were in Kingston in a little under half an hour, pulling up on Lily's drive minutes later.

'Got the key,' Sarah called, tipping it out of the yellow plant pot by the pond. She let them in, the smell of incense almost knocking Tess giddy.

'I hope that stuff isn't burning while she's out,' Tess complained. 'The amount of junk in this place, it'd go up like a tinder box.'

'I'll make sure she's done her fire safety awareness course,' Sarah promised. She led the pair into Lily's front room, then pushed open the door to the cloakroom where she'd hidden from Elma Chew. The bear was on the floor inside the door, exactly where she'd left it.

'Here . . .' Sarah picked it up and tossed it to Jerome. He pulled his keys from his pocket and flipped open a miniature penknife.

'Whoa,' Sarah said, holding up her hands. 'Do you need a concealed weapons permit for that thing?'

Jerome pulled a face at her. 'If you want to discuss concealed weapons . . .'

'That's enough,' Tess snapped. 'Open the bloody bear, Jerome.'

He slid the penknife in between the stitches and pulled upwards, the threads snapping one by one. The back of the bear split open, and Jerome went to put his fingers inside.

'Stop!' Tess snapped. She pulled a pair of gloves from the small handbag she was carrying. 'Use these.'

Jerome put the gloves on, then felt inside the small teddy bear. He was frowning – had they been wrong? Then his face broke into a grim smile as he fished the small plastic bag, filled with white powder, out of the inside of the bear.

'Well,' Tess said, 'I think this explains the sudden popularity of these small fluffy bears.'

'And I'm pretty sure it explains who killed Rupert Millington,' Sarah added. 'And why they wanted to frame Lily.'

'It does?' Jerome looked perplexed, but Tess was pretty sure she knew what Sarah was going to say.

'Lily gave a drug-filled teddy bear to a little boy who died not long afterwards,' Tess said. 'I think it's fair to say that we know why "donation" money was frequently making its way into Truly Fletcher's bank account. Richard Johnson-Wells was incredibly convincing, I must say, but it would be a coincidence that Leodora's lover happened to lose the post-mortem of the child Rupert was being blackmailed over. I can't see what Babette's involvement would be, unless she was letting Rupert use the farm to store the drugs. Perhaps that's how her cows were poisoned?'

'You'd better call it in,' Jerome said. He turned to Sarah. 'And you need to call your mum and get her back here. If Truly Fletcher is killing the people she believes are responsible for her son's death, the person who gave him the bear would be pretty high up on the list.'

Tess left the room to ring the station while Sarah dialled Lily again.

'No answer,' she said. 'She said she'd had a weird message and that she was going to sort something.'

'A weird message?' Tess asked. 'Did she say who from?'

'No,' Sarah replied, thinking of where she'd heard that ding-dong before. 'But I know where she is. And she's in trouble.'

Chapter Forty-Nine

Lily pushed open the door to the shop, setting off the little ding-dong that made her smile. So few shops had the proper ding-dongs anymore. She hung up on Sarah as Truly looked up from behind the counter and smiled at her.

'Lily, thanks for coming.'

Lily nodded, glancing outside the window. She should not be here, in Lewes, streets away from the police station. But Truly had said it was an emergency, that it was about Rupert. 'What is it, Truly?'

Lily looked over the beautiful gifts Truly made by hand. The shelves were looking sparser these days, but then who could blame the poor girl if she hadn't been working as hard, after what had happened to little William. Such a tragedy. Thinking of the boy made her think of Sarah's frantic phone call ten minutes ago. Why had she been so wound up about that bloody bear? Lily had forgotten it was even in the house – it certainly hadn't been kept as any kind of a souvenir, like Sarah had suggested. And so what if half the village had them? She didn't know why Rupert was investing in the soft toy market in the first place but it was none of her business.

'It's, well, it's a bit delicate.' Truly looked embarrassed. 'It's about Rupert. About what happened to him. Would you mind if we went out the back? It's a bit more private.'

Lily felt the dread that had been lurking inside her rise up. What did Truly know about Rupert?

'Of course, love,' Lily said, following Truly through to the back of the shop. The back door was open, and Truly's studio sat at the end of a patch of garden. 'This is perfect, really, for you, isn't it? Lucky to get a shop you can set up like this.' She was babbling, trying not to belie her nerves. Whatever Truly said she would have to deny, plausibly. If she knew what Rupert had suspected about the gifting tables . . . well, best just to see.

'Absolutely,' Truly replied, leading her out into the garden area. 'This studio has been a lifesaver. After what happened to Will I found it so hard to be at home, I spent a lot of time here.'

'I'm so sorry about what happened to your son,' Lily said. She stepped into the studio and was surprised at how spacious it was. Just a long table in the middle, and a huge, impressive-looking kiln at the end.

'Are you, though?' Truly asked from behind her. 'Are you *truly* sorry?' She gave a tinkling laugh at her own joke and Lily frowned. She began to turn around when she felt a sharp sting. She gasped, not sure of what was happening, why this young woman had just scratched her, or what with.

'Rupert said he was sorry,' Truly said. 'Then when I told him that wasn't good enough – that I was going to tell the police what he'd done – he threatened me. Said, with my record he'd make sure everyone thought I'd bought the drugs that killed Will.'

'Drugs?' Lily said, confusion clouding her thoughts. Things had started to go blurry. What was happening to her? Had Will Fletcher died from drugs? That wasn't right, was it?

'Drugs,' Truly repeated. 'Drugs Rupert and you filthy whores were pushing around Lewes and Brighton. You and Babette. You're not sorry yet, Lily.' From out of the darkness that clouded her vision she heard Truly's voice say, 'But you will be.'

Chapter Fifty

Jerome pulled up outside the shop on the high street and took off his belt.

'Wait!' Tess said, grabbing his arm. 'We have to wait for Walker. He said we weren't to go in until uniform arrive. They will be here in minutes.'

'You can wait,' Sarah said, flinging open the door. 'I'm going to find my mum.'

She jumped out of the car and flew into the shop. The bell clanged loudly and Sarah regretted running in so hastily. She needn't have worried though, the shop was empty.

She let herself behind the counter and peered through the door behind it into a corridor and what looked like a staff room beyond. The fire door leading outside stood open. Sarah went over to the fire door and peered around the edge. In the garden area out the back there was a large summerhouse-style hut. Sarah thought it looked like a studio maybe. She wasn't afraid to admit that she'd hoped that Tess and Jerome were going to follow her in, despite their bosses' orders, but she understood why they couldn't. She'd messed up Tess's career enough as it was.

As she was about to move towards the door to the studio, she saw movement out of the corner of her eye, from behind the left side of the building. Jerome's head appeared over the wall at the far end, then his entire body, in one fluid and quite sexy movement. Either there was something to climb over on the other side or he'd just vaulted a six-foot wall.

'Bins,' he mouthed, and despite the tension, she smiled. He motioned for her to get back and let him go in first, but she shook her head. She wasn't waiting outside. Besides, if she was going to walk into a situation where she was basically bait, she was going to need Jerome fully intact behind her.

Sarah put her hand on the studio door and was about to push when she saw her sister's head appear on the other side of the wall. She gave a small nod and Tess nodded back. She knew that trying to stop her was futile. Sarah pushed open the door.

The scene in front of her took a moment to take in. Lily was lying in front of an open kiln, the fire inside roaring. The room wasn't hot yet, the fire hadn't been on long. Sarah had time to register that this was the perfect way to burn Rupert Millington's body before a sharp pain coursed through the side of her body. She stumbled to one side, thinking she'd been punched. Wow– that hurt. Sarah pressed a hand to her side and felt warm blood. Not a punch then, she'd been stabbed. She tried to turn to face her attacker but pain coursed through her and she fell to her knees, trying to hold in the blood that was seeping through her clothes, between her fingers, everywhere. *That is a lot of blood*, was her last thought before she closed her eyes.

Chapter Fifty-One

Tess heard her sister cry out in pain and tried to pull herself over the wall from the small recycling box she'd been standing on, but it wasn't high enough.

'Jerome!' she shouted, but he was already running towards the studio. Tess looked around, desperate for a way of getting herself up and over, on to the bins on the other side.

Please God, let Sarah be okay, she prayed. *And I'll go to the gym every day and get arms like Jerome's and never not be able to get over a wall again.*

With a cry of exasperation Tess ran back around to the street, back to the shop front. She flew in through the door, a sharp pain shooting through her hip and she barely registered that she'd banged into one of the stands, sending it flying and scattering trinkets everywhere. She carried on running, through the back door behind the counter and into the garden where Jerome had Truly Fletcher on the ground in handcuffs.

'There was someone else,' he gasped. 'Ran past me when this one ran at me. Sarah's inside, I think she's hurt.'

Tess didn't need to make a decision between running after whoever else had been in the building, and running towards her sister.

Inside the studio was flaming hot. Sarah lay on the floor of the studio, blood blooming around her in a thick red pool. Tess fell to her side and looked for where the blood was coming from, pulling off her jumper to stem the flow. She found the knife wound in her sister's side and pressed her jumper to it, fumbling with her other hand for her phone to dial 999. Looking around wildly she saw Lily lying in front of a roaring furnace, either unconscious or already dead.

'Nine nine nine, which service do you require?'

'Ambulance!' It took the longest second of her life for the call to connect. 'This is Detective Sergeant Tess Fox. I'm at Truly Yours in Lewes High Street and I have two people hurt; one has been stabbed and is losing blood fast, I can't confirm the status of the second victim right now. Police are already on their way—' She paused as she heard a commotion from outside the studio. 'Police are here. We need an ambulance, now.'

'An ambulance is on the way, Detective.'

Tess had answered the ambulance service's questions a million times, but never as a relative of one of the victims. Suddenly, she knew how people on the other side of these scenes felt; the frustration, the desperation. Armed response moved into the studio, officers everywhere fanning out to search. One ran over to Lily.

'Is she alive?' Tess yelled. 'Is she alive?'

As the paramedics rushed in Tess was pulled backwards, away from her sister, away from Lily without knowing if either of them would live or die.

As the adrenaline was replaced by shock and fear, Tess felt a hand on her arm and turned to see Jerome at her side. She collapsed into his arms and began to sob, not knowing or caring who saw her tears. Jerome guided her out of the studio to allow the officers to secure it as a crime scene, and into the garden where Walker was waiting for them. Tess looked up at him, waiting for the bollocking to start.

'Are you okay, DS Fox?' he asked, and his concern was almost worse than his fury. Tess wiped the tears from her face.

'Sorry, sir, just shock.'

'Morgan, take Tess home. Suspect is in custody, we can take your statements later.'

'No, sir,' Tess started. Walker held up a hand but she carried on. 'There was someone else—'

'DS Morgan has already told us, we've got officers out looking now. We can do this without you for a few hours.'

'I'm not going home. I want to be in on Truly's interview. Please. Sir.'

Walker looked as though he was about to object. Tess hoped he wouldn't, she didn't want to have to pull the 'I told you so' card about Fletcher and the blackmail. Maybe he realized that because he sighed and nodded.

'I'm leading. But you can sit in. Come on.'

Chapter Fifty-Two

Truly Fletcher looked even smaller sitting in an interview room next to her burly lawyer, an unsmiling man with a bald head who looked more like a doorman at a nightclub than a criminal defence lawyer. When Tess and Walker entered the room she didn't look up from the piece of skin she was picking at on her thumbnail.

They sat down opposite her and Tess took their suspect in as Walker went through the official stuff for the tape. Despite her pallid, thin face and her sullen expression, there was still a hint of the beautiful woman Tess had seen in the photo. It was clear, though, that the loss of her son had taken its toll.

'Who was with you at the studio this afternoon?' Walker cut straight to the chase. They needed to know, because Truly didn't have a visible spot of Sarah's blood on her, and no knife had been found at the scene which meant that she probably hadn't been the person to stab her. Their perpetrator was still on the loose, and very dangerous.

'There was no one else.' Truly shrugged. Her lawyer muttered something to her and she shook her head.

'So you stabbed Sarah Jacobs?' Walker asked. Truly nodded.

'Yes.'

Tess ground her teeth. Who was Truly covering for?

'Why?'

'Because she came in when I was about to kill Lily Donovan.'

'Can I get a minute with my client, please?' Truly's lawyer interrupted.

'You've had plenty of time before we started,' Walker said. 'Ms Fletcher is aware of her rights. Why were you going to kill Lily Donovan, Ms Fletcher?'

Truly looked up at DI Walker and for the first time, Tess could see the murderer behind those eyes. The rage that simmered there was frightening.

'Because Lily Donovan gave my son a bear filled with cocaine, and it killed him. And I wanted her to die for it.'

Tess had known that was what Truly believed but it was still a shock to hear it coming from her mouth. She hated that she couldn't defend Lily without arousing too much suspicion from Walker. There would be no evidence that Lily was involved in the drugs that Rupert had been supplying, Tess would have to let the investigation take its course.

'If you believed Lily Donovan was responsible for your son's death, why didn't you tell the police?'

Walker had been briefed by Tess about the lack of post-mortem available on William Fletcher, and the affair between the man who should have conducted it and Leodora

Millington. On the drive to the station Tess had explained about the drugs they had found in Lily's bear, and where she had got that bear from.

'Because Rupert Millington told me that if I went to the police he would tell them that I'd bought the drugs from him. You probably know by now that I have a criminal record for possession of cocaine. We both know who would be believed. If I took him down he would take me down with him.'

'But he still paid you every month.'

Truly gave a strange sound that almost sounded like a laugh. 'Yeah. Well, by blackmailing him he knew I was in even bigger trouble. Besides, I think the horrible bastard actually thought that he would be more valuable to me alive and out of prison.'

'But you still killed him.'

Truly nodded. 'I was always going to kill him. The money was a bonus.'

'The money linked you to Millington,' Tess spoke for the first time. 'It was a risk.'

Truly turned her gaze on Tess, who felt as though every inch of her was being scrutinized by the other woman. Truly's lip curled. 'What exactly do you think I was risking, detective? I only stayed alive to get my son the justice he deserved.'

'And Babette Ramsey?' Walker said. Tess knew he was rushing things now, but she also knew why. Truly could clam up at any moment and their interview would be over. He wanted her to admit everything on tape before that happened. Tess wanted this done as quickly as possible, too – she needed to get back to the hospital.

'Oh yeah, Old Widow Ramsey. How do you think she kept that farm going after Walter put a shotgun in his mouth?

Not by being Farmer of the Year, I'll tell you. I wondered if she might confess to the drugs, after her cows "accidentally" ingested some of her supply. But she kept shtum.'

'So you killed her.'

Truly raised her eyebrows. 'I thought Lily Donovan killed her?'

'We know how you tried to frame Mrs Donovan,' Tess informed her. Not strictly true, Sarah had been rushed to hospital before she could tell them, but Tess was confident she knew and would tell them when she woke up. *Please let her wake up.*

'Good for you,' Truly said. She shrugged. 'I don't care what you know.'

'What we don't know, is who stabbed Sarah Jacobs,' Walker said again.

'I told you,' Truly said. 'I did.'

'We know that's not true, Truly. Who was with you? Why are you protecting them?'

Truly looked at her lawyer who looked like he'd basically given up at this stage. There are some people who can't be helped.

'No comment,' she said. 'I'm not saying anything else.'

Chapter Fifty-Three

Lily sat in the corridor of the hospital, waiting as six people fought to save the life of her youngest daughter, while her eldest awaited trial for murder. How had she made so many mistakes? How had her daughters' lives come to this? One might be dead before she was thirty-five and the other in prison for the rest of her life. She wished Frank was here. She needed someone to share the blame, and the guilt. Only this had happened without Frank around at all. Lily had got Sarah involved in this: if she hadn't asked for Tess's help that night they might never have known she was even in Kingston. She hadn't needed Tess to prove her innocence – the police would have figured out that she didn't kill Rupert Millington. She'd asked for Tess because she knew the girls had found one another again and some stupid part of her thought she might be able to be a part of that. Now look what she'd done.

'The Sarah Jacobs fan club is causing quite the stir out in the waiting room,' Tess's voice interrupted her thoughts.

'For someone who's not supposed to have any friends, there are a lot of people waiting for good news.'

'We don't have any news yet,' Lily told her, her voice shaking slightly. 'She lost a lot of blood. They're operating.' She moved her head too fast and winced.

'Should you even be here?' Tess asked. 'Looks to me like you should be in one of those beds yourself.'

'They're not getting their hands on me until they've saved Sarah,' Lily said. Tess smiled.

'You know there's more than one doctor here? It's called a hospital.'

'All right, smartarse. Whatever Truly injected me with knocked me out, but it didn't kill me, did it? So I'm going to sit here until I know that Sarah is OK.'

Tess sat down next to her. 'Fair enough,' she said. 'I'll join you, if that's okay?'

Lily nodded. 'Not quite the girls' night I had planned, but apparently my daughters don't do anything so mundane as facepacks and Netflix.'

Tess laughed. 'No, you're right about that. Sarah's really something, you know? She's strong. She'll be fine.'

They sat in silence for a few minutes. Lily found every second excruciating.

'Did you arrest Truly?' she asked. She'd woken up in the back of an ambulance, no idea what had happened after Truly had injected her with something that had knocked her out. She hadn't found out about Sarah until Tess had showed up at her bedside, then tried to stop her taking out her cannula and going to find out where her daughter was.

'We got her. She came out of the shop, ran at us waving

a gun. Jerome tackled her, I disarmed her. By that time the patrol cars were there and we arrested her.'

'Well, thank goodness for that,' Lily said. 'At least she can't hurt anyone else.'

'It's not quite that simple,' Tess said, and Lily's head snapped up.

'What do you mean? Surely you have enough evidence – she stabbed Sarah!'

Tess shook her head. Lily frowned, confused.

'Sarah walked into the pottery studio and was stabbed in there. Truly came from behind us, from the shop. She had no blood on her, and the knife is nowhere to be found. Truly didn't stab Sarah.'

'Then who the hell did?'

'That's what we're waiting to find out. I need a statement from you. Forensics are printing the studio. Hopefully we'll get another set of prints, or Truly will talk. She's making no comment at the moment.'

'Did she kill Rupert?'

Tess nodded. 'We think so. The bear you gave to her as a present for William was stuffed with cocaine. We believe that William ingested the cocaine after the bear split open, and that Truly called Rupert for help because she knew he'd wanted the bear back. We don't know how much Leodora knew, but it was her boyfriend who ruled William's death SIDS. If we can get him to talk, that will give us motive, then it's just a case of piecing together the rest of the evidence. It makes sense that Truly would blame Rupert for her son's death.'

'She thought Babette and I were involved too.'

Tess nodded. 'We think, unfortunately, Babette might have

been. We think the lights were some kind of a signal set up between them – that Rupert had them on a timer, that's why they carried on after he died, but the configurations could be changed. One of the letters in Babette's house looks like a key: static means no pick-up, flashing means they meet in the fields between his house and the farm to make a drop. We know from Martin that she had a box of the bears from Rupert's garage; someone has been sent to the farm to pick them up and find out if there are drugs in them too. It seems like Rupert has been supplying every housewife in the village in more ways than one.'

Lily snorted. 'I knew he was a prick.'

Tess stood up. 'Are you going to be okay while I go and let the others know she's still in theatre?'

'Of course I will, I'm not some senile old woman.'

Tess smiled. 'Anything but.'

But as Tess walked back down the corridor, Lily wished she wasn't leaving her on her own.

Chapter Fifty-Four

A continuous beeping sound pushed its way into Sarah's dream. There had been people, lots of them, wearing different faces that they would take off and change every few minutes. Tess was there, and Lily, Jerome, Wes, Gabe and Mac. Wes's watch began to beep.

'It's time to go,' he said. 'Sarah? You have to wake up. Sarah. Wake up.'

Her eyelids began to flutter open and she heard his voice again – louder this time and more insistent. 'She's waking up! Get a doctor, she's waking up!'

She tried to speak but her throat felt ragged, like someone had shoved sandpaper down it. She was clearly in hospital – that was the beeping sound she had heard – but her mind wouldn't produce the date, or what had happened to her. She grasped for the last thing she remembered, being with Tess and Jerome at Tess's house, looking through the pile of evidence. A picture of a bear? Oh God. It all clicked into place in an instant. Truly, her mother . . .

'Mum?' she croaked, although it made her throat burn. 'Mum?' She eased her eyes open and Lily's face was the first thing she saw. Relief flooded through her body like adrenaline. 'You're okay,' she croaked.

'You called me mum!' Lily was beaming, and tears were running down her cheeks.

'Don't . . . get . . . used,' Sarah tried but it hurt too much. She closed her eyes again and leaned back against the pillow, hearing the sounds of doctors and her sister's voice, her mum demanding that no one crowded her. She wanted to ask whether they had caught Truly and Harriet but everything felt so heavy. Maybe just a little more sleep.

The second time she woke there was only the face of a woman she didn't recognize standing over her. 'I made them all wait outside,' she said. 'You need some more rest. I got you ice chips but they melted, you've been asleep a while.'

'Water,' Sarah croaked, and the woman helped her to sip at the melted ice chips. The relief she felt as the cold water slid down her throat was indescribable. 'Thank you.'

The third time, she was able to ask to see her mother and Tess, and her throat no longer felt like it was being torn from her neck each time she spoke. The doctor fetched the two women and they pulled up chairs next to her bedside.

'Did you . . .?'

'We got her,' Tess said, before she could finish asking. 'Truly.'

'What about Harriet?'

Tess's face froze, then evolved into a picture of horror. 'Harriet? Harriet was the one who stabbed you?'

'I was stabbed?' That explained the intense pain in her side. Sarah hadn't been able to stay awake long enough to find out exactly what Harriet had done to her.

'You've been in surgery for hours,' Lily said. 'She damaged a kidney. You'll live, though.'

Tess was already on the phone, speaking urgently. She hung up and dialled again, spoke to someone else. Sarah lay back on the pillow, exhausted.

Chapter Fifty-Five

'But why?' Sarah asked, when Tess returned to tell her that Harriet had been arrested. She had a hazy recollection of why Truly had killed Rupert Millington, and maybe Babette. But she hadn't expected to see Harriet there that day. 'Why was Harriet involved?'

'Harriet and Truly are sisters,' Tess said. 'Baby William was Harriet's nephew. Add that to the fact that Rupert ripped her husband off and almost cost him his business . . .'

'Not sleeping together?'

'She says not,' Tess replied. 'There's no indication that they were having an affair.'

'But the love potion?' Lily said.

Tess smiled. 'Probably an early attempt to poison Rupert and frame you,' Tess said. 'But she must have got the dosage wrong. Leodora remembers Rupert getting a bit sick around that time but we'll never prove it unless she admits to it. We could do with knowing how they killed Babette,' Tess said. She had a concerned look on her face. 'But I don't want you to strain yourself.'

Sarah shook her head. 'Ask Wes. We figured it out together. He'll show you.'

The doctors did a fair bit of complaining, but they allowed Tess, Lily and Jerome to gather around Sarah's bed while Wes carried in a paper mache replica of Babette's door.

'What?' he said, seeing the look on Tess's face. 'We've had some downtime at work.'

'The question of how Babette's killer got out of the room,' Wes said, 'Is elementary. She walked out of Babette's door.'

'While Tess and Martin were stood outside it?'

Wes shook his head. 'At least five minutes before, if not earlier,' he said. He picked up his phone and pressed 'play'. Babette's voice filled the air. 'Lily, no!'

'Recording,' Sarah said. 'Played through the Alexa. Babette was already dead.'

'So we weren't hearing her voice,' Tess said. 'Just a recording of it?'

Wes nodded. 'Exactly. Sarah measured the distance, if they were in the next room, or possibly the room opposite depending on how strong the phone's Bluetooth was. Then when you ran in with Martin, they just had to sneak out of the house the front way. They probably almost ran into Sarah.'

'And the locked door?'

'I thought you'd never ask.' Wes propped up the paper mache door. There was a key hanging slightly out of one side of the lock with a thin piece of string. 'If the key on Babette's side was balanced in like this, it wouldn't stop the other key,' he produced a second key, 'from fitting in like this, and locking the door from the outside. Then, you just pull the key in further with this string . . .' He pulled the string gently, and it slid back into the lock. 'Then burn the end—'

'Oh no you don't.' The doctor walked in just as Wes was pulling out his lighter. 'They're just going to have to take your word for it.'

'That's where the ash came from,' Sarah said. 'We think the plan was to frame Lily, then kill her and burn her body in the kiln so it looked like she'd gone on the run.'

'All of Rupert's drug empire, and therefore everyone involved in William's death, taken care of, as far as they were concerned. They thought Leodora had no idea.'

The doctor looked at her sharply.

'Okay, time's up. Everyone out. Sarah needs her rest, and you lot have barely slept all night either.' She wrinkled her nose in Wes's direction. 'Or showered. Go away, the lot of you. She's going to live, give her some peace.'

There were groans all round but they acquiesced. As they left, they each squeezed Sarah's hand in turn and her eyes filled up. Bits of her crew, bits of her family, and here they were together, to support her. Her mum was the last to go, kissing Sarah on the forehead gently.

Epilogue

It had been two months since the attack on Lily, and Sarah's stabbing. Truly and Harriet had remained silent, but the evidence against them had mounted up, and the CPS had charged them both with the murders of Rupert and Babette, and the attempted murder of Lily and Sarah.

Julia's court appearance had happened whilst Sarah was in hospital, but Lily had attended and reported back. She had been remanded without bail until her plea hearing, where the judge would set a trial date. Lily had insisted to Sarah and Tess that Frank was Julia's father, and Sarah didn't have the heart to ask her if she was certain that Julia was the little girl Lily had given up all those years ago. Yes, she'd seen her as a child, and Julia looked a lot like both Lily and Sarah, but there was always the chance she was a cousin, or in fact a complete stranger with a coincidental resemblance. Sarah was still trying to convince Tess to get hold of Julia's DNA for a full test against hers and her mother's.

'So you say, *I bet you can't drink those three.*' Sarah pointed at the smaller tumblers filled with water. 'Before I can drink these three—' She indicated the pints. 'Only rule is we can't touch each other's glasses.'

'Fine,' Lily said, looking at the three small glasses in front of her. 'Go.'

Sarah began to down her first pint. Lily picked up the first glass and emptied it, then, before Sarah could place her empty pint glass over her third – still full – tumbler of water, she snatched the other two up, one in each hand and downed them both. Sarah's mouth fell open in amazement.

'You knew the trick,' she said, screwing her nose up in disappointment. Lily laughed.

'I was Frank Jacobs's wife once upon a time,' she said. 'You'll have to try a bit harder than that to pull a fast one on me.'

'You weren't Aubrey Taylor's relative, though, were you?' Sarah said, avoiding Lily's eye. 'You never had relatives that lived in Lewes.'

Lily bit her lip. 'How do you know that?'

'That night we broke into Rupert's house, I found his research. Did he blackmail you into having sex with him?'

It was Lily's turn to look away. 'I told you, I'm not sorry he's dead.'

Sarah had suspected as much but the confirmation that her mum had been blackmailed into sleeping with that awful man felt like a punch in the stomach. 'Mum . . .'

'Sarah!' The urgent shout came from the top of the stairs.

'Tess?' Sarah shouted back. 'Everything okay?'

Her sister's face appeared at the door of the hidden room. 'You have to see this.'

She passed her phone to Sarah. A man stood on the steps of Brighton Police Station as cameras flashed in his face.

'Good afternoon,' Frank Jacobs said, smiling at the camera.

Sarah stared at the screen, then blinked a few times and looked again. The date on the screen was today, and her father was alive.

'I'm afraid that news of my death has been greatly exaggerated,' on-screen Frank said.

'He always wanted a chance to use that line,' Sarah muttered, before she slumped over in a dead faint.

Acknowledgements

Thanks as always to my agent Laetitia Rutherford – ten years, eleven books, two children each, one global pandemic… we've been through it all! To Ciara, Megan and Annie who, let's face it, we all know run the agency, and to Rachel for making sure my books are read around the world.

Thank you to all at HQ who took a chance on Sarah, Tess and their motley crew. To the dream team of Cicely Aspinall, Seema Mitra, and Becci Mansell, as well as Charlotte Phillips for the most gorgeous covers I could ask for. Thanks also to Jon Appleton and Michelle Bullock.

To the residents of Lewes – I apologise for infiltrating your truly amazing bonfire night celebrations for my research, and thank you so much to all who chatted to my husband and I, and made us feel so welcome. Any mistakes made are completely my own, and any names used of present-day society members are fictional.

To my amazing children and long-suffering husband, sorry about the state of the house during deadlines, again. Thanks for putting up with me, love you always x

Find out where the page-turning Impossible Crimes series began…

DI Tess Fox's first murder scene has two big problems. One, the victim was thrown from the balcony of a flat locked from the inside. Two, Tess knows him.

But the biggest problem of all is Tess's half-sister, Sarah. She has links to the deceased and has the skills and criminal background to mastermind a locked-room murder. But she's a con-artist, not a killer.

When two more bodies turn up, Tess now has three locked room mysteries to solve and even more reason to be suspicious of Sarah. Can she trust someone who breaks the law for a living, even if she is family?

'A tasty whodunnit' *The Sun*

Available now in paperback, ebook and audio

ONE PLACE. MANY STORIES

ONE PLACE. MANY STORIES

Bold, innovative and
empowering publishing.

FOLLOW US ON:

@HQStories